THE SUITE LIFE

PORTIA MACINTOSH

Boldwood

First published in Great Britain in 2024 by Boldwood Books Ltd.

Copyright © Portia MacIntosh, 2024

Cover Design by Alexandra Allden

Cover Illustration: Shutterstock

A CIP catalogue record for this book is available from the British Library.

Paperback ISBN 978-1-80426-709-7

Large Print ISBN 978-1-80426-710-3

Hardback ISBN 978-1-80426-711-0

Ebook ISBN 978-1-80426-707-3

Kindle ISBN 978-1-80426-708-0

Audio CD ISBN 978-1-80426-715-8

MP3 CD ISBN 978-1-80426-716-5

Digital audio download ISBN 978-1-80426-713-4

Boldwood Books Ltd
23 Bowerdean Street
London SW6 3TN
www.boldwoodbooks.com

For Joe – extra thanks for this one

1

This wedding is going to ruin me.

Honestly, you know weddings are going to be expensive, and they're worth it, right? But it is only when you start planning one that you realise just how expensive they're really going to be. Everything is so expensive – more so than it would be if it were for a big birthday party, for no reason at all – and it's not so much that there are hidden costs, just completely random and unexpected ones.

Flowers – yeah. A cake – of course. A dress – obviously. Chair hire – what? Honestly, I'm getting a stitch thinking about it even now. I thought it was a joke when the wedding planner started banging on about chair hire. These venues – these super-duper expensive venues – don't always come with chairs. They'll take care of the food, the tables, the curtains that will cover the walls (for some reason it's cool to cover the walls with curtains) but not the chairs, God forbid, you think they just have chairs lying around? They do, but you have to hire them, and so people typically hire them from somewhere better – great ones. Expensive ones!

But the reason this wedding is going to ruin me is because it's a destination wedding – that's a wedding and a holiday, rolled into one – and not just anywhere with a bit of sea, sand and sunshine, oh no, this one is in Hawaii.

'A destination wedding is an absolute dream come true,' Lucy gushes, her eyes sparkling with excitement. 'The idea of getting married on a picturesque beach, celebrating with everyone you love, having your photos taken as the sun sets over the horizon. It's so romantic, isn't it?'

Lucy, my older sister, is clearly on a different page to me.

We're in what is thankfully a relatively quiet bar – that's me, Lucy and the other key players in this wedding – talking about the wedding, because the wedding is the most important thing, the wedding to end all weddings. Wedding, wedding, wedding. Honestly, I am sick of hearing, saying and even thinking the word: wedding.

'Oh, absolutely!' Nina replies. 'I've always believed that everyone should get married abroad, preferably on a Tuesday.'

I raise an eyebrow as I stare at her, waiting for what she just said to make sense, or for her to explain what she means. A Tuesday?

'If the wedding is abroad, and on a Tuesday, then you will be able to tell who is willing to make the time and the effort to be there,' she explains. 'Only truly committed friends and family members would make the effort to be there. You'd find out who your real friends are, and only those who are worthy would get to enjoy your special day – no freeloaders who just want a bit of food and to get drunk while you pay for it.'

I purse my lips to stifle a chuckle. The concept of throwing a weekday wedding as some sort of litmus test for friendship is a bit extreme, even for Nina.

'I'd never thought about it like that,' Lucy muses.

'Probably because it's not realistic,' I can't help but chime in.

'People have jobs and homes and kids and responsibilities and commitments – all sorts of reasons why they can't just bob to Bali on a weekday.'

'We're all making the effort for Hawaii,' Nina reminds me.

We are, and it really is an effort.

'Plus, this is already an exclusive wedding, at an exclusive location,' Lucy reminds her.

Inwardly, I can't help but roll my eyes. An exclusive wedding. Okay, I will admit that the Grand Palm Resort is an exclusive hotel, everyone has heard of it, whether they've been or not – because even rich people feel like paupers there, in comparison to those in the luxury suites, but my sister is delusional if she thinks anyone is actively trying to wangle an invitation to her wedding. She is my sister and I love her – I would travel to the moon to see her get married, if that's what she wanted – but I'm having to use precious holiday days to take the week off work, and plane tickets to Hawaii aren't cheap, nor are the cheapest rooms at the Grand Palm Resort, and then there's all of the usual expenditure that comes with a wedding – see what I mean, about how this wedding is going to ruin me?

Rick, who has never been one to keep his true feelings to himself, sniggers.

'You know, it's daft, really.' He starts swirling the ice in his drink. 'The way women take weddings so bloody seriously – too seriously, even. And, Nina, come on now, that's manipulative, crazy-woman talk. Weddings should be simple.'

'Not all women are like that,' I remind him, annoyed at his stereotypical viewpoint.

Rick is very much a lad's lad. To him, women are women, and they're emotional and crazy and obsessed with weddings. Okay, sure, women can be those things, but we're complex creatures, with layers and layers of different traits and desires. I hate when men lump us all together as a bunch of girly crazies. In my experience, men can be much worse.

'Yeah, Rick, Gigi definitely isn't in that category,' Nathan pipes up, jumping to my defence. 'She's always said she wants something small, just close family and friends at the registry office, followed by a laid-back party. Nothing grand. That's what I've always wanted too.'

Nathan and I talked about our wedding on several occasions – usually when we were in bed at night, being goofy, having a laugh, chatting about anything, everything and nothing. We would always agree that, no matter what, we didn't want a big, flashy wedding. Each time we had the conversation, the relief I felt was immeasurable. Well, most people do want a grand wedding, whereas I would cringe at the idea of all eyes being on me. Honestly, I don't know where people find the self-confidence to walk down the aisle. But I'm the kind of girl who would pull a sicky from school, if I knew I was going to be given an award during assembly that I would have to walk onto the stage to collect – walking down the aisle is like that, but worse, because you have to do it in a special dress, that everyone is probably judging, that usually features elaborate details and parts that are ripe for an epic wardrobe malfunction. I just know that I am the sort of girl who would trip over her train or, worse, reflect the light off her sequins and somehow cause a fire that burns an entire church to the ground. Okay, maybe that's extreme, but why chance it?

'Well, Nathan, as the best man and not the groom, thankfully you don't get to call the shots,' Lucy playfully reminds him. 'And Gigi's the chief bridesmaid, so I know she'll go along with whatever I want.'

Nina, who's been sitting quietly since I disagreed with her weird Tuesday wedding theory, can't help but pull a face. You can tell she's livid about not being chosen as Lucy's chief bridesmaid because she isn't making any sort of attempt to hide how she feels – it's the scowls, the passive-aggressive comments, and the near constant pointing out how she could do a much better job than me at almost everything. Nina is Lucy's friend and colleague, but I'm her sister, and in the sisterhood hierarchy I'm obviously going to take the top spot – even if Nina might actually be able to do a much better job than I could.

I'm here, despite the unresolved awkwardness that none of us are mentioning, and I'm doing my best. Not being wedding-minded, and never having planned one before, this is all new to me, but Lucy isn't just my sister, she's my best friend too – I couldn't imagine doing all of this, in these circumstances, for anyone else.

'Well, you're out of luck, if you don't want attention on you at your wedding,' Nina tells Nathan, her mouth twisting into a strange smile. 'When you get married, your bride is going to be the most jaw-dropping, show-stealing bride in the history of weddings.'

'Yeah, I know I'm really lucky,' Nathan says with a smile. 'I guess, on that day, I'll be so happy, I won't care if everyone in the world is watching.'

'Honestly, mate, I'm worried about you guys stealing the show at our wedding,' Rick tells him playfully. 'You might just be bringing the most impressive plus-one anyone here has ever met!'

'Yeah, seriously, so impressive,' Nina adds. 'You guys will be the couple no one can take their eyes off – never mind the bride and groom.'

Everyone at the table laughs, but it doesn't take long for the atmosphere to turn awkward as, one by one, they all realise what they are saying. Their chuckles die down, and one by one, everyone averts their gaze, looking anywhere but at me.

Ahh, the elephant in the room – the one who was absolutely

not invited to this super-exclusive wedding, but is almost certainly going to be my plus-one – the fact that Nathan and I broke up last year, in November, and now he's dating someone who is just *so* impressive, irritatingly so, because I just cannot compete. Oh, and not that it's a competition, but the fact that he has moved on with so much style (and so soon after our split – a matter of weeks, as far as I can tell), and I haven't, is starting to make it look like I'm still hung up on him. I don't even have a plus-one to take to the wedding, which is always there, in the back of my mind, because I am going to look so tragic, being the only single person in the wedding party, while the man I thought I was going to spend the rest of my life with sits loved-up across the table.

It's an unavoidably complicated situation. Lucy's fiancé, Rick, is Nathan's best friend (which means Nathan is his best man too), and since I'm Lucy's sister and chief bridesmaid, we all have no choice but to play nice. As the wedding day approaches, it's becoming increasingly evident that we're going to have to spend more and more time together, and I can't put into words how much I hate it. How am I supposed to move on from him when he's still knocking around?

In desperate need of a breather, I make my excuses, telling the group I'm going to the bar to get another drink. Hopefully, while I'm away, they can all whisper together, about how so, so sad it is that I'm single, and how they should all try harder not to make me feel bad. Honestly, I hate the idea of them all pitying me, but if it happens behind the scenes, and it makes it less awkward for me in person, then I'm all for it.

As I walk away from the table, I can't help but feel a knot in my stomach, knowing that this is just the beginning.

I sit down at the bar, briefly taking shelter from the shitstorm back at the table. The dim lights and quiet chatter are a welcome escape from the increasingly awkward vibe back there.

The friendly barman flashes me a knowing grin as he serves another customer. I wonder if you have to be attractive to be a barman, or whether it just helps. Eventually, he lands in front of me and takes my order.

'Why the long face?' he asks, his smile cheeky, knowing what a cliché line he's delivering.

I wonder how often people actually give him an honest response?

'I'm the chief bridesmaid at a destination wedding where my ex-boyfriend is the best man, and to make things even more uncomfortable, he's bringing his new celebrity girlfriend.'

'Yikes,' the barman replies, but his curiosity is piqued. 'Who's his girlfriend?'

'Sunshine Greene,' I tell him with a sigh so deep I almost take the mats off the bar.

'Wow, she's hot,' the barman blurts – almost involuntarily.

Don't worry, I'm used to that reaction. Sunshine was a contestant on *Welcome to Singledom*, the reality TV dating show where they stick a bunch of young, attractive singles on an island who have to couple up while trying to survive in a *Big-Brother*-meets-*Survivor* situation. I used to be a fan of the show, in fact, I watched the series Sunshine took part in – and hilariously I even made Nathan watch it with me, even though he hates stuff like that. Sunshine actually made show history, by being the only bombshell islander whom every single man was willing to leave their partner for. Not all that long after we broke up, Nathan met her through the PR firm he works for. How was I ever going to be able to compete with that?

Realising his reaction might not have been the ideal one, the barman quickly backtracks and stammers an apology.

'It's fine. I'm used to it,' I inform him. 'Really. I mean, being still single while he's moved on, everyone around me seems to think there's no chance I'll find a date for the wedding. I couldn't look or feel any more tragic – especially not to that lot – so, unless you want to slip me your number, when you bring me my drink, to show them that I'm not completely undesirable to everyone...'

I'm joking – well, half joking, at least – but I notice a glimmer of something in the barman's eye.

'A barman giving you his number won't impress them, trust me,' he replies. 'But I do have an idea. Go sit back down with your friends. I'll bring you a drink.'

I smile, nervously excited, keen to see what the barman has up his sleeve. I make my way back to the table and sit down with the others. They're all back to general wedding chat now, rather than the part that highlights my own tragic situation.

I am just about to get lost in my thoughts when the barman joins us, bearing a tray with my drink and a folded piece of paper. He hands them to me with a grin.

'The guy you were talking to at the bar wanted me to give this to you,' the barman tells me, quietly, but still ensuring that my friends can hear him. 'It's his number.'

The barman makes his exit, clearly pleased with his work. I look at the piece of paper, then at my friends, and I can't help but smile as I notice that everyone around the table has turned their attention to me. Then they look over at the bar and notice a handsome, dark-haired man in an expensive-looking suit. Oh, this is so satisfying. I can tell by the look on their faces that, even if it is only for a split second, they're impressed, maybe even a little envious. There is a hot man at the bar and he's seemingly given me his number. I'm young (ish), free and single. I can take numbers from hot men. Nathan is in a relationship so, in theory, his days of getting a buzz like this are over.

Their admiration soon crumbles as the man is joined by a woman, clearly his wife. The light catches the shimmer of her wedding ring as she places a hand on his face to kiss him, confirming their connection. The atmosphere at the table turns awkward, and the room suddenly feels smaller, and warmer, and if the ground could just open up and swallow me whole, that would be great. I'm almost certainly heading down that way eventually anyway.

'Wow, what a creep,' Lucy blurts.

'Yeah, that's not on,' Rick adds. 'Someone should say something to him.'

Nathan, ever the gentleman, stands up, his chair screeching loudly against the floor.

'I'm going over there,' he announces. 'His wife should know. He's not messing her, or you, around like that.'

Oh, great, now everyone feels sorry for me again. Also, more pressingly, this poor man is totally innocent of any wrongdoing, and Nathan marching over there is only going to cause a big mess and, ultimately, more embarrassment for me.

I rise from my seat, clearing my throat, searching for the words and the confidence to nip this in the bud.

'Wait, it wasn't him who I was talking to at the bar,' I insist. 'You guys have got the wrong end of the stick. That guy is good, he hasn't done anything wrong, don't go talk to him.'

'Then who were you talking to?' Lucy asks.

All eyes shift from me to scan the quiet bar, searching for the mystery man who sent me his number. Luckily there is another lone man sitting at the bar. Unluckily this man is a dishevelled-looking bloke in his sixties. He's propping up the bar – actually, technically the bar is propping up him. He's necking shot after shot as he scowls blankly into space. He's clearly having a bad day – perhaps even worse than mine, although with each second that ticks by, I only seem to make the competition stiffer.

'Oh,' Lucy says simply.

Nathan sits back down again.

'Okay, well, as I was saying about the food…'

It's hilarious, isn't it? Just when I thought things couldn't get any more tragically comical, my life finds a way to outdo itself. This wedding is shaping up to be an absolute nightmare, and it's only just begun.

2

'Okay, Gwen, what are we doing today?' I ask, raking my fingers through her long black hair as I make eye contact with her in the mirror.

'You know, I think it might be time,' she announces with an optimistic smile. 'I think I'm ready to go back to blonde.'

Gwen is a regular client of mine and, while we may well be one of the best hair salons in London, we cannot work miracles. I remember, the very first time she sat down in my chair, I explained to her that her box-dyed black hair wasn't going to be transformed into Barbie-blonde locks after a few hours in the chair. The thought of it being a process, with multiple steps, wasn't something she was into. Well, people want to leave the hairdressers looking amazing, right, otherwise was it even worth staring at your potato-like face for hours? I don't know why it is but, for some reason, everyone looks awful when they're staring into the mirror at the hairdressers, questioning if they have always been so ugly – I know I look like a potato, especially when I'm all wrapped up in foil, but then as soon as the stylist is done, boom, it's a miracle transformation. The most attractive you will ever feel is standing there, getting your 'after' photos taken for the stylist's portfolio. It's just a fact. I mean, I'm a hairdresser, totally capable of styling my own hair, but sometimes I get one of the others to give me a blow-dry, just so I can get that salon-fresh confidence boost.

'It's not going to be that easy, unfortunately,' I say, trying to keep my tone patient, even though we've had this conversation several times before. 'You've got layers of black dye to contend with. We'll have to strip it out, bleach it, tone it, and it's going to take multiple sessions. Your hair might not even survive it all.'

'But you know what you're doing,' she insists.

'But, even so, with hair you just never know,' I reply. 'Slow, steady and cautiously is the only way to go, if you don't want orange hair or breakage.'

'Okay, fine, fine,' she says with a sigh. 'Just, okay, see how blonde you can make it today.'

'I can see how light we can make it,' I reply. 'It might not be what you want, but it will be a step towards it.'

'Yeah, fine, fine,' she says, batting her hand like she's waving me away to get on with it.

I always thought being a hairdresser would be such a glamorous job. I loved the idea of styling the rich and famous, seeing my work on TV and in magazines, and I was probably about thirteen when I started having my own hair highlighted (hello, chunky blonde and red highlights of the nineties), but I loved visiting the salon, soaking up the atmosphere. I knew I wanted to work in one and, boy, have I found a great one. It makes where I used to go when I was a teen (Angelz, with a Z) look like someone's living room with a sink in it.

Honestly, when you walk through the doors here at Tom Olsen Hair, you are entering a safe space. People don't just come here for a new hairstyle, it's like a contemporary café (we're all trained up on the espresso machine – only the best for our wealthy and often famous clients, of course) and a therapist's office rolled into one. You can ask advice, bitch about people you don't like – and you never know who will be in the chair next to you. But while it is glamorous to be a client here, working here doesn't exactly come with the same level of sparkle. I seem to spend my life buying black clothes because the ones I wear don't last all that long before I stain them with little flecks of lightener, and despite this being one of the few industries where the customer definitely isn't always right, I often find myself having to talk people down from requests that will quite literally have them tearing their hair out whenever they touch it.

Sometimes I'm not surprised Nathan left me – the girl behind the chair – and wound up with Sunshine Greene – the kind of girl who sits in one. Ever since Sunshine was on *Welcome to Singledom*, her star has just kept rising and rising. Young people worship her – not that I'm not young, I'm well aware that being in my early thirties is very much still young, but Sunshine is an icon to young girls in their teens and their twenties. They all want to be like her, to be popular on Instagram, to collaborate with brands.

If I were to compare us for a moment... pretty much every single thing that Sunshine posts online goes viral, with the likes and adoring comments flooding in. I went viral once, when I was caught on the big screen at a football match, seemingly picking my nose (in my defence, it was summer and a tiny fly flew up there).

Sunshine is an investor and designer at fast-fashion retailer ABO. I suppose I too am an investor at ABO, in a way, because I am almost always waiting on refunds for items I have returned from orders that I couldn't really afford.

And then there is just how effortlessly stylish she is. My style has been described as effortless too, just, you know, when effortless means without effort. Sunshine is like caviar. I genuinely am a potato in comparison – and I thought Nathan was a potato kind of guy. He has expensive taste, sure, don't we all (at least try to), but he also tends to prefer the simple things in life. He always acted like he was actively turned off by clout-chasing influencers – people online who would say and do all sorts to get attention – and he's always looked down his nose at reality TV. That's what makes it hurt all the more, than he must really love Sunshine, to pull such a 180 on everything I thought he believed in.

'I'll go get your colour mixed up,' I tell Gwen, who is already engrossed in something on her phone.

I walk across the busy salon towards the back room where we mix the colours.

The salon itself is a sleek, modern place, filled with high-end decor and chatter from the well-heeled clientele. Owned by Tom Olsen, one of the top stylists here, it's no wonder so many people come here again and again. Tom is the only person I trust to do my blonde balayage, and I can only afford him because I get staff discount. Honestly, the clientele here have more money than sense – sometimes literally, in the case of Gwen, who would happily see me make her bald at her own direction (but then completely hit the roof after, obviously).

Inside the back room I find Tom himself and Zoe, another stylist, having a chat as Zoe cuts lengths of foil.

'So, come on, how were drinks with your ex last night?' he asks me, cutting to the chase, always one to lap up the gossip. I suppose, being a hairdresser, you get a real appetite for it.

'Oh, only about as awkward as you can imagine it being,' I reply. 'I somehow managed to make it look like I was flirting with a man old enough to be my dad. They must think I'm so desperate for a plus-one for this wedding. I couldn't have made myself seem more generally undesirable.'

'Gigi, you are not undesirable,' Zoe corrects me firmly. 'Don't be so hard on yourself. You just need to find a decent date for the wedding. A really decent one.'

'How hard can it be?' Tom says. 'I'd go with you, just for the free holiday.'

'Hmm, except, not only are you married, but Nathan knows you and that you are my boss,' I remind him. 'I don't think Nathan or your wife would be impressed with that one.'

'Fair point,' he chuckles. 'Well, why not try Matcher? You could advertise yourself as a free holiday to a luxury resort in Hawaii. Trust me, you'd have more blokes than you could get through in a night.'

I snort as I shake my head vehemently. I really can't see a dating app like Matcher being the answer to my prayers.

'No way, Tom,' I insist. 'Matcher is already a nightmare without adding crazies looking for free holidays to the mix.'

'Ignore his ideas,' Zoe says with a roll of her eyes. 'Just keep putting yourself out there, Gigi, and stop looking so hard. True love will find you.'

'Except she doesn't need true love; she needs a truly impressive date,' Tom replies. 'Sunshine Greene is hot, and every guy wants her, every girl wants to be her. She needs something serious to compete with that.'

'Okay, okay, I get it,' I reply with a laugh.

I mean, it's all true, and it's not exactly funny, but I can't deny the sheer absurdity of the situation.

'I'd better get back to my lady,' I say with a sigh. 'We're going from jet black to ash blonde.'

'Of course you are,' Tom says, laughing me out of the room.

Tom is right. What I need is not any old plus-one for this wedding, but a super-special one, someone who is going to make Sunshine Greene look like a nobody. Easier said than done, though, right?

Ah well, if all else fails, I suppose there is always Matcher, even if inviting someone insane to the wedding is the last thing I want to do. It is still on the list, though.

3

Arriving home to the comforting aroma of Mum's cooking wafting through the air is something I could get used to – well, I suppose I am used to it now, whether I want to be or not. Yep, I'm back living with my mum and dad, the undynamic duo, who are – it turns out – really appreciating having me living back at home with them because my mum says it gives her something to keep her busy and my dad says it makes Mum cook better food. I like to think they enjoy my company too but no one has said that out loud yet.

Living here is not exactly where I thought I'd be at this stage in my life, but hey-ho, life can be like this sometimes, right? And all you can do is head back to the nest and regroup before you head back out into the big bad world again. I had hoped that I would've flown the nest again by now, given that I moved in here in November, post-break-up, and we're now in April, but finding somewhere that I can afford on my own in London, that isn't awful, that isn't a million miles from where I work, is proving rather difficult. There's also the fact that, if I'm being totally honest, I do feel comfortable here. I've got my feet under the table. With Mum in full-blown nurturing mode, almost all of the 'adulting' is off my plate. I know, it sounds bad, but I'm finding that, while I'm at work, all of the washing, cooking and cleaning is taken care of, so all that's left for me to do is turn up, eat dinner and then watch hours of quiz shows with my dad – just like I did when I was a teenager.

This house – a detached on a picturesque new-build estate – isn't the house I grew up in, my mum and dad bought it a few years ago. In a way that feels better than if I were staying in my childhood bedroom, because that really would feel like a regression.

The house is set across three floors and with my parents preferring to sleep on the second floor, they have assigned me the top floor all to myself. There is a bedroom – the biggest bedroom in the house – complete with its own stunning en suite. Obviously I would rather circumstances were different generally but, looking at things simply, this is easily the nicest bedroom I've been able to call my own.

Thinking back to when I was a kid, I don't know how the four of us coped in our old three-bed house, where scheduling bathroom time was always a military operation. It's only when you're trying to share one bathroom between four people on, say, a morning when everyone is getting ready to go out for the day, that you really test every organisational skill you have. Lucy and I were always arguing over the bath, fighting over who got to use it first, and whoever was going second would always be watching the clock like a hawk. That was probably the only thing we used to fall out over though (well, that and maybe occasionally because we would borrow one another's clothes without asking), we've always been like best friends.

I'm almost scared to admit it, but I'm enjoying the break, and after a bad break-up and getting shafted by all of the knock-on bullshit that comes with it, it's nice to cosplay as a teenager again.

If there is anything positive to take away from this ordeal it is knowing that, in the future – and brace yourselves, because this is low-key depressing – I'm going to make sure I always have a plan of action that stops me ending up out on my arse. Yeah, I know, it's not ideal to go into a relationship thinking about what you will do if it all goes tits up, but living with Nathan in his apartment meant that when we broke up his life (apart from my presence) stayed otherwise identical, but for me I became homeless, I didn't have the funds or the foresight to find somewhere else, so here I am.

I should also probably stop calling it a break-up, as though it was at all mutual, because the reality is that I got dumped.

Nathan, in his infinite wisdom, decided that the spark had gone from our relationship, and that we weren't right for each other. I found it interesting, mainly because I never considered us to have that elusive spark. Nathan wasn't a sparky kind of guy.

When we first met, sure, I was drawn to his brooding, strong, and silent demeanour, thinking it made him seem mysterious and sexy. However, it turned out, he was just generally moody, enjoying his own space and peace and quiet – which is not all that sexy, but everyone is entitled to their boundaries. That's why seeing him with a shiny young thing like Sunshine is so surprising. I accepted Nathan for who he was, loving him regardless, for four years. But he seems to think love is something more spectacular and less comfortable. Perhaps it is.

The main reason things are so shit post-break-up is just how much things have changed for me. Nathan may be basking in Sunshine but I'm very much out in the cold. Socially I'm suffering, feeling a big hole in my life, missing the days when we were the fab foursome – me and Nathan, Lucy and Rick. We used to spend so much time together. Now – ha – now Sunshine has replaced me. I can tell that Lucy feels bad about hanging out with her but I've always encouraged her, telling her it's fine, because it's not her fault, and it's not Sunshine's fault. But now I'm a double whammy of both awkward around Nathan and no longer part of a couple –

so couply activities are definitely out. You really don't miss couples' bowling until someone takes it away from you.

Ted, my parents' Labrador, greets me by the door. What I would give to be with someone who was essentially Ted in man form – he's so sweet, so loyal, always so pleased to see me. I drop to my knees and ruffle his ears and he frantically tries to kiss me. Again, if only I could find myself a man like this. I promise him I will take him for a walk after dinner before I follow my nose to the dining room. Dad is in his seat, at the head of the table, while Mum is putting the finishing touches on the table settings.

'Perfect timing, I'm just about to take the chicken out,' my mum, Shirley, says as she spots me.

The smell of my mum's cooking greets me like a much-needed hug. Then, of course, my mum heads over to give me an actual hug.

Despite being in her sixties, she defies the usual image of someone her age. There's a genuine youthfulness about her that I secretly hope runs in the family – maybe I've inherited some of those genes if I'm lucky (although historically, I never am).

'What's on the menu tonight?' I ask, taking my usual spot next to Dad.

'Chicken in white wine sauce,' Dad replies, playfully rolling his eyes into the back of his head. 'Home is where the heartburn is.'

Alfie, my dad, is also in his sixties but isn't exactly passing for younger like my mum is. In fact, he seems to be on a mission to set about proving the opposite. There's a cute and charming quality in the way he's eagerly embracing his twilight years a bit sooner than expected. Retired and living his post-work life to the fullest, Dad's hobbies include fishing, gardening, and not only listening to the radio in his shed but actively getting into arguments with it. It's like he's fully made peace with his inner grumpy old man, though, truth be told, he's more laid-back than grumpy. I'm pretty sure that he survives on a mixture of oxygen, my mum's cooking, and telling dad jokes.

My mum smiles proudly as she places the food down on the table. The rich aroma of her famous chicken in white wine sauce fills the room, making my stomach do a happy little dance. Honestly, this is the post-break-up life.

'How was work, love?' my mum asks as she serves up the vegetables.

'Oh, fine,' I reply. 'The usual, really. Is it just the three of us tonight?'

Lucy has been dropping by for dinner more and more as the wedding is fast approaching – kick-off is in less than two weeks. We've all been talking about it for so long, it's hard to believe it's almost here.

'Yes, just us,' Mum confirms. 'How are you feeling about the wedding?'

'Yeah, can't wait,' I reply, putting on my bravest of brave faces. 'I'm really looking forward to it.'

If only my tone matched the enthusiasm I'm desperately trying to convey. It's not that I'm not happy for Lucy and Rick, of course I am. I was previously really looking forward to their wedding, when everything was fine and the wedding gift I was taking them didn't come with a barrel full of awkwardness.

'Did you manage to book a single, er, a room for yourself, love?' she asks, quickly changing her choice of words as she goes.

A single room for a single girl, because the room I was originally staying in was booked by Nathan over a year ago, for the two of us, but now obviously he's sharing with Sunshine.

'Yeah, all sorted,' I reply, giving my best reassuring smile.

Mum nods, taking her seat, and you can tell by the look on her face that she's trying to work out how to say the other thing that she wants to say. I already know what it is, but even having that extra time doesn't help me come up with a decent answer.

Ted grumbles from under the table.

'He's hungry,' Dad points out.

'I know, I was going to feed him, but – have you seen the dog bowl?' she asks him.

Dad smiles to himself smugly for a second.

'No,' he blurts in disbelief. 'I didn't even realise he could.'

Mum sighs so deeply it blows the dad joke right out of the room.

'So, are you bringing a plus-one to the wedding?' she asks, trying to act like she's not all that bothered if I answer at all.

'Obviously not,' my dad answers on my behalf. 'She's not going to take someone she's just met, is she? And we know she isn't seeing anyone.'

I shoot him a look, feigning offence.

'Oh yeah, how do you know?' I half ask, half protest.

'I know because you live with us,' he reminds me. 'You never go out, you never bring anyone home. Unless it's one of those internet boyfriends...'

I have no idea what he means by the term 'internet boyfriend' but I can't say I'm not into it – it sounds like it might be preferable.

I laugh it off.

'Guys, look, you don't need to worry about me,' I insist. 'I am actually really looking forward to the wedding – and the trip to Hawaii – and my plus-one situation is all taken care of – in fact, my plus-one is a surprise, so you'll just have to wait and see.'

'Ooh, who could it be?' Mum says excitedly.

'You'll just have to wait and see,' I repeat myself cryptically.

I mean, that's not untrue, my plus-one is going to be a surprise. For them and for me.

4

'Okay, lovely, I'll get a towel on you, then you can head back to the chair,' I tell my client as I finish rinsing her hair at the sink. The water cascades down, carrying away any remaining traces of conditioner. I wrap her hair up in a towel before grabbing another one to dry my hands.

The salon is busy today, alive with the gentle hum of hairdryers, the snip of scissors, and the usual lively mixture of conversation.

As I get to work on detangling my client's hair, I catch fragments of conversation floating around the salon. One of the things I love about working here, with so many different and interesting clients, is listening in on their conversations, like episodes of a podcast that I can tune in and out of, depending on which one interests me.

'That's wild,' Zoe exclaims.

'It's a funny coincidence,' Tom replies. 'I wonder if she knows.'

Our eyes meet as I continue my work – it's always fun brushing out the backcombing after a full head of balayage.

'Gigi, have you seen the news today?' Tom asks me.

'Nope,' I reply firmly, shaking my head. 'I'm on a full news and social media self-imposed blackout.'

'Wow, really?' Reanna, one of the new trainees, interjects with curiosity, her voice squeaking with disbelief.

Reanna, with her multicoloured hair and Gen Z directness, radiates self-confidence. I often wonder if I was born ten years later if I would have that generation's natural self-assurance. I could really do with some at the moment.

'What, completely? Still?' Zoe chimes in. 'So you won't have heard that The Burnouts are doing a reunion tour and a new album?'

'No, but thanks for telling me – I loved The Burnouts,' I confess with a smile.

'I think my mum loved them,' Reanna adds.

Yikes, that makes me feel dated.

'I loved them too,' my client adds, jumping into the conversation. 'That Dylan – phwoar.'

'Yeah, but apparently he's a good boy now,' Zoe replies. 'So my fantasy of him pulling me from the crowd and making mad, passionate love to me backstage feels pretty dead in the water.'

I smile. That's another thing I love about working here – every day is a laugh. It reminds me of school sometimes, all of us going through the motions, doing our work, but having a genuine giggle doing it. I actually look forward to coming to work each day.

'So, why are you avoiding the news and your socials?' Reanna asks, clearly puzzled why someone would do such a thing.

'Because her ex is dating Sunshine Greene,' Tom tells her, unsuccessfully stifling a grin.

I give him a dirty look as he wanders off to answer the salon phone.

Reanna's eyes widen in disbelief.

'No freaking way,' she exclaims. 'I'm dead.'

'Yep, it's hilarious,' I reply with a sarcastic chuckle. 'My ex left me for the most perfect woman on the planet – har-har.'

Reanna seems genuinely sympathetic.

'No, for real, that is pretty savage,' she points out.

'Have you thought about what you're going to do about the wedding?' Zoe asks me.

I head over to them, to nab some heat protection from Zoe's station.

'My plan is still to find an impressive date for myself,' I confess, not sounding at all confident about the plan. 'I just have no idea how I'll do that.'

'I know a guy,' Reanna says simply.

'You know a guy?' I echo.

'Yeah, you know Doctor Mad? I know him,' she reveals, and by the tone of her voice, I imagine I'm supposed to know who he is too.

I stare at her, processing the information, but I can't find a file on anyone called Doctor Mad in my brain. I'm going to have to own my uncoolness and confess.

'I don't know who that is,' I admit.

'You don't know Doctor Mad? He's a YouTuber,' Reanna replies, taking her phone from her pocket, and tapping it with her insanely long nails. 'His channel is so good. Here, look...'

She holds up the phone for me and Zoe to see.

'Oh, wow, he's cute,' Zoe says excitedly.

Doctor Mad – which I'm assuming isn't his real name – is in his late twenties, with a trendy modern mullet and a nose ring. It's a look that definitely works for him.

Reanna may not have the sound on, but the scene of him at a table with four other guys, laughing and joking, makes him look like a lot of fun.

'Wow, is that how many views he gets?' I blurt out, my eyes

widening at the impressive number displayed on the screen as Reanna closes the video.

'Yep,' Reanna replies with certainty. 'He's a big deal.'

'How do you know him?' Zoe asks curiously.

'He's my brother's best mate,' she reveals proudly, 'and the last time I saw him, he was ranting about how hard it is to find a nice, normal girl now that his account has blown up. Want me to set you up with him?'

'Oh, I don't know about that,' I reply hesitantly, laughing it off.

'Go on,' Zoe encourages me with a mischievous glint in her eye. 'This is exactly what you need – imagine turning up to the wedding with someone like him – a YouTuber is way cooler than a *Welcome to Singledom* contestant.'

'I need to dry my lady's hair,' I tell them with a smile, heading back over to my chair.

'Come on, Gigi, give him a chance,' Reanna persists. 'Let me drop him a message.'

I wince as I feel myself coming around to the idea.

'Okay,' I reluctantly agree. 'Do it, before I can change my mind.'

'What is she doing?' Tom asks as he joins the conversation.

'I'm drying my lady's hair,' I inform him, changing the subject.

'And she's going on a date with Doctor Mad,' Reanna adds, smiling widely as she taps away on her phone.

'What?' Tom blurts out. 'Doctor Mad? How?'

'Reanna knows him,' Zoe explains.

'Well, can you get him to come here, for his hair?' Tom suggests. 'It can't hurt to have more high-profile clientele.'

'And they are the only ones who can afford your prices,' Zoe jokes.

I leave them to their playful banter and get back to work. As I dry my lady's hair, I can't help but fantasise about turning up to the wedding with a cool YouTuber on my arm. Even if people haven't heard of him, I would only need to mention what he does, and his hits would speak for themselves, right? Nervous energy surges through my veins, making my hands feel shaky, but not for the typical reasons people worry about before a date. Sure, I want him to like me – well, I need him to like me. The thought of moving on for real churns my stomach, but an impressive no-strings wedding date is just what I need.

Assuming Doctor Mad says yes, of course.

5

'So, are you a real doctor?' I ask jokily.

I'm sitting in a restaurant, a funky burger place I haven't been to before, across the table from Doctor Mad, whose real name turns out to be Lewis.

The place is super-cool, with graffiti-style murals on the walls, mismatched furniture, and an array of quirky decorations everywhere the eye can see. Neon signs add a vibrant glow to the room, and the menu is filled with creative burger combinations that were almost impossible to choose between. It's the kind of place where the vibe is just as important as the food.

'No, not a real doctor,' he replies with a laugh.

So far, I've learned that making videos is Lewis's full-time job, and he's clearly way into it because he gets so excited when he talks about it, and he hasn't really asked any questions about me yet, preferring to talk about himself. If this were a real first date, and I could afford to be choosy, Lewis wouldn't be doing all that well so far. But the night is young, and the food is imminent. It would have to be one hell of a bad date for me to walk away from the double cheeseburger and sweet potato fries I've ordered. I can practically smell it coming.

'Reanna said you do hair too,' Lewis eventually says, turning the conversation to me.

'That's right,' I reply.

'What do you think I should do with my hair next?' he asks me. 'I thought I might do a video where I let someone shave my head, for charity maybe.'

And the topic of conversation is right back to him again.

As Lewis messes with his phone, I look around the room to see if the food is on its way. It says a lot – and none of it good – when the food is more exciting than the person you're sitting with. Sure enough, a server is heading our way with two large plates.

'Nice one,' Lewis says as she places the plates down in front of us.

'Yes, thank you,' I add.

God, it smells good. I grab a sweet potato fry and dip it in some tomato sauce before popping it in my mouth. Wow, it's glorious. Just the right combination of crispy on the outside and fluffy on the inside.

Lewis removes the top from his burger and begins to peel the slice of cheese off from on top of the meat. I watch him, captivated, as he pops it in his mouth before returning the lid to his burger.

I cock my head and narrow my eyes as I watch him flag down a server.

'Excuse me, this is supposed to be a cheeseburger,' he tells her, 'but there's no cheese on it.'

'Oh, I'm so sorry, let me get that sorted for you,' she says, her expression apologetic, as she takes his plate back to the kitchen.

I just stare at him for a moment.

'Can I have a chip?' he asks me, offering no explanation. 'I'm starving.'

I nod towards my plate, by way of saying yes, because I can't get any words to come out of my mouth.

'Thanks,' he replies.

I pick up my burger and take a bite. It tastes just as delicious as it looks with meat cooked to perfection, partially melted cheese, and pickles, which I know some people hate, but I love them.

Eventually, the server returns with Lewis's burger and sets it down in front of him.

'Here we go, so sorry for the mix-up,' she tells him.

'No problem at all,' Lewis replies. 'Cheers.'

I eat a couple more chips, trying to relax. But then I notice Lewis, once again, remove the top from his burger, peel the cheese away, eat it, and then return the lid.

My jaw drops as I watch him flag a different server down. Is he fucking serious right now?

'Excuse me, pal, this is supposed to be a cheeseburger, but there's no cheese in it,' he tells him.

'Sorry, bud, I'll get that sorted for you,' the server replies, taking Lewis's plate and dashing off to the kitchen with it, keen to sort the problem.

Lewis smiles to himself.

'Another chip?' he asks me optimistically.

'Sorry, what are you doing?' I can't help but ask.

'I'm seeing how much free cheese I can get,' he replies, as though it's a perfectly normal thing to say, and he's confused as to why I'm even asking.

'Why?' I blurt, my eyes wide, my voice a little manic.

'Pranking is my thing, it's my brand,' he tells me, as though I should already know that fact. 'This is the kind of thing my fans love to see me do – I've got to keep the content coming, I have a schedule.'

I follow his gaze as it briefly flits to his phone, which I notice is standing up against his water glass, facing him.

'Are you filming this?' I ask in absolute disbelief.

'Yeah,' he replies – again, like it's a totally normal thing to do. 'My phone films me, and this pin badge on my jacket is actually a camera. Check it, but don't make it obvious.'

I peer down the lens of the camera that is hiding behind the metal pin badge – of an old-school camera, which is almost offensively on the nose – and then look at him again.

'I can blur your face in the video if you don't want to be in it,' he tells me, as though that's a reasonable thing to say too.

'Yeah, please do,' I insist firmly. 'This definitely isn't my brand.'

'Fair enough,' he replies as he looks over my shoulder, waiting for his burger to return.

I pick up my burger and take another bite, intending to make short work of it and then make an excuse about needing to go home early. Lewis and his pranks are absolutely not my cup of tea at all, in fact, I feel so uncomfortable. These poor people are just trying to do their jobs in a busy place – they don't need someone like Lewis coming in, acting the clown, making everything harder than it needs to be. Is this funny? Like, is it actually funny to anyone? Sometimes I'm never quite sure if I'm just getting older, or if stuff like this doesn't appeal to anyone – then again, with the views he gets, there clearly is a market for it.

While Lewis may well be an impressive date to take to Lucy and Rick's wedding, he would probably just mine it for content and ruin the whole thing. I would never take a chance with Lucy's big day like that, no matter how much I want to show Nathan that I've moved on, and I can bag myself impressive dates too.

As Lewis's burger is returned to him, and I watch as he once again begins the ritual of removing the cheese, I sigh to myself.

Nope, this isn't going to work. Not at all.

6

'Wait, what?' Tom says, disbelief etched across his face as he hovers his scissors tentatively above his client's head.

Even the man in his chair, who is currently mid-haired, joins the collective stare-down, his eyes locking on to mine in the mirror. Ah well, at least my disastrous date was good for something, it's keeping everyone entertained today. I've got everyone around me on the hook, waiting for the next instalment of the cringy saga.

'Oh, no, you heard me right,' I say, adding a dash of theatrical flair. 'He kept asking, again and again, for more cheese in his burger. Eating it, then asking again, and again, and again.'

'Well, yeah, that's his vibe,' Reanna chimes in, bobbing her head with an air of nonchalant wisdom. She seems mildly surprised that the rest of us aren't connecting the dots. 'He makes funny videos, but he's a prank artist at heart, so it's a big part of his content – *obviously*.'

'On a date, though?' Tom says, his scissors still in suspense.

'I guess it's a great cover,' Reanna explains with a shrug. 'Makes it look more legit, you know?'

'So, what did you do?' Zoe, who is currently sitting in his chair, asks. She literally moves to the edge of her seat as she waits to find out.

'I ate my burger – obviously – and then I made an excuse that I had to go,' I say. 'I put down some money for my food and then I got the hell out of there.'

'I've seen a video where he and his mates took turns kicking each other in the nuts to see who was the last man standing,' Tom's client tells us. 'He won.'

'Well, thank God you didn't sleep with him, then,' Tom jests, his scissors snipping through the air. 'It sounds like his equipment has taken a beating.'

I can't help but wince at the vivid mental image.

'He probably would have filmed it for his channel,' Zoe adds, her tone a mix of humour and horror.

'Yeah, just pranking you throughout,' Tom chips in, his banter doing little to ease the cringeworthy scenario playing out in my mind.

'I'm sorry it didn't work out, Gigi,' Reanna says sincerely. 'I tried.'

'You did, thank you,' I assure her, appreciating the effort. Her heart was in the right place, even if Lewis did turn out to be a bit of a nightmare date. She's his friend, how was she to know what he would be like in that sort of setting? Like, if I set someone up on a date with a friend who was a surgeon, I wouldn't expect them to bring a scalpel and cut them open between courses.

'So, what's the plan now?' Tom asks curiously.

I sigh as Zoe, Tom and his client all look at me expectantly. I do think it's funny how, whoever is in our chairs when we are chatting becomes a sort of extension of us, bringing them into the conversation. Sometimes it's useful, to have that hive mind – in fact, it was one of Zoe's clients who alerted Erin (one of the other stylists here) to the fact that she couldn't eat gluten, just by overhearing one of her conversations.

'I have no idea,' I admit, my mind trying to block the cringy flashbacks from my date last night. It is probably worth pointing out (and this is something I'm only just realising myself now) that last night was my first date since Nathan and I broke up. I suppose it didn't feel like a real date, because the plan is to find a plus-one, not a boyfriend, but still, it has definitely put me off the idea of moving on.

'The chances I'll find a date – a really good one – in a matter of days are slim,' I tell them. 'I mean, the chances I could find any date don't seem ideal. Perhaps I could go alone, hold my head up high, show them that I don't care?'

'Yeah, that could work,' Zoe chimes in encouragingly. 'You don't need a man.'

'Do you think?' I glance at Tom and Zoe, hoping for a confidence boost, but their expressions aren't exactly reassuring.

'I know, I could see if I've got any high-profile clients coming in over the next week,' Tom suggests. 'And if not, I could see if any of them would be willing to move their appointments – we could orchestrate your very own meet-cute.'

'Wow, Tom Olsen, hairdresser *and* matchmaker,' Zoe teases, a playful smile on her face. 'That could be a good idea, though. Tom definitely knows some people. You just need to catch their attention.'

'Right, yes, because of all the people in this salon, I'm the one who turns heads,' I quip sarcastically. 'Not any of the gorgeous women who work here, or the stunners that come here only to leave looking even more attractive than when they came in.'

'Some people are into all sorts,' Tom jokes, his humour trying to help me through my self-deprecation.

'Which is his rude, jokey way of saying: don't be so hard on yourself,' Zoe adds, always the voice of reason. She pauses as she thinks for a moment. 'Have you thought of going to any celebrity hang-outs, or anywhere rich people hang out?'

'Yeah, here's the thing about that, how is a nobody like me going to get into the kind of areas where celebrities or rich people hang out?' I say, pointing out the flaw in her plan.

'I'll have a think,' Zoe declares confidently.

'And I'll see who I can scramble,' Tom adds, his commitment evident. 'We've got your back, Gigi.'

'Thanks,' I say, laughing it off, but with a hint of genuine gratitude too.

I'm so fortunate to have the support of my friends, but the reality is sinking in, and it's not looking good. For any of this to work, I'm going to need more than just creativity and a bit of charm, what I need is some luck – something that is definitely in short supply for me this year.

And, if I can't manifest some good luck, then the only other thing that could work is a miracle. It really will be a miracle, if I don't wind up at this wedding alone.

7

As we take in aisle after aisle of another department store, I run my hands across yet another rail of brightly coloured sarongs. It's only April, so summer hasn't exactly arrived in London yet, but the shops are stocked so that people can prepare for their holidays, which is lucky for us, shopping for the last bits we need for Hawaii. We know exactly what we need so we're on a mission, weaving our way through displays of sundresses, bikinis, and sandals, picking up last-minute essentials, and trying not to get distracted by shopping for things we don't need. Of course, we keep failing, getting distracted by brightly coloured things, testing perfumes, and trying things on.

Lucy's fingers dance over the array of swimsuits, her eyes lighting up at the tropical prints and bold colours on offer.

'What about this one?' she asks – briefly breaking from talking about the wedding – as she holds up a playful bikini adorned with pineapples. 'It's perfect for Maui, right?'

I laugh.

'Very bridal,' I tease.

She grins, tossing it into her shopping basket, and then her attention is captured by a rack of sunglasses. She grabs an oversized pair – the kind celebrities like to hide from the paparazzi behind – with smoky brown glass and gold details. She puts them on and looks at them in the mirror, striking a serious pose.

'No photos, no photos,' she says, like a Hollywood starlet. 'At least I'm not going to need these at the resort.'

'Why, have you developed UV-resistant eyeballs?' I joke, not entirely sure what she means by that.

'Very funny,' Lucy replies as she returns them to the rack. 'No, because the resort is so exclusive. The press aren't allowed anywhere near, and the guests know that discretion is key – not that it's a problem for me and you but, honestly, Sunshine is so relieved. We really lucked out with where we chose. She might not be coming if we were getting married somewhere she could be mobbed. I just want everyone to feel comfortable on my big day.'

I can't help but let out a little sigh, an involuntary response to the mention of Sunshine, Nathan's new flame. I don't mean for Lucy to notice but she does.

'Are you really okay with all of this, Gi?' Lucy checks, sincerity in her eyes.

I offer her a reassuring smile.

'Absolutely,' I tell her firmly, keeping my smile fixed in place. 'It's your big day, and I'm genuinely looking forward to being a part of it. Okay, it's been a bit tough since Nathan and I split, and the idea of him and Sunshine being there isn't exactly at the top of my wish list. But I understand that he is Rick's best friend, so he should be there. I want you two to have the most amazing wedding, and forget about my drama, because that's not what this trip is about. As long as you and Rick are happy, that's all that matters to me.'

Lucy seems a little comforted by my words, but I can tell she's still worried.

'Promise me, Gi?' she persists. 'You're my sister and I love you to bits. My wedding day wouldn't be right without you being a part of it – and actually enjoying it, obviously.'

I give her a reassuring squeeze on the shoulder.

'One hundred per cent,' I insist. 'That's why I'm trying to find myself the perfect beach hat – it's the only thing I don't have. Then I'll be destination wedding ready.'

Lucy laughs.

'Mum and Dad mentioned that you're bringing a mystery plus-one,' she says. 'Am I allowed to know any more detail than that, or is it a surprise for me too? You don't have to tell me. Genuinely, you could turn up with one of my ex-boyfriends, and I wouldn't care. All I care about is that you enjoy this day as much as I do. I've been really worrying about it. It's a relief, if you are bringing someone, if I'm being honest.'

Ever since Nathan and I broke up, Lucy has reassured me that it didn't matter when I decided, that I would be welcome to bring a plus-one, because she would be ordering extra meals and keeping extra spaces at one of the guest tables just in case, because she wanted to make sure that anyone who wasn't certain if they could come could make up their mind at the last minute. So, knowing that I don't need to tell her for the numbers, what's the sense in owning up to her that I don't have anyone to bring with me? Look at her face, you can tell how relieved she is that I might be finally moving on from Nathan. I don't have the heart to take that away from her, all I can do is play along.

'Just wait and see,' I tell her with a smile. 'It can be a surprise for you too!'

As her relief shifts to genuine happiness, I know that it was the right thing to do, to string her along for a bit longer. She wraps her arms around me in a tight hug.

'Thank you,' she says into my shoulder. 'I want this to be perfect for you too.'

But as Lucy pulls away, I notice a shift in her expression. Happiness flickers into something more vulnerable, and before I can figure out what's going on, tears brim in her eyes.

'Hey, what's up?' I ask her.

'I'm just... I'm so glad you're happy and moving on,' she blurts. 'I've been so caught up in planning and making sure everything's perfect that I haven't checked in on you. I'm sorry, Gigi. It's the best wedding gift you could give me, to know that you're bringing a date. I want you to enjoy every moment and not worry about anything else.'

'Oh, well, I guess I'll return that expensive gift I bought you two,' I joke, lightening the mood.

'Don't you dare,' she replies, laughing through her tears.

'How are you feeling about the wedding?' I ask her, because it's always worth checking.

It's a relief when her face lights up.

'I'm really looking forward to it,' she says. 'I'm not nervous at all, and now that I know you're happy, everything's fallen into place. I can't wait to marry Rick. I can't believe it's happening!'

'Well, there you go,' I tell her. 'It's all going to be great. Why don't we take a break from shopping, and go and grab a coffee and a slice of cake?'

'I would love that,' she says, wiping her tears away. 'Sorry for the dramatics. I just feel like a huge weight has been lifted off my mind.'

'Don't apologise,' I say with a smile. 'Come on, let's go.'

We're in the Olive Strand department store, known for its award-winning café, so we can pause what we're doing and take a break. I need a breather, to be honest, because putting on a brave face is exhausting.

One thing I am certain of is that Lucy cannot find out that I don't have a date, not yet. Fair enough, if I don't find someone to take, she will find out eventually, but we'll be in Maui for a week before the big day, which should give me a chance to show her that I can be around Nathan and Sunshine and be absolutely fine with it. The last thing I want, right now, is for her to be worrying about me, when she should be looking forward to her big day.

But, just in case all of the above doesn't work, it's probably best I keep trying to find someone to take with me, because that's the easiest way to get through all this.

Wow, I knew weddings were stressful, I just always thought if one was going to stress me out, it would be my own.

8

As I push my way through the salon doors, bum first, carefully clutching my handbag, my phone and my iced coffee, I'm surprised when I spin around to see Tom waiting to greet me. He never greets me at the door on a morning, especially not with a big dumb grin on his face like he has right now.

'Good morning,' I offer with a laugh, amused by... whatever it is he's doing.

'Oh, Gigi,' he says with a suspicious grin. 'I have the answer to all your problems.'

Yep, that's cryptic enough to be terrifying.

'Oh, really?' I reply, widening my eyes for dramatic effect. 'How so?'

Tom taps his nose before walking away, smiling widely to himself.

I guess I'll worry about that later at some point – yet another thing to schedule. And to think, I was actually going to get a decent lunch break today.

I shrug it off for now and head to the back room, putting down my bag and jacket before taking a big drink of my coffee. Lattes all winter and then, as soon as there is a sniff of sunshine, I switch to iced coffees again. I can't start my day without one or the other, though. The thought of running around this place all day, without a few shots of caffeine in me, sounds impossible.

I head back to reception where I find my first client of the day, pop star Kelly Parker, here for her latest transformation. She's a regular of mine – in fact, she almost feels like a friend. She even follows me on Instagram. That's when you know you have a great stylist/client bond.

I greet her with a smile.

'Hey, Kelly,' I say, kissing her on both cheeks.

'Hi, babes,' she replies. 'I couldn't be more ready for this – look at my roots.'

She pulls off her trendy trucker cap to reveal hair that, to be honest, most people would be over the moon with.

'What are we thinking today, Kelly?' I ask, eager to get started, as I lead her over to my chair.

'Well, I'm thinking with summer coming up, it might be nice to go a bit lighter,' she says. 'Maybe some blonde highlights?'

'I think that would look gorgeous,' I tell her.

It's amazing how many people lighten and darken their hair with the seasons. It's great, though, it really feels like you shake up your look, and the ritualistic part of it is exciting. I get giddy for summer or Christmas accordingly.

'I'll go mix your colour,' I tell her. 'Can I get you a drink?'

Kelly flashes her water bottle at me.

'I'm good, thanks,' she says with a smile.

I mix the colour and cut long lengths of foil to accommodate Kelly's super-long hair, and then head back out.

When I return, I find Tom deeply engaged in what seems like his favourite pastime – interrogating clients about their holiday plans. I can't help but chuckle; it's the cliché hairdresser's question, and Tom executes it with the precision and seriousness of a seasoned professional.

'I'm going to LA for a few months, but just for work,' Kelly tells him.

'I wish I could just go to LA for work,' he says with a sigh. 'I'm stuck here. Gigi is going to Hawaii.'

'Oh, really?' Kelly says.

'Yeah, for my sister's wedding,' I reply, realising my voice isn't laced with the level of enthusiasm you might expect.

'Oh,' Kelly says simply, picking up on a vibe.

'Her ex-boyfriend is the best man,' Tom tells her. 'And his new girlfriend is Sunshine Greene.'

'Yikes, that's tough to top,' Kelly replies, clenching her jaw.

'It's actually impossible to top,' I tell her. 'I even went on a date with a YouTube prankster, in an attempt to turn up with a date who might be even a little bit impressive, but it was a disaster. Do you know how hard it is, to find a date with an impressive CV?'

I've just realised how stupid that sounds.

'Wait, of course you don't, you're Kelly Parker,' I tell her, pointlessly, laughing at myself.

'Actually, I do,' she replies as she grabs her phone from her bag. 'Have you heard of One in a Mil?'

'I haven't,' I reply.

'It's a dating app, strictly for celebrities, high-profile individuals, high-net-worth/high-flying businesspeople,' she explains. 'Basically, you have to be very famous or very rich to use it.'

'Oh, perfect for me then,' I joke sarcastically.

Kelly laughs.

'It just might be,' she replies. 'I'm here in your chair for most of the day, right? What if I change my display name and profile pic on the app, so that it looks like it's your profile? It's not like I'm using the app at the moment. I mean, who's going to notice?'

'Who's going to notice that I'm not rich or famous?' I say. 'Anyone with eyes?'

'Airdrop me some photos of yourself,' she demands. 'Actually, I'll just pick some from your Insta. In fact, take a selfie with me too. I'll put on your profile that you are a hairstylist to the stars, because that is true.'

I laugh.

'Do you really think this will work?' I reply.

'Let's give it a go and see,' she says. 'Can I chat on your behalf?'

'Go for it,' I reply. 'I'm probably at my most charming when I'm someone else.'

'Look, this isn't necessary,' Tom interrupts. 'I've got a genuine celeb coming in, any minute, and I'm going to set Gigi up with him.'

'Well, you do that, and I'll do this, and we can see who finds her the better date,' Kelly suggests with a grin.

'Game on,' Tom replies, before heading back to reception.

Game on? *So* happy they're finding my love life so entertaining. But if either of their plans come off, I might be on to something good.

Kelly leans back in the chair, a mischievous glint in her eyes.

'Oh, playing matchmaker for someone else is ten times more entertaining than looking for love for yourself,' she tells me. 'Been there, done that, swore off dating anyone remotely rich or famous ever again. Don't let me put you off, though – this is exactly what you need.'

I just laugh.

'It's fine,' I tell her. 'My situation is... unique. And I would rather you do it for me than I do it for myself. Honestly, the idea of rich and famous people judging me, considering if I'm worthy – it gives me this funny feeling in my stomach.'

'Don't you worry, babes,' she says, waving my worries away

with her free hand. 'I'm crafting your image, as a stylist to the stars, and it's your photos. Technically, it's all true. You might not be splurging on private jets, but you're certainly a star in your own right. Anyone who swipes right on you is doing it for you.'

'Okay,' I reply, unconvinced, as I get to work on her hair.

I try to keep stealing glances at her phone screen but Kelly is like lightning on that thing, swiping at warp speed. I'm just going to assume it's going well.

I hear the door open and then the sound of Tom's voice as he greets his client, so I whip my head around like an owl.

'Kane, hello, mate,' Tom says.

'All right,' Kane replies.

Tom greets the thirty-something man, shaking his heavily tattooed hand.

Kane is tall, with broad shoulders, and a rugged handsomeness that screams rock star.

His jet-black hair falls over his shoulders, a stark contrast to his pale skin which seems to be largely covered with tattoos. He has a lip ring, a nose ring, and more rings in his ears than I can count. His dark eyes hint at a mysterious intensity. They're almost mesmerising.

I watch as Tom leads him to a chair.

'Is that who he's setting you up with?' Kelly asks.

'I guess so,' I reply. 'Do you know who he is?'

'Yeah, he's from a metal band – Chillz, I think they're called,' she tells me. 'I met them once. One of them put the moves on me. Not this one, though. I think it was the singer.'

'Lovely,' I say, raising an eyebrow.

This should be interesting.

'Gigi, do you have a minute?' Tom calls out, beckoning me over.

'Good luck,' Kelly says through a stifled chuckle. 'I'll carry on trying to sort you out a decent date.'

Approaching Tom, I offer a curious smile.

'Yes?' I say simply.

'Gigi, this is Kane, he loves metal music,' Tom introduces with a hint of mischief. 'And I was like, do you know who else loves metal – the biggest metal fan I know – Gigi!'

Kane's lips twitch into a smile, which makes his lip ring move in a way that I'm sure would drive me mad if I had one.

'Really?' Kane says.

'Oh, big time,' I confess – of course, I'm lying. And Tom knows I'm no metal fan. I can't believe he thinks this is going to work.

'Favourite band?' Kane asks, and I momentarily falter, caught off guard by his intense gaze and the fact that I don't think I know any metal bands.

'Aside from yours?' I say with a smile, stalling, trying to buy myself some time.

I notice Kane's T-shirt peeking beneath his leather jacket.

'Probably Megadet,' I confidently declare.

'Megadeth?' he says back to me, assuming he must have misheard me.

Yep, that makes more sense.

'Yes,' I say, trying to maintain my confidence.

Kane smiles widely as he opens his leather jacket to show me his T-shirt.

'Wow,' I exclaim, 'I have that same one at home.'

'Don't tell me this square makes you boring for work?' Kane teases, a playful grin on his face.

He's obviously picking up on the fact that I don't look very metal right now, because I don't now, and I don't ever. I don't know what else to do apart from play along.

'Yep, the loser,' I reply. 'I, obviously, dress much differently – more like you.'

'That I would like to see,' Kane responds, a twinkle in his eye. 'Do you like Kronk Red Meat?'

Is that a band? A food? Something else?

'Do I like Kronk Red Meat?' I repeat back to him with a scoff. 'Er, what do you think?'

Kane's smile somehow grows even wider.

'Of course,' he says. 'I'm going to see them tonight with some friends. Do you want to join us?'

'Oh, Gigi, you would love that,' Tom encourages me. He's also making it impossible for me to say no.

'I would,' I say, injecting genuine enthusiasm into my tone.

Kane is good-looking, he's in a band – this could work.

'Sick,' Kane says. 'Give me your number before I leave, yeah?'

I smile as I head back over to Kelly. There are butterflies in my stomach and a million questions swirling around in my brain – the most important one being: how am I going to pull this off?

Tom quickly catches me up, a triumphant smirk playing on his lips.

'Boom! I've sorted her a date, with a celebrity,' he gloats to Kelly, his voice hushed yet brimming with smug satisfaction.

'So have I,' Kelly replies through a smirk, never one to be outdone. 'One that could walk through a metal detector without setting it off.'

She proudly shows us her phone screen, revealing a photo that momentarily leaves me speechless.

'Oh my God, that's...' I begin, struggling to find words.

'Yep,' Kelly proudly confirms. 'Celebrity chef Roscoe Morrow. And you're having dinner with him – today. He's opening a restaurant at the end of the week, it's not far from here, and he's there today. He says he wants to prepare a tasting menu, for just the two of you.'

'She can't tonight,' Tom says, sounding like my disapproving dad. 'She's going on a date with my guy.'

Kelly laughs, rolling her eyes at Tom as she taps away on her phone.

'Why would Roscoe Morrow want to do that for me?' I can't help but ask.

'I've been flirting up a storm with him, so make sure you're super flirty with him in person too, he's really into it,' she tells me. 'And... yep... he's at the restaurant all day. He says you can go for lunch instead.'

I instinctively look to Tom for his approval – it really does feel like he's my dad now.

'Okay, because it's an emergency,' he reluctantly agrees, adopting a tone that adds a touch of paternal disapproval. 'But hedge your bets, go on both dates – I'm confident mine will be better.'

'I'm definitely going to win this one,' Kelly declares with a smile.

So my love life really is a game now – cool.

Wow, I guess celebrity dates are like buses. You wait around forever and then two come along at once. One of them has to be decent, right?

9

I pinch myself as I stand outside Roscoe Morrow's highly anticipated restaurant, Mare Segreto. I can't believe I'm actually here.

The name of the restaurant hangs above the door in huge silver metal lettering, set against a vibrant blue background that gleams in the sunlight, almost like the ocean does.

I can tell, just by looking at the shiny new exterior, that this place is going to be pure luxury, and oh-so expensive, and here I am in my lightener-flecked work clothes, on what is supposed to be a date with a TV chef. The odds don't feel like they're in my favour, and I couldn't feel less like a catch right now, but I need to back myself.

One of the pros about working in a salon is that I had a whole team of people with the skills to glam me up a bit, ahead of my lunch date, so my hair and make-up looks fabulous. There wasn't much that could be done for my boring, plain black work clothes, but Kelly did insist I borrow her Balmain leather jacket, to 'elevate' my look a little. I'm nervous, sure, and out of my depth? Definitely. But it's amazing how much more confident I feel, for having nice hair, flawless make-up, and a fancy jacket. It's almost like I'm in disguise or armour – like I have some kind of inexplicable tactical advantage, by not being my usual self.

I check my reflection in the large floor-to-ceiling windows, which are blocked by signs teasing that the restaurant is 'opening soon'. It's a deliberate tease, preventing any curious onlookers from sneaking a peek inside, and here I am, getting to waltz straight in – assuming I'm not being catfished, of course, because this just doesn't feel like the sort of thing that happens to me.

I let my imagination run away with me, wondering if this is somehow some kind of elaborate Doctor Mad-style prank, but then the double doors to Mare Segreto swing open, and out walks the man himself, Roscoe Morrow.

As he flashes me a warm, welcoming, made-for-TV smile, I instantly relax – but just a little. I need to be on the top of my game today, I can't afford to relax too much.

Roscoe stands tall, with a posture that is almost exhausting to look at, radiating an air of sophistication that complements the sleek exterior of his restaurant. His neatly trimmed beard adds a touch of rugged charm, and his blue eyes, sparkling with genuine friendliness, instantly make me feel welcome. His salt-and-pepper hair exudes an air of distinction, complementing his perfectly tailored chef whites. He looks every bit the part, and I can now officially add chef to the list of professions I find sexy – come on, a person who cooks food, how am I only just realising that's just my type on paper?

'Gigi?' he checks with a smile.

'Yes, hello,' I reply, offering him a hand to shake, like a total dork.

Roscoe laughs.

'Come inside,' he says, ushering me through the door, closing it quickly behind him before a passer-by can sneak so much as a peek inside.

The inside is just as shiny and new as the exterior, with the silver and blue theme carried throughout. The windows look even bigger from the inside, blocked up like they are now – this place is going to be bathed in natural light when it eventually opens.

With an effortless charm that could win over Gordon Ramsay in a heartbeat, Roscoe leads me on a tour through his new restaurant. I wonder how many people have seen it so far? This feels so intimate and special. Honestly, you would never get a date like this on Matcher – I would say I'll always use this new app from now on, but of course I'm not rich enough to be on it, so this is my one shot at dating someone who isn't going to take me to Nando's.

'Welcome to Mare Segreto,' Roscoe tells me as he guides me through the bar.

I'm relieved to hear him say the name of the place out loud before I had the chance to mispronounce it and embarrass myself.

'It's stunning,' I reply, twirling around on the spot, taking it all in.

Everything looks perfect, which makes me think the big opening must be any day now.

'I'm trying to do something special,' he explains. 'It's not just about the food here; it's an immersive experience.'

'Well, I'm excited that I get to try it,' I say sincerely.

'And I've got the best seat in the house ready, just for you,' he tells me with a proud grin.

After a brief tour, Roscoe leads me into a small, separate room.

'The pièce de résistance,' he announces. 'The chef's table.'

A large table sits in the centre of a room that is tastefully but simply decorated on all sides except one. The table faces a huge set of glass sliding doors that look directly into the kitchen, almost like looking at a huge cinema screen live-streaming the heart of the action.

'Wow,' I blurt.

'It's really something, isn't it?' he says. 'I wanted my guests to be able to see what was going on but, behind the glass doors, you still get the ambience of the restaurant. No kitchen noises, or smells, just luxury. It's not just about the delicious dishes; it's about the entire experience.'

'It's honestly incredible,' I insist.

'Well, madame, if you would like to take your front-row seat,' he says playfully, in his best French accent. 'I can learn more about a woman from watching her eat than I can asking her questions, so how about I whip up your lunch, before you start grilling me, hmm?'

I laugh. I'm a sucker for a pun.

'Okay, sure,' I say excitedly. Well, I am starving.

I take my seat at the centre of the large table as Roscoe disappears behind the glass to do his thing.

Genuinely, it's like being at the ballet, watching him effortlessly dance his way around the kitchen. Dinner and a show – which sounds like exactly what he's going for.

I relax into my plush chair and I still can't believe my luck. A private dining experience, in a yet-to-be-launched restaurant, being cooked for – and waited on – by a renowned celebrity chef. If money could buy an experience like this, I know I wouldn't be able to afford it. This is like my own personal heaven, and Roscoe is even more gorgeous in person. I know that I've been pretty one-track-minded, wanting nothing more than to find a date for the wedding, but... I don't know... maybe moving on might not be so bad after all. Well, I'll have to do it sooner or later, won't I, it's not like Nathan is going to come crawling back (and, even if he did, I should tell him to piss off, right?), and I don't want to be alone for the rest of my days. If I am going to move on, well, perhaps it should be with someone like this? Someone who will sweep me off my feet and show me that they're not all bad, that dating isn't terrifying, and who knows? I might just find myself having fun.

Roscoe joins me again, presenting me with my first dish. It's a work of art, a delicate creation with vibrant colours and intricate details, oh-so fancy, and I have no idea what it is. Still, I can't wait to try it.

'Here we are,' he announces.

'Oh, wow,' I say, not playing it cool at all as I grab my cutlery.

Roscoe takes a seat next to me, sitting sideways so that he can face me. He places an elbow on the table and rests his head on his hands as he gives me a look.

'I honestly don't think there is anything sexier than watching a woman eat,' he says, his voice low and soft. It almost tickles.

'Well then,' I say, trying to muster up a little seductiveness of my own. 'I might just be the love of your life.'

I pop the first bite into my mouth, ready to be wowed, but something isn't right.

The taste registers, and it's unmistakably seafood – the one thing I can't stand. Panic sets in; it's like I'm frozen in time, my tongue rejecting the unwelcome flavour. Across the table, Roscoe gazes at me expectantly, waiting for the positive reaction he's expecting. Oh boy, he's going to be waiting a long time.

I always feel silly, admitting to other grown adults that I don't like any seafood because it makes me seem like a kid that doesn't want to eat their vegetables but something about it just gives me the ick. Which, yep, sounds childish, so there's no way I can admit it now – definitely not to a chef, and especially not to the chef who just prepared it for me.

With no idea what else to do, I knock over my glass of water, to create a distraction.

'Don't worry, I'll grab something,' Roscoe says, ever the gentleman.

I smile, trying to disguise the fact that the food is still in my mouth.

The second he is out of the room I open my handbag and, no, I can't just spit it in there, can I? Before I have to make the tough call, I notice the answer to my prayers: poo bags. Living with my parents means that I take Ted for lots of walks, and I always seem to have poo bags in every bag, coat and trouser pocket I own. I've never been more grateful.

I spit my food into one and then scrape the rest of the food from the plate into there too. I drop it in my handbag and return to a normal, neutral-looking position just as Roscoe arrives back with paper towels.

'Sorry,' I tell him. 'I think I just got overexcited about the food.'

'I can see that,' he says happily. 'You cleared your plate – wow, you even ate the garnish.'

'What can I say, I'm a hungry girl,' I reply.

'You enjoyed it then?' he checks.

'Oh, I loved it,' I lie. 'It was really impressive. The flavour, honestly, I'm speechless.'

Roscoe smiles, genuinely flattered, encouraged by my enthusiasm for his food.

'What could you taste?' he asks curiously.

The sea. Nothing but the sea.

'Ah, well, I was going to ask you that,' I bullshit further. 'Am I detecting a secret ingredient? What is it?'

Is it the sea?

'Ah, now that would be telling,' he says with a wink. 'But, between you and me, I put extra passion into my cuisine, when I'm preparing it for someone special.'

'You know, they say the way to someone's heart is through their stomach,' I say with a smile, settling down a little, now that the fish dish is out of the way.

'Well, I know other shortcuts to the heart,' he tells me, narrowing his eyes, his mouth lightly curling into a smile. 'But, for now, we can focus on the food. I wasn't expecting to be preparing lunch for a beautiful woman today. It's a nice distraction, I'm hardly even thinking about how terrified I am, about the opening this week.'

'A beautiful woman?' I repeat back to him, flattered. 'Flattery will get you everywhere. So will food – you're a double threat.'

'In that case, let me fetch your next course,' he says, dashing back through the glass doors, clearly keen to impress.

My gosh, I dodged a bullet there. Whatever Roscoe brings out next is going to be all the better for not being whatever that was. I should have known it was out of my comfort zone when I realised I couldn't identify what it was.

I could weep with relief when he brings me my next dish – a miniature version of a full English breakfast.

'Oh, wow, I've never seen such a beautiful full English before,' I say, studying the delicate and colourful arrangement – it's like nothing I've ever seen before. 'And somehow it doesn't look bad for you at all!'

Roscoe grins, clearly pleased with my reaction.

'That's the beauty of Mare Segreto,' he explains. 'The theme automatically makes all the dishes healthier.'

'How so?' I ask curiously because, whatever witchcraft it is, I need it in my life. Unless, of course, he's the same as my mum, who claims everything is healthy if she cooks it in the air fryer. Somehow I doubt that, though.

'Seafood is generally considered a healthier option,' he explains. 'So, by incorporating it into various dishes, we add that touch of healthiness to every creation.'

My heart stops.

'Wait, this is seafood?' I check, gesturing down at the cooked breakfast foods in front of me.

Even I can hear the hint of alarm in my voice, so I offset it by smiling like a maniac.

'Yes, of course,' he replies. 'Everything we serve is seafood, presented as other foods. You would never know, would you? Were it not the theme of the restaurant.'

You would if I'd taken a bite.

'Unbelievable,' I tell him. 'Good work.'

'Thanks,' he says. 'Dig in.'

I pick up my knife and fork and hover them over my plate. Think, Gigi, think.

'Oh, no,' I say, dropping my cutlery theatrically, taking my left hand in my right hand and holding it out in front of me. 'It's my late auntie's ring, I've lost it.'

Roscoe's brow furrows with concern.

'Did you definitely wear it today?' he asks.

'I wear it every day,' I lie. 'Oh, now that I think about it, I remember hearing something hit the floor when I was waiting outside, I never considered that it could have been me who dropped something.'

'Don't worry,' he reassures me. 'I'll go look.'

Wow, he really is great. I almost feel bad for deceiving him but, come on, he isn't going to be very happy if I tell him I think his food is vile.

With Roscoe out of the way, I fill up another poo bag and drop it into my handbag.

Roscoe returns, a slightly worried expression on his face. Yep, I feel terrible.

'I couldn't find it,' he tells me.

'It's okay,' I reassure him. 'I'll check back at work. I might have taken it off there.'

He softens into a smile.

'You've cleared your plate again,' he says happily.

'Yes! It was delicious, but I'm actually so full now,' I tell him as I rub my stomach for effect.

'Are you sure?' he replies. 'Because I made a special dessert, just for you. I thought we could share it, and then maybe you can interrogate me. I think I've seen all I need to see here.'

He smiles – of course he does, because he thinks he's found a girl who loves his food so much she clears her plates in minutes.

Dessert is definitely something I can do, and I am starving, for obvious reasons.

'Oh, go on then,' I say with a bat of my hand. 'You've twisted my arm.'

'I'll be right back,' he says.

I sigh. At least I know dessert will be good but, as for what will happen if I get a second date, I'm not sure how exactly I'll walk this one back. I'm not going to count my chickens yet.

Roscoe returns with a beautiful cupcake with hints of pink and expertly piped buttercream on top. Starving, I smile at the sweet treat before grabbing it and taking a big bite.

As the flavour registers on my tongue, Roscoe's smile turns mischievous.

'As I'm sure you've already guessed, it's a smoked salmon and cream cheese cupcake,' he says proudly.

The strong, smoky taste of the salmon hits me like a tidal wave and the fact that it is masquerading as something sweet pushes me over the edge.

'I'll be back in a minute, not feeling too good,' I mutter, trying to hide my panic, before bolting to the toilets.

Once I'm out of sight, I hastily spit the unwanted seafood

cupcake into my hand, because that's just the kind of classy date I am.

Inside the ladies' loos, I spit into the sink repeatedly, desperately attempting to rid my mouth of the lingering fish taste. Swilling water around my mouth provides some relief, but I'm almost tempted to stick a bit of liquid soap in there – can it really be worse?

After what feels like an eternity, I return to the table. Roscoe's face looks like thunder, a storm brewing behind his eyes.

'Sorry,' I tell him, mustering up my best unwell-person impression, like I'm a kid trying to blag a day off school from my mum. 'I haven't been feeling myself today. I'm a little sick – but it definitely wasn't the food.'

'I know it wasn't the food,' Roscoe says, his tone suddenly completely different. Oh, he seems mad.

For a second, I just look at him. He eventually breaks the silence by dropping the poo bags full of food down on the table in front of him.

'I know it wasn't the food because you didn't eat any,' he clarifies. 'Your phone was ringing in your bag – a few times, back to back, and I was worried it might be urgent so I was going to bring it to you.'

He hands me my phone, and then my bag, and it couldn't be more obvious that he's giving me my cue to leave.

I silently take them from him and head for the door. Unsurprisingly, he doesn't even say goodbye.

Back out in the street, I realise that the calls were from my mum, so I call her back to make sure everything is okay. Now I know that it's my mum, I'm not worried. She often calls a few times if I don't pick up – and oftentimes she just calls me by accident, because she never remembers to lock her phone screen.

'Hello, darling,' she says as she answers.

'Hi, Mum, did you want me?' I ask. 'I've just seen your calls.'

'Oh, sorry, everything is fine, I was just in the area and I thought I would see if you fancied some lunch,' she suggests.

'Yes,' I say, a little too quickly. 'I'm starving.'

I make a plan to meet my mum and, thankfully, I have plenty of time left in my break. Well, the last thing I want to do is head back to fess up that it all went disastrously wrong, and I really am hungry.

Ha, and to think, I was worried about what I would do if we had a second date. The chance would be a fine thing.

10

What does a generally bland dresser wear to a metal gig? It sounds like the set-up to a joke but, genuinely, I want to know.

I mean, I don't think I'm bland, obviously. I love clothes – shopping, wearing things, trying different looks. But my preferred colour palette is muted, and I'm not exactly a provocative dresser – I don't have the confidence for that. But, by metal standards, the browns and greens you'll find in my wardrobe are more 'lady of the manor' than Children of Bodom – can you tell I've been googling metal bands? I even put a metal playlist on, while I was getting ready, but only for about five minutes before I gave up and stuck on some Taylor Swift instead.

Tonight I've got my date with Kane, from metal band Chillz, and he is expecting someone who looks the part to turn up. Genuinely, the only thing that is remotely metal about me is my fillings.

I stood in front of my own wardrobe for ages and, unsurprisingly, didn't find the black leather or silver chains I was hoping I might've had but had somehow forgotten I'd bought.

Desperate times call for desperate measures, though, and after my date with Roscoe was such a disaster, my date with Kane tonight feels like my last real chance. I'm pulling out the big guns – if pulling out the big guns means I am rifling through my mum's wardrobe, which I'm almost certain it doesn't.

I used to do this when I was a kid, I would go through her clothes, trying all sorts of things on, looking myself up and down in the mirror and laughing. It was like a time capsule, with things that were decades old, that even my mum wouldn't wear. Thankfully, it still is.

I've opted for a black lace tutu dress (a really cheap one, that she bought in a fancy dress shop, to wear to an eighties party that she went to as Madonna), a cropped fur jacket that has seen more decades than I have, and a pair of red-tinted glasses that I found in a drawer on my dad's side.

I look myself up and down in the mirror. Bloody hell, I look like Elton John. Perhaps I'll ditch the red-tinted glasses.

The frills of my dress bounce almost comedically as I move, making my way back to my bathroom, where I put on even more make-up, hoping lots of black eyeliner and red lipstick can pick up the slack. I flick my eyes out at the sides, in at the corners, and even draw on a few bonus flicks below my eyes – I'm not sure what they're supposed to be, but they're not coming off now.

I had the sense when I arrived to tell my mum and dad that I was only popping in and out, so said hi and bye, safe in the knowledge that it's TV quiz show prime time and that I should be able to make my way out unseen. The last thing I need is to have to explain to them where I'm going, or why I'm dressed up like this – I'm not even sure what I would tell them.

I make it to the door with only Ted noticing. He wags his tail at me but I can tell there's a tone; even the dog is judging me.

With a deep breath, I open the front door, making a quick escape into the cool night, but I celebrate my stealthy exit too soon.

At the bottom of the driveway, who do I run into but Nathan, because an ex-boyfriend would be the worst person to bump into dressed like this, so of course that's what's happening. And I thought trying to explain this to my *parents* might be the worst thing I could imagine right now.

'Hello, Nathan, how's it going?' I say brightly, because if I don't mention how I'm dressed right now, perhaps he won't either.

'Hey, it's going good, I'm meeting Rick and Lucy to have dinner with your parents, Sunshine is away at the moment,' he explains, and then, without taking a breath, 'Where are you going dressed like that?'

'To a metal gig,' I say simply, as though it's the most normal thing in the world for me to say.

Nathan's jaw doesn't get the memo.

'What?' he replies in disbelief. 'Why?'

'I like metal,' I reply, again, casual as you like.

'Since when?' he says.

'Since always,' I tell him. 'Perhaps you don't know me as well as you think you do.'

Nathan laughs.

'It's nice that we can still get on,' he says with a smile. 'Do you have to get straight off? Can you join us for dinner first?'

'Dinner?' I scoff in disbelief. 'That doesn't sound very metal.'

'Even Ozzy Osbourne has to eat,' he replies, his smile optimistic.

'Sorry, I've got to go,' I say. 'I'm in a bit of a hurry.'

And with that, I dash off, before anyone else can see me. I don't even dare to look back at Nathan, but I can tell you almost certainly that he's still laughing at me.

11

I can safely say that metal is so not my genre. It's not that I have anything against it; it's just that some people were made for listening to quirky pop queens and sad boys with acoustic guitars, and others were made for gigs where they fire 'blood cannons' and dance with the idea of devil worshipping. I'm sure that last part was a joke, but you can never be too careful. The thrashing guitars, the pounding drums, screaming men – it's all a bit much for someone whose usual idea of heavy is turning the volume up on Lewis Capaldi. It's just not for me.

The music's been so loud that I haven't had much chance to talk to Kane – which is probably for the best, because, come on, what am I going to say to him? But he has been getting close, placing his hands on my hips, dancing with me in whatever way you can plausibly dance to a band called 'Kronk Red Meat'. Thankfully he didn't say anything about my outfit, or my make-up, so I assume I'm blending in – but I suppose it's impossible not to blend in, in a room where everyone stands out, if you get what I mean.

Now, the show's over, the music has stopped, and the lights are on. I feel all sweaty, but, thankfully, if my make-up has run, I figure it'll only help me to fit in more.

'Did you enjoy that?' Kane asks me, his own eyeliner smeared across his face, and he runs his hand through his hair to remove the last of the bright red 'blood' confetti.

'Oh, I loved it,' I say, and it could not be a bigger lie. '*Loved it!*'

It was like being inside a blender, in fact, it's only now that the music has stopped that I can hear my ears quite literally screaming for help.

'Favourite song?' he asks.

Okay, so, I expected this to happen, and so I made a point of remembering one song title – to be honest, it was pretty much the only one I could understand the title of, even if I couldn't make out any of the lyrics.

'It was 4G,' I say proudly. 'Love it. It's my favourite.'

'Really?' he replies, his eyebrows raised. 'What do you love about it?'

'I just love it,' I say as confidently as I can – does anyone love 4G? 'I really love what it's about.'

Kane smiles and nods approvingly – I guess I picked his favourite song too. It's about time I had a bit of luck.

'Do you want to go backstage?' he asks.

'I would absolutely love that,' I lie through my teeth, but you know, I'm here now, and I think it's going well?

'Great, let's go,' Kane says, leading the way with the confidence of someone who knows he can go anywhere he wants here. I suppose I forget that he's famous because I haven't heard of him before.

Kane flashes a backstage pass, which I guess he's had stashed in his pocket, like a magician holding an ace up his sleeve, and as if by magic the burly bouncer steps aside to let us past.

I step into the backstage room, and instantly, it's like I've wandered into an alternate universe where everyone is considerably more metal than I could ever be. Leather, spikes, and tattoos as far as the eye can see, and I'm here in my mum's old Madonna costume, and a fur coat that I'm starting to worry might be real, in which case I deserve to have blood cannons shot at me.

'Back in a minute,' Kane says over the music.

'Okay,' I say, feeling a little bit like a lamb to the slaughter (which might actually be a good thing here?) standing on my own.

The room is a sensory overload of pure metal. It's dimly lit, but I can see that the walls are plastered with faded concert posters and graffiti that tell the tales of countless bands that have been here before. The air is thick with the scent of sweat, adrenaline, and all of the other smells you might expect to smell in a room full of musicians and their friends.

A worn-out leather sofa, patched with duct tape, is apparently the perfect surface for snorting things off, if you're ever wondering. It hadn't ever crossed my mind but now you know.

I'm not entirely sure what to do with myself, standing here alone, although I am mentally writing a list of what I don't want to do.

I decide not to move, or talk to anyone, or eat or drink any of the food lying around, because these all sound like ways for me to get myself in trouble.

Time crawls by (although probably only a couple of minutes go by), and eventually, Kane reappears.

'Come on, this way,' he instructs, a mischievous glint in his eyes. 'I've got a surprise for you.'

I smile nervously, following him into the next door.

I stop in my tracks at the sight of a naked man with long, sleek black hair, his hands on the hips of the also naked woman in front of him, thrusting away at her – to the beat of the music, I think, which is undeniably impressive. The woman screams with delight as she runs her hands through her short pink hair.

'I thought we could join them,' Kane says with a hopeful smile.

Why on earth would he think that?

'When you said your favourite track was Fourgie, and why you loved it…'

My ears stop working, refusing to listen to another word Kane says, as I realise my mistake. The song isn't called 4G, it's called Fourgie, and I can't say I'm familiar with the term but, now that I know what I'm hearing – and what I'm seeing – I think I can guess.

'Oh, that's so sweet,' I say, as though he just gave me a bunch of flowers, because of course I do. 'But I've just had a call from my mum, to say my auntie isn't well, and that I need to go see her ASAP.'

Yep, I'm resurrecting my dead auntie (the one who gave me the fake ring) who never actually existed to begin with.

'Oh, shit,' Kane says. 'Is there anything I can do for you?'

'No, no,' I insist, a little too quickly. 'Stay here, have a nice Threegie.'

I cringe. I don't think that's a thing.

'I'll see you later,' I tell him before I make a dash for it.

Honestly, just when it's starting to feel like progress, and that I might be able to bag myself a date for the wedding, it turns out I've actually secured myself three. Three would be too many. It wouldn't be the vibe I was going for.

Ah well, back to the drawing board.

12

Tom stares at me blankly. I stare back at him. I don't know what to say any more than he does.

I've just spent the past few minutes filling Tom and Zoe in on my date with Kane last night and, unsurprisingly, they are in a state of shock.

'Wait, what?' Zoe eventually breaks the stunned silence. She leans closer, as though she might have misheard me.

'Oh, you heard me right,' I reply.

'Blood cannons?' Zoe continues, her disbelief turning into a mix of horror and fascination.

Tom's eyes widen to the point where it briefly changes his hairline.

'That's your takeaway from this?' Tom asks her. 'Not the orgy?'

'Well, I've heard of orgies,' Zoe points out. 'Not that I've ever been to one.'

She gets that disclaimer in there like lightning.

'God, and I thought the Roscoe story was cringe,' Tom points out.

'Well, you know me, I don't like to disappoint,' I say with a laugh, bowing for comedic effect.

'So... last night... you didn't?' Tom checks curiously.

'No, Tom, unsurprisingly I didn't,' I answer with a sarcastic level of casualness. 'That's not really why I was there, and I don't think rocking up to the wedding with three dates, looking like horny pall-bearers, is going to hit the spot, do you?'

Tom bursts into laughter, appreciating the unexpected turn of the conversation. There's nothing like a joke to take the edge off a shock.

'I'm sorry there's no time for me to find you someone else,' he says, still chuckling.

'Please don't apologise, and definitely don't try to find me someone else,' I insist, only half joking. 'I'm not sure I can keep up with your clientele.'

'I won't know where to look the next time I cut his hair,' Tom muses out loud.

'Just be sure to warn me when he's coming in, so I can hide behind the boxes in the storeroom,' I suggest.

'So, how long are you in Hawaii, before the wedding?' Zoe asks, getting the conversation back on track.

'My flight is tomorrow, and then we're there for about a week,' I reply.

'So maybe enough time to find yourself a holiday romance?' Zoe suggests optimistically. 'You never know who you might meet. Surely it must be easy to get someone already there to go to a wedding with you?'

'I mean, you say that, but look at how terribly I'm doing here,' I remind her. 'Lewis – AKA Doctor Mad – really was well and truly crackers. Kane thought an orgy might be a good first-date icebreaker. And then, even with someone like Roscoe, who seemed great – not only did I manage to tank the date completely – by being myself – but he's already messaged me and asked me for Kelly Parker's phone number because he saw her on my profile. Part of me wonders if he was only feeding me to get to her.'

'It's a tale as old as time,' Tom jokes.

I sigh dramatically.

'At least you get a holiday,' Zoe adds optimistically. 'You're going to Hawaii tomorrow. The only place I'm going tomorrow, other than work, is the dentist. At least you're not me, being told to lie back and open wide.'

'She almost was last night,' Tom jokes, shaking his head. 'An orgy. Bloody hell.'

I see my first client of the day arriving so I go to greet her in reception. One more day of work, and then it's off to Hawaii for the wedding. I'm absolutely dreading it.

13

The plane hums with anticipation as I navigate my way down the aisle – well, it's either that, or it's me shaking.

Lucy and Rick's destination wedding comes with a silver lining – if the opposite of a silver lining is a huge financial burden – free plane tickets for the VIPs in the wedding party. As sister of the bride, and chief bridesmaid, I am very happy to have made the cut.

The wedding planner who booked my ticket told me I would be sitting in what I am told is 'premium economy' which, other than sounding like a bit of an oxymoron, is double the price of regular economy.

As I realise I am at my assigned seat, I take a look around. Initially, the seat appears like any other, kind of like what I imagined economy would look like. I'm hoping that there are some secret bells and whistles here that I'm yet to learn about, that are going to elevate (no pun intended) my flight to the first of several eye-wateringly priced upgrades.

I sink into my seat and turn my gaze towards the window, looking out at the runway, on the dry land that I love so much.

Flying itself doesn't bother me, but there is something about the take-off and landing that pump me full of anxiety. Once I'm up there I'll be fine, so long as I push from my mind just how high up in the sky we are (until it's time to come back down, obviously) but until it's time for take-off, I'll be a wreck.

I find myself fidgeting with the zip on my handbag. Back and forth, again and again, trying to focus on the rhythmic movement in a poor attempt to distract myself.

'Still a nervous flyer then?' Nathan's voice snaps me from my thoughts.

I twist my neck in the direction of the familiar voice, and there he is, casually settling into the seat next to mine.

'I guess we gave the wedding planner the same time slots,' he points out with a smile. 'Flying through the night, to land in the morning? Great minds.'

'Yeah, I guess so,' I reply, still a little stunned to find him here, next to me. 'I was hoping I would be able to sleep for most of the flight.'

'That's my plan too, so we're lucky we're sat next to one another,' he replies, still smiling away, like this isn't weird at all.

As we settle into the seats, I chew my lip thoughtfully. Nathan's comment about me still being a nervous flyer is an interesting one. It makes it seem like we were together a long time ago, as opposed to just last year. Yes, of course I'm still a nervous bloody flyer, nothing has changed in recent months – why would it? His choice of words suggests that Nathan views our relationship as a more distant memory than I do. It makes sense; after all, he's moved on.

'Where is Sunshine?' I ask, my voice casual. God, please tell me she isn't coming to sit with us. I don't think I can stomach hours on end of close quarters with those two.

'She's catching a later flight,' Nathan replies. 'She's always so busy with work. She's in Rome or Paris at the moment – I forget which. Wherever she is, she's making her way to Maui from there.'

'Cool,' I say simply, trying to come across as though I don't have any thoughts or feelings on the matter.

'Isn't it mad,' Nathan continues, seemingly oblivious to any potential discomfort or awkwardness that might exist between us. 'We always said we'd love to go to Maui for our honeymoon – and here we are.'

'Oh, my goodness, are you two off on your honeymoon?' an excitable flight attendant interjects, having overheard a snippet of our conversation.

'We're…'

'We are,' Nathan answers, talking over me.

'Oh, well, you two deserve something special,' the flight attendant gushes, clearly delighted at the thought of having newly-weds on board. 'Once we're up in the air, I'll bring you some drinks.'

'Aww, that would be lovely,' Nathan replies appreciatively, looking at me. 'Right, Gigi?'

'Right,' I agree with a forced smile, playing along with the unexpected charade. What on earth is he playing at?

As soon as the flight attendant is out of earshot, Nathan leans in and lowers his voice.

'If they think we're a couple, we'll get free stuff, so play along,' he insists.

'Okay,' I reply, bemused, struggling not to pull a face. It's probably best if I just humour him, I just want this flight to go as quickly as possible.

'It's a life hack that Sunshine taught me,' he explains with a wink. 'That or pretending to get engaged – that always bags you freebies too.'

'Right,' I say, rolling my eyes at the term 'life hack'. I'm sick of hearing the term because it's rarely an actual hack, and is more often just straight-up being deceitful or it isn't a hack at all, it's just doing normal things.

I'm anxious throughout the safety demonstration because, for some reason, it worries me even more that there is a plan for if things go wrong, than if there were no plan at all. It's almost as though they're expecting it – even though, deep down, I know that they are not.

The moment the plane begins its ascent, my anxiety intensifies. I push myself back into the seat, and my fingers grip the armrests so tightly my knuckles begin to turn white.

It surprises me when Nathan reaches over, takes my hand in his, and squeezes it reassuringly.

'It's all going to be okay, I promise you. I'm here for you,' he says in a calming voice.

I sigh gratefully, feeling a bit better thanks to his unexpected support, but at the same time it only serves to remind me of what I'm missing. But what am I missing really? Is it having someone who is there for me, who makes everything feel okay, or am I missing Nathan?

Sometimes, I can't be sure.

14

A driver takes us from Kahului Airport to Wailea, which is thankfully only a short drive across Maui. Honestly, any journey feels like a breeze when you've just endured a long-haul flight with your ex-boyfriend, quickly followed by a medium-haul one. I swear, the flight from LAX to Maui felt even longer than the one from London to LAX – I think it's because my tolerance for Nathan has almost completely run out. I'm grateful that the last leg of the journey is a simple drive, sparing me from another short-haul flight to complete the set – I've had my fill of air travel for the day.

Finally, the car pulls to a stop outside the Grand Palm Resort. Stepping out into the warm Hawaiian air, I take in my beautiful surroundings – right now I'm only in the carport, where people are dropped off, and I'm already in awe. Dare I say it, the flying feels worth it already, because something about the atmosphere here just relaxes me.

Nathan and I stand to the side as our bags are swiftly loaded onto a trolley, ready to be transported into the hotel lobby. I watch as Nathan tips the driver. Then he turns to me.

'You can give me half later,' he says. Classic Nathan – he's always been tight, even though he has plenty of money.

I bite my tongue. You would think he would be more grateful, after all, I did let him keep the lavish double room we booked here together, so that Sunshine could share it with him. I, on the other hand, had to secure myself a relatively last-minute booking – the cheapest room available, it turns out. Only I could book an expensive week in paradise and end up in the only cheap and cheerful option they have – the price certainly wasn't cheap or cheerful. Lucky me.

'They forgot one of my bags,' Nathan declares with a tut, his eyes scanning the area for the nearest employee.

'Oi, you,' he calls out, flagging over a man in a white shirt. I can't help but cringe at the way Nathan is talking to him. 'One of your colleagues just took our bags, but he forgot this one, take it, will you?'

The man just laughs, and Nathan's frustration intensifies.

'You think it's funny?' Nathan replies furiously. 'I want to speak to your boss – *now*.'

'Okay, well, you'll have to hop on a flight back to England, mate,' the man replies, his accent instantly giving him away as someone from the London area. 'I don't work here.'

Oh, God, I didn't think I could cringe any harder.

Right on cue, another employee with a trolley appears, ready to load it with the man's bags – the man who is so very clearly a guest.

'Come on, let's go in, I'll just carry it,' Nathan tells me, his face an especially intense shade of crimson.

I begin to follow Nathan, making eye contact with the random man as I pass him.

He gives me a cheeky wink. I can't help but smile back at him, silently expressing solidarity because I'm no stranger to Nathan's attitude problem, before following Nathan into the resort.

Wow, the Grand Palm Resort is even more beautiful inside – and yet I still feel like I'm outside, thanks to the open bifold doors that cover most of the walls, and all of the greenery dotted around. The lobby is as grand as the name suggests, decorated in warm creams and brown tones, finished off with fascinating artworks and sculptures. I can't wait to explore every inch of the place.

Nathan steps up to the front desk to check in first – ever the gentleman.

I quietly wait my turn, but then I notice the woman behind the desk nodding in my direction.

'Would you like an extra key card for your partner?' she asks.

'Oh, no, she's not with me,' Nathan insists, a little too firmly for my liking. 'She's not my partner.'

I can't help but pull a face at his choice of words.

Nathan takes his key card, tells me he'll see me later, and then heads off. My God, I hope I'm not flying home with him at the same time too because his presence alone was enough to keep me feeling stressed out.

'Can I check in, please?' I ask the woman behind the desk.

'Of course,' she replies. 'Sorry for the mix-up. Can I have your name, please?'

'Gigi Marsden,' I tell her.

'Sorry?' the woman behind the desk replies, and I can't help but notice a flicker of something in her eyes – panic, maybe, although perhaps I'm being paranoid.

'Gigi Marsden,' I repeat, saying it much slower this time, making sure that every syllable is clear.

'All right, Ms Marsden, I'm just looking at the room we have you in, and, unfortunately, I don't think we're going to be able to put you there,' she says, making me feel instantly anxious and imagining the worst. Isn't this all just so on-brand for me?

'No?' I respond, attempting to maintain an air of calm that I have absolutely no right to possess.

'No, but not to worry because, though we are fully booked, we can upgrade you,' she explains, sounding a tad too rehearsed for my liking. I saw the look on her face, and I've been 'upgraded' before when really it was just a cover-up for a mix-up with the bookings. I'll bet it's the oldest trick in the hotel book, they act like they're doing you a favour, but in reality, they're just scrambling to cover up a hiccup. I'm not buying it, not for a minute. I will, however, take it, silently, because as I keep reminding myself, I have no other choice. It's my sister's wedding, so I have to be here, doing and enduring whatever needs to be done/endured.

'Please, take a seat for a moment,' she says as she gestures towards a nearby seating area.

I do as I'm told, my mind racing with visions of where this unexpected upgrade might lead me. I can't shake the suspicion that, despite her reassuring tone, I might end up sleeping under the stars with nothing but a beach towel for comfort.

The woman at the front desk calls out to a staff member named Keanu. He joins her behind the desk, and they exchange hushed words, occasionally nodding in my direction. Alarm bells start ringing in my head – something isn't quite right, I can just feel it.

After a brief exchange, the woman hands Keanu a key card, and he heads over to me with a warm smile.

'If you would like to come this way, please, Ms Marsden,' he says.

'Okay,' I say – because what else can I say?

I follow him, nervously trailing him through the hotel, my fake smile fading as the feeling of unease builds inside me.

Keanu swipes his key card, and we enter what I assume is my room – except it isn't, it's just a lounge – a really nice lounge, but a lounge nonetheless.

For a moment I just stand there, waiting for an explanation, hoping they're not about to ask me to sleep on the sofa until they sort out a real room.

'Nice, huh?' Keanu says, breaking the awkward silence.

'Yeah, it's lovely,' I agree, but not so lovely they can store me here indefinitely.

'As you can see, this is the lounge,' Keanu explains. 'If you look round here you will see the kitchen area. Those windows, over there, are actually doors, which fully open out over the private pool area. And of course your bedroom and bathroom are upstairs.'

'What?' I blurt, confused.

'Sorry, Ms Marsden, have I forgotten something?' Keanu asks, sensing my unease.

'No, no, sorry,' I respond, unsure why either of us is apologising, or what on earth we're talking about, to be honest. 'Where is my room?'

'This is your suite,' Keanu clarifies with a smile. 'Your bedroom is upstairs.'

What? No! I can't believe it. An upgrade to a suite? And calling this a suite is an understatement. This is a house! A sprawling, luxurious open-plan living space, a bedroom upstairs, and did he just mention a private pool? My jaw is on the floor. Could I finally be getting a bit of good luck?

Hilariously, since my date with Doctor Mad, I find myself regularly questioning if everything is a prank now – jazzed to have that new dimension to my anxious thoughts – but I'm here, and they're saying my name, and it's really happening.

'Okay,' I eventually say, my tone surprisingly muted given the circumstances, my mind still trying to get things straight. 'Cool.'

Keanu hands me the key to the suite along with something called a gold card.

'This gold card gets you into the exclusive areas of the resort – only our very special guests have these,' he explains. 'It's mostly celebrities and high-profile individuals.'

'And me,' I quip in disbelief.

Keanu laughs warmly.

'Yes, of course. But we're very exclusive; everyone is very private,' he insists. 'You won't have any trouble here.'

'I'm sure I won't,' I reply. 'I'm in paradise.'

'I will leave you to settle in. But if there is anything you need, that phone by the door can connect you to a twenty-four-hour concierge service – nothing is too much trouble,' he tells me.

'Okay,' I reply, still slightly dazed. 'Thanks.'

It's not that I'm ungrateful, I just can't believe I'm here.

Now that I know that this lounge is *my* lounge, I'm blown away by it. It has the same cream and brown tones as the lobby, giving it that same luxury hotel vibe, and yet I don't feel like I'm in a hotel at all. This really does feel like a house.

Looking out of the bifold doors, I can see the private pool area Keanu was talking about. The pool glistens under the Hawaiian sun, surrounded by lush greenery and comfortable loungers. It's huge, and there isn't a person in sight.

I make my way upstairs with an excited spring in my step, keen to see my sleeping arrangements for the next week. The bedroom is even nicer than I expected – and after seeing downstairs, I was expecting big things – boasting huge floor-to-ceiling windows that showcase the pool area below and extend the view to the sandy shores of the beach. I don't know why but it always makes me happy to see the sea. The room is absolutely flooded with natural light, casting a warm glow over the gigantic bed.

I lie back on the bed, wiggling myself into a comfortable spot – not that it takes me more than a few seconds. Glorious doesn't even begin to describe it. This is a dream, a far cry from the sad single-girl room I was expecting.

Maybe, just maybe, my luck really has changed. I could certainly get used to it.

Yep, this will do. This will definitely do.

15

I saunter into the hotel restaurant fashionably late – except I don't saunter, I do that awkward fast walk that probably isn't any speedier than normal walking, and I'm not fashionably late, I'm just late. Oh, but doesn't the former sound more befitting of someone who is staying in a suite? My beautiful, gorgeous, sexy suite is the reason I'm late, in a roundabout way, because I fell asleep on that bed pretty much instantly and I didn't wake up again until my mum called me, to make sure I was here. I threw on a dress – a cream sundress, that I was so sure would look good, but in hindsight I am probably too mucky for – a pair of heels and another layer of make-up, to hopefully cancel out the old one that isn't looking great after hours on planes followed by a nap.

Oh, great, everyone else is here already – well, everyone who is a key part of the wedding party. The handful of others who are making the trip for the wedding are coming later in the week.

Lucy and Rick are sitting at the centre of the table, almost as though they're rehearsing for the top table on the big day. Then, next to Lucy we have our parents, and then Nina.

On Rick's side there is his brother, Alfie, who is sadly the only

close family member who will be here. I don't know all the details
but his parents were the kind of rich where a private jet was one of
their main modes of transportation – one day they went up, but
sadly they never landed. It was when Rick and Alfie were kids, and
thank God they weren't on the plane, but I know it's left them both
with a fear of flying, and I'm not surprised – as someone with a
fear of heights, I know how terrifying it is, facing your phobias.
That's why it's such a big deal, that they're here, in Hawaii, for the
wedding. If the two of them are willing to spend all that time on a
plane, just to give Lucy the special day she has dreamed of, then I
can certainly put up with my ex, and his new girlfriend.

Speaking of the devil, Nathan is sitting next to Alfie, and then
finally Sunshine is sitting next to him. There is only one seat left at
the table, for me, right opposite Lucy and Rick, but sadly it leaves
me sandwiched between Nina and Sunshine. Amazing, my own
personal hell.

'Hey, everyone,' I announce myself with a smile.

Lucy, Rick, and the others respond with varying degrees of
warmth. Obviously my parents look pleased to see me, Nina less so
– a combination of the two of us never really getting on and her
bitterness around me being chief bridesmaid – and Sunshine is
shooting me daggers, just like she always does when she sees me.
Honestly, I should be the one who is hostile to her, not the other
way round.

'Oh, that's okay,' she says, feigning nonchalance, 'I can just
finish telling my story later.'

'I didn't realise you were telling a story,' I say, reminding myself
not to apologise. I'm trying to apologise less because I do it all the
time, even when something isn't my fault. I apologised to a door I
walked into the other day.

If this weren't the only unclaimed seat, I would sit anywhere
else.

'Sorry I'm late,' I say as I take my seat. 'I'm not in the main hotel; I'm out in the grounds, so it's a little trek.'

'That's okay. I was just talking about my trip to Paris, doing some promotional photos for my new fashion range,' Sunshine says, making it all about her again.

Sunshine looks like the ultimate influencer. Every part of her look is meticulously curated to reflect the latest fashion and beauty standards – the good and the bad. Her long brown hair is so sleek and shiny, she keeps a year-round tan, and her make-up is always flawless. Her body is perfect, in every way, some of it natural and some of it not, but all of it together just makes her this girl-next-door type that everyone seems to love. It's a shame she's not very nice.

It's also a shame that she appears to be wearing the same dress as me, except hers looks more expensive, is shorter, and generally shows more skin. It makes mine look like I went to a shop for older ladies, while she picked up hers in the teen section of some designer store. I guess there's nothing I can do about it now. That's what I get, for daring to be more bold with my holiday outfits.

Sunshine gets back to her story and, the more she talks, the less I want to hear.

'So, there I was in this quaint little patisserie in Paris, you know the kind, so charming, with a view that most people only get to see in the movies...'

Sunshine glances around the table, ensuring she still has the undivided attention of everyone here. Everyone seems impressed – or at least they're pretending to be. Even I do it, when she's telling a story, but it would be rude not to, surely? Even though she mostly just brags, or mildly rubs in my face that my ex-boyfriend is hers now.

'I ordered the most stunning dessert – a raspberry rose macaron tower – you can see it on my socials,' she continues. 'Anyway, the waiter who brought me it, he was like: you're never going to eat all that, are you? Obviously he said it way more French. And I said: yeah, of course. And then he told me that I was probably the prettiest girl who had ever eaten there. So, yeah, that's the story.'

Don't roll your eyes, don't roll your eyes, don't roll your eyes.

'Oh, wow,' Lucy says, doing her best to seem interested. She waits a few seconds before turning to me. 'Did you get here okay, Gi? Nathan said you were on the same flight.'

'Yeah, it was fine. I was okay,' I say.

'Why wouldn't you be?' Nina asks curiously, sensing that we're talking about something she doesn't know about.

'Gigi doesn't like flying,' Lucy explains, giving me an understanding look. 'Or heights generally.'

'Well, that's just silly,' Sunshine chimes in, her tone dismissive. 'What do you think is going to happen? I take flights all the time – sometimes multiple flights per month – do you think I'm going to be in a plane crash?'

No, but I'm not exactly opposed to the idea.

'Do you remember crying when we went to Switzerland?' Nathan says, laughing to himself, like he's recalling a fond memory.

'The oxygen masks dropped,' I point out in my defence.

'By accident,' Nathan replies.

'Which we didn't know until *afterwards*,' I clap back – for what it's worth.

'So, who is looking forward to the wedding?' Lucy asks, changing the subject. 'Other than me and Rick, obviously.'

'I can take or leave it,' Rick jokes, shrugging casually.

'Yeah, right,' Alfie, Rick's brother, interjects with a playful smirk. 'She's got you wrapped around her little finger. You would be lost without her.'

'Yes, I suppose I would,' Rick admits. He wraps an arm around Lucy, planting a sweet kiss on her cheek.

A waiter silently distributes menus around the table as we all coo at Lucy and Rick's PDA. I notice when he gets to me that he gives me a warm smile, so I smile back.

It's lovely here this evening. Outdoor dining is one of the best things about going on holiday somewhere warm. The breeze keeps creeping past and is just enough to keep us cool on a warm evening like tonight. String lights delicately drape above us, illuminating the night with a soft, warm glow, but if you look closely you can see that the sky is full of stars.

'So, what is everyone having?' Rick asks the table.

'I think I'll have the tuna,' Dad announces. 'Gigi, fancy the tuna?'

Dad knows I hate seafood so I pretend to stick my fingers down my throat, making a sicky noise.

'Gigi hates fish,' he tells everyone, to make sure it is a joke for absolutely everyone.

Flying, heights, fish – I am such a catch. Oh, God, no, I'm not making dad jokes, that one was an accident.

'You hate fish?' Sunshine squeaks – she obviously finds this one even more unbelievable than flying.

'Yeah, tuna especially, though,' my dad answers for me. 'She says it's a bit off-key.'

Sunshine looks at me.

'What?' she asks.

I look to Dad, because I have no idea what that means either.

'She finds it off-key,' he says again, slower this time. 'Because you can't tuna fish.'

Lord. Have. Mercy.

'Ridiculous,' Lucy says with a laugh. 'Well, there are two things I can't choose between.'

'So let's get both and share,' Rick suggests.

'Aww, babe,' Lucy says, kissing him again.

'We really have bagged ourselves some great ones, haven't we?' Sunshine says – clearly devastated that we haven't been talking about her for a few minutes – with a gleam of satisfaction in her eyes as she takes Nathan's face in her hands and kisses him on the cheek. Nathan, of course, smiles in acknowledgement. He never seems to stop to think whether or not any of this might be awkward for me.

'I arrived at our room to find out that this one had arranged for a bouquet of flowers for me,' she continues, sighing contentedly.

My mum lets out a sigh.

'Oh, give over,' my dad says to her jokily, noticing her reaction, before turning to address the table. 'She's always complaining that I don't buy her flowers – I didn't even know she sold flowers.'

Everyone laughs. Dad's on top form tonight.

My mum may roll her eyes but there's no way she would have married my dad, and stayed married all this time, if she didn't like his naff dad jokes.

My parents share a knowing look and you can just see the love that they have for one another flowing back and forth between them.

'Forty years together,' Dad says, raising his glass, a playful smirk spreading across his face. 'I would've gotten less for murder.'

Mum playfully swats him.

'And yet I'm the one who has often felt like my life would be more peaceful if I committed it,' she jokes right back at him.

'Aww, we'll be made up, if we're together as long as you guys are,' Lucy says as she squeezes Rick's hand on top of the table.

'Yes,' Sunshine says as she turns to Nathan. 'I hope we'll be celebrating milestones like that someday too.'

'Okay, you guys being all loved-up is making me miss my

boyfriend so much,' Nina chimes in. 'I can't wait for him to join us in a few days.'

All of a sudden it feels like everyone's eyes are on me, the only person who hasn't said anything – AKA the only single person at the table.

'I have a suite,' I blurt – in lieu of a significant other.

'What?' Mum says.

'A luxury suite,' I clarify. 'Over two floors, with a kitchen and its own private pool area.'

'How have you got a suite?' Nathan asks, almost accusingly.

Ha. I wish I knew.

'It's your new fella, isn't it?' Lucy practically sings. 'Your mystery wedding date. Wow, he must be minted if he can afford a suite here!'

I just smile and tap my nose.

'Can we see it?' Dad asks eagerly. 'Can we use the pool?'

'Dad, there are so many pools here,' Lucy reminds him with a click of her tongue.

'Yeah, but Gigi's sounds better,' Dad insists.

'I have a gold card too,' I add, actually loving being the centre of attention for once.

'What?' Sunshine asks, almost enraged.

'It gets you into the exclusive areas of the hotel,' I explain, enjoying the satisfaction of being one step ahead.

'I know what it is,' Sunshine claps back. 'I asked for one, but they said that I didn't qualify.'

What? That's even better! Smugness washes over me. It's a sweet victory, even with Sunshine sitting here with my ex-boyfriend. I have a gold card, and she doesn't – from the look on her face, I reckon she would probably trade Nathan with me for it.

The waiter returns with a bottle of champagne, showing it to me.

'Ms Marsden, compliments of the Grand Palm Resort,' he says.

Oh my God, what is happening? I don't know if I want to laugh or cry or both.

'Aww, thank you,' I say casually, keen to keep my cool new image. 'Can I share it with my family and friends?'

'Two more bottles are on the way,' the waiter replies.

'Oh, wow,' Mum says. 'Whoever this new fella of yours is, he must be something special.'

'I honestly cannot wait to meet him,' Lucy says giddily.

It's funny she should say that because I can't wait to meet him either.

16

Waking up in the bed of my dreams, in the nicest suite I've ever seen, I stretch and yawn, feeling the soft sheets against my skin.

I slept with the window open, allowing the gentle Hawaiian breeze to sweep in, making the sheer net curtains dance in the air. I can't help but sigh, already convinced that this suite life is something I could get used to.

I've never really had a space truly to myself before. I've moved from my family home to live with housemates, then I moved in with Nathan, and finally I moved back in with my parents again. I've never been able to just do anything I wanted. I should walk around my suite naked. Because I can.

With a cheeky grin, I decide to go for it. My T-shirt drops to the floor, and for a brief moment, I feel like I'm performing a striptease for myself. It's silly, but I blush. Okay, now I'm naked. What next?

I think I'll head downstairs, make myself a cup of tea, and sit on the sofa and drink it. Just me, naked, in my suite, with a cuppa. Like a slightly sad, vaguely horny version of Cluedo.

I manage to walk halfway down the stairs before I notice

Keanu, the hotel employee from yesterday, standing there staring back at me.

'Shit,' I blurt, legging it back up the stairs, retreating to the safety of the bedroom.

What do I do, do I hide in here forever or... No. I should just face the embarrassment head-on, go down there and face him like the strong, independent woman I'm pretending to be. Let's nip this in the bud like adults.

I throw on a robe and head down the stairs again.

There he is, still standing there, holding a newspaper like a shield.

'I... I was supposed to bring you your newspaper,' he stammers, offering the paper as a peace offering.

'It's fine, honestly,' I reassure him, taking the paper. It seems like it's business news – he needn't have bothered.

'I'm so sorry for flashing you,' I add, feeling my cheeks growing redder.

'No, I'm the one who is sorry,' he insists. 'I thought you were sleeping, and I didn't want to wake you, so I thought I would leave the paper on the table. Please, don't tell anyone.'

'I'm more embarrassed than you are, believe me,' I tell him. 'I'm not going to tell anyone.'

I can see a wave of relief wash over him.

'Thank you so much,' he says. 'If there is anything I can do for you while you're here, please just let me know.'

'Can you make me forget that I just did that?' I quip, trying to lighten the mood. 'Honestly, it's fine, thanks for the paper.'

Keanu can't flee the scene fast enough.

I decide to laugh it off, shaking my head as I drop the newspaper down on the table – well, if it doesn't have pictures of celebrities on the front, and salacious headlines, then I'm not really interested.

Instead, I'll head upstairs and put on some clothes – lots and lots of clothes – and then head out to meet my family for breakfast.

Oh, and I'll try not to flash any more hotel employees while I'm on my way.

17

Something seriously strange is happening.

I had an amazing night's sleep – something I haven't been getting all that often recently, either down to my life just generally feeling like it has fallen apart or the fun fact that I can hear my dad snoring through the bedroom floor – but then how could I not, in my super-king bed, in my suite? The suite life definitely suits me, it turns out. Who knew?

That's not the strangest part of the morning, though. What's weird is that, ever since we came down for breakfast – me, Lucy, Rick, Nathan and Sunshine – I haven't been able to shake this feeling like the entire world is revolving around me. No, I'm not just being big-headed, because I'm in a suite (although I suppose I am, just a bit), it's like... you know in *The Truman Show*, how everyone in town, and everything they are doing, is all about him? I'm not joking, from the moment my bum touched the seat, it's been like the 'Be Our Guest' scene from *Beauty and the Beast*. Everyone who works here is being so nice to me, so accommodating, so attentive. I'm not complaining, I just don't understand.

None of my tablemates do either, evidently, because they're

watching everything almost suspiciously. Even Lucy, who I know loves me very much, has this look etched on her face, showing that she can't understand why this is happening.

'Did you win the lottery or something?' Rick half-jokes, raising an eyebrow.

'Not that I'm aware of,' I reply with a chuckle.

'Good morning, Ms Marsden,' a waiter says as he places a plate down in front of me. 'A fruit platter, to start your day.'

My jaw drops at the stunning arrangement of fruit, laid out by colour, like a delicious-looking rainbow. It all smells so fresh that I can practically taste it. My mouth is watering – usually this only happens at breakfast time if there are pastries, or I'm still asleep.

'Can I get one of those?' Sunshine asks him.

'Of course, ma'am, the breakfast buffet is right over there,' the waiter tells her.

My God, if I could bottle this feeling, and sell it, I would be incredibly rich and it would explain why I was getting such special treatment.

'Okay, when do we get to meet this mystery man?' Lucy asks. 'Honestly, I'm thinking about him more than I am Rick.'

'Thanks,' Rick jokes sarcastically. 'She's right, though. When we got in bed last night, it was all she wanted to talk about.'

'We didn't give it a second thought,' Sunshine says, although the look on Nathan's face maybe suggests otherwise. 'But you might as well tell us who it is. We'll find out eventually.'

'I'm keeping my cards close to my chest for now,' I say cryptically.

'He's your date to the wedding, we should know something about him,' Sunshine says.

'Can we maybe get a few clues?' Lucy suggests.

'My lips are sealed,' I reply.

'Surely there's something you can tell us?' Sunshine pushes on and, for the first time, I notice a hint of disbelief in her voice. 'He's starting to sound too good to be true.'

All at once my body shuts down. I can't speak, I can't move, I can't think. I can't... I can't just blurt the same old 'wait and see' line because Sunshine is on to me, but I can't offer up anything else because this incredible mystery wedding date is a figment of my imagination.

I need to do something, not just sit here like a lemon. Every second I don't say something only makes me look more and more sus, and the look on Sunshine's face is seamlessly blending into a smirk, like she's caught me out.

'Excuse me,' a man's voice interrupts us.

'Great timing, can I get another coffee?' Nathan says, offering the man his cup.

'I still don't work here, mate,' the man replies with a good-natured grin.

Oh, for goodness' sake, how has Nathan managed to mistake this man for a member of staff for a second time? It was cringe enough yesterday but now it's just plain embarrassing. He doesn't even look like a waiter – was Nathan this much of an arsehole when we were together, or has Sunshine 'elevated' his social status to the point where he thinks he can treat people however he wants?

The man, who is actually quite good-looking now that I'm thinking about it, remains unoffended by the mix-up. He has dark, tousled hair that falls effortlessly, framing a face that blends rugged handsomeness with a cheeky softness. He's tall – well over 6ft, but he only seems more imposing given that he's standing and we're all sitting. Nathan would always say that he was 6ft when he wasn't, but men often say that, don't they? As though lying about a few inches here or there will sway us. I don't mean that as raunchy as it sounds but, however you read it, my opinion holds up.

'Can I borrow you?' he asks me.

I'm taken aback, although lord knows why, because Hawaii Gigi is the main character, apparently.

'Yes, sure,' I reply.

I'm not one for going off with strange men but I'm relieved to be able to duck out of the conversation about my date.

We walk away, away from the prying ears of the breakfast table, eventually taking shade underneath a large palm tree. He offers a warm smile, and I return it, curious about what he wants to discuss.

'That girl doesn't let up, does she?' he says, laughing to himself.

I give him a bemused look.

'The one with the brown hair,' he prompts me.

I can't help but smile, because this honestly never happens.

'Do you know who she is?' I check, half expecting everyone in the world to know about Sunshine Greene. That's usually how it goes, but he looks genuinely clueless.

'No, who is she?' he replies.

Music to my ears!

'She's my ex-boyfriend's new girlfriend,' I tell him, leaving out the part about her being a sort of celebrity. It's bad enough that she's so beautiful.

He raises an eyebrow.

'That guy is your ex?' he says in disbelief.

I nod.

'Yep.'

He lets out a low whistle.

'Man, I thought he was just like your dickhead brother or something like that when I saw you with him yesterday,' he explains. 'Not that I would've told you he was a dickhead, if he was your brother but, seeing as he's your ex, I'm sure it's fine – and I'm sure you know.'

I burst into laughter. Just when I think things have reached peak awesome, I meet a guy who not only thinks Nathan is a tool, but he's never heard of Sunshine.

'Wait, sorry, but... who are you?' I ask, trying to make sense of the situation.

'I'm Donnie,' he says casually. 'You?'

'I'm Gigi,' I reply, still processing the fact that this stranger is talking to me like he knows me. 'I just... what did you want?'

'I don't want anything,' he insists. 'I was sat at the table next to yours, alone, so I couldn't help but overhear your conversation, and that girl was on to you.'

'On to me?' I say.

'Yeah,' he replies. 'I rumbled the fact that you don't have a date for this wedding pretty much right away but, as your conversation was going on, I could tell she was picking up on it too.'

Okay, it's scary how on the money he is.

'Sorry if I'm overstepping the mark,' he says, realising the audacity of his intervention. 'This is the problem, when you're bored on your own, it makes you nosy. But you sounded like you were in a tight spot, so I thought I should intervene. I would hope someone would do the same for me, if I were in a similar spot. Not that I can imagine being in a similar spot.'

I laugh. This is so ridiculous, but I'm really grateful.

'Thank you,' I say sincerely. 'That's surprisingly and disturbingly accurate.'

'Yeah, you're welcome,' he says. 'If I were you, I would go back there and join in on whatever the conversation has changed to, and keep it off your wedding date.'

'Yeah, thanks,' I reply. 'I'm thinking my date might be too ill to come; I'm just leaving it long enough to tell them for it to be believable.'

'Or there are plenty of men knocking around the resort who

would love to go to a wedding with you,' he points out. 'I'm sure you can find someone. Anyway, I'll let you get back to your breakfast.'

Donnie heads back to his table so I rejoin my family. He was right – the conversation has moved on. What I need to do is keep my mouth shut and my head down. Maybe he's on to something about the resort, too. There must be someone here I can take to the wedding. I'll start looking today.

18

The poolside bar is swimming in sunlight and is already packed with people, most of them set up for the day, lounging by the pool, either topping up their tan or shading themselves under the dreamy cabanas.

The atmosphere is alive with chatter and ambient music. There are people in the pool – the main pool, not my fancy private pool, which is something I never thought I would be able to say – but the vibe is so chilled out. There's no screaming or splashing – it's nice.

The bar is beautifully decorated with tropical flowers and there is fruit pretty much everywhere, which leads me to believe that the cocktails here are not only healthy, but part of my five a day.

I take a seat on one of the plush cream-cushioned bar stools and grab a menu. I'm wearing another sundress that I stupidly bought when I thought that Hawaii Gigi should be more bright and out there. It's a light-yellow dress which, now that I'm out in the daylight, I am realising leaves nothing to the imagination. You can see my lime-green bikini through it from a mile away. Still, it's too late to worry about it now, all I can do is own it. Perhaps it will make me seem like I'm super confident and comfortable in my skin. I'm not, but I'm sure half of the battle with being confident is convincing other people that you feel it.

I face out from the bar, over the pool area, as I go to choose a drink but, instead, I find myself surveying the other guests, trying to pick out of them instead.

It's so strange, and I feel like a bit of a predator, but I need to find myself a man. Not just any man, though, oh no, someone who comes across as impressive enough that they could be the person keeping me in the lifestyle I am accustomed to. Yes, I am accustomed to this lifestyle already, after only one day.

I turn back to face the bar, my eyes scanning the list of drinks, trying to pick just one that I fancy, but with every single one sounding delicious, that five-a-day joke I just made might become a reality.

I look up to see the barman, just as he places a cocktail down in front of me.

'I saw you browsing the menu so I thought I would help you out,' he tells me. 'I thought you might like this one.'

I smile at him, then at the drink, because that's normal.

Inside the tall glass, the liquid shifts in colour, from turquoise at the bottom, through different colours of the rainbow, finishing with a delicious-looking shade of magenta at the top. It reminds me of the colours I've seen already here, the sea, the sky, the sand, the sunset last night. It really is a masterpiece, topped off with a sugared rim and a huge chunk of pineapple.

'Thank you,' I say, raising the glass to my lips.

Oh, my goodness, it smells like everything. Passionfruit, coconut, mint, heaven. It's the kind of drink that, if I weren't already in Maui, would most definitely transport me here.

I take a sip and, wow, I expected it to taste good but this is something else. I assume it's alcoholic but you would never know from the taste, there's no sharpness to it, no bitter aftertaste. It's just a big fruity glass of holiday. I love it.

I don't know which drink it is, but the barman made a good choice for me – if only picking a man was this easy.

As I turn back around on my stool, surveying the pool area like a hawk in search of its prey, a man around my age approaches me. He's broad-shouldered, with a shock of auburn hair. He's definitely rugged, and unsteady on his feet, it would appear.

'Hello,' he says, greeting me with an unmistakable Glaswegian accent. 'Are you a Brit?'

'How did you know?' I reply with a smile.

'Your pale skin and the fact you're hitting the drink before lunch,' he points out with a chuckle. 'Not that there's anything wrong with that. I started drinking yesterday afternoon – I haven't stopped yet.'

'Nice,' I reply simply.

If I didn't believe his words then his breath would almost certainly confirm his alibi. I can smell the booze on him from here. If it were possible to get drunk from second-hand drinking, then I would be positively tipsy right now.

'I'm Gary,' he introduces himself. 'Gary Garrie – so good, they named me twice.'

I can't help but laugh, although I'm not sure if he's joking.

'I'm Gigi,' I say politely.

'What are you doing here? Are you here alone?' he asks curiously.

'I'm here with my sister, for her wedding,' I explain. 'The whole family is here. You?'

'I won a competition,' he slurs. 'And I'd just lost my job anyway, so I thought, fuck it, I'm going to Hawaii. It's bloody expensive, though, isn't it?'

'It really is,' I agree.

'Anyway, I'm off to find my room,' he announces with a scratch of his head. 'Wherever it is. Maybe I'll see you later.'

'Yeah, good luck,' I reply with a polite smile.

As he stumbles off, it's clear that Gary Garrie is neither wedding date material nor someone who can help me bag myself one by propping up the bar with me.

As I take a big gulp of my cocktail, I can't help but wonder if this whole ordeal is utterly ridiculous. What the hell am I doing – what am I hoping will happen? If there ever was a moment to back out of this silly charade, to come clean and admit the truth, it's probably now. But, damn, the thought of confessing is almost more embarrassing than the entire charade itself. I can't walk it back now, not without looking even more tragic than if I'd just decided to go to the wedding alone to begin with.

My options are seriously limited. I could find someone to take with me, but that's quite obviously not something that's coming naturally to me, or I could claim that my supposed date got held up and couldn't make it, but Sunshine is already suspicious, and getting caught in the act would surely be the most humiliating outcome of all.

The truth is, I need a date – not just to save face, although that's certainly up there, but because I genuinely want one. The idea of being the lone singleton amidst all the couples on the dance floor during the bride and groom's first dance is tragic. Bloody hell, if Lucy plans to throw her bouquet, she may as well just hand it to me, to save us all some time.

I need to find someone, but who will fit the bill? There are so many people here but it feels like searching for a needle in a haystack, trying to find a date for the wedding, with a personality and a success record like mine.

The barman places another cocktail in front of me, with a

charming smile on the side. This time it's a long blue drink with a white foamy top.

'Another drink,' he tells me. 'Glasses don't run empty on my watch.'

That's good, because they always run empty on mine.

I return his smile and thank him for my drink. I should probably drink them a little slower, if he's going to keep them coming at this rate.

'Do you need my room number or for me to pay, or something?' I ask.

'No, no,' he assures me. 'No charge.'

I thank him again, but something is up, because I've definitely seen him taking payments from other people while I've been propping up the bar. I highly doubt it's because he fancies me. Gosh, you don't think he feels sorry for me, do you? I quickly push that thought from my head. Even considering it is knocking my confidence.

As I sip my drink, I overhear a man talking on the phone as he sits down next to me.

'...I've been on the phone to Geneva, and they're not having it,' he says with a scoff.

He's got a seriousness about him, and he lacks that chilled-out holiday vibe most people seem to be giving off, but his bright blue eyes seem to give off something soft and approachable, behind his strictly-business exterior. His accent is American, unmistakably, but I can't tell you where he's from exactly.

'...I bet my Aston Martin he doesn't,' he laughs into his phone. 'Anyway, we've got a meeting in two hours, so we'll see. Talk soon.'

Hanging up, his gaze shifts towards me, and our eyes meet.

'You'll be amazed how many people come here for work,' he says with a smile, nodding towards his phone. 'Are you here for business or pleasure?'

'My sister's wedding,' I reply.

'So neither then,' he jokes.

'It is feeling that way, from time to time,' I admit with a laugh.

'Can I buy you a drink?' he asks.

'You can try,' I joke. 'They just keep getting put in front of me.'

'You're a big shot then, huh?' he replies. 'Only the big shots get the special treatment.'

'Oh, no, not at all,' I insist.

'Sure, I'll believe you,' he says with a wink. 'Me neither.'

'You're important enough to be here for work,' I point out.

'Yeah, but I would rather be getting wasted and going to a wedding,' he confesses. 'I don't get much time to hang out.'

'We're hanging out now – kind of,' I say, daring to flex my flirting muscles.

'We are,' he agrees. 'I suppose there's no reason we couldn't have some fun.'

'Gigi, hello,' a voice interrupts us.

I turn to see Donnie approaching the bar.

'Hello,' I reply.

'Can I borrow you?' he asks.

Again?

'I'm just, er...'

'Just for a minute,' he tells me casually.

'Back in a sec,' I assure... the man whose name I've just realised I don't know.

'Okay, what's up?' I say through a laugh as Donnie pulls me to one side. Again.

'Nothing, I'm just saving you from that guy,' Donnie replies.

'And what makes you think I need saving?' I ask through a frown.

I'm a strong, independent woman. I don't need a man to save

me (I do need one for a date, though, haha, what a ridiculous person I am).

'Oh, right,' Donnie says sheepishly. 'Sorry, I jumped to... well, the best conclusion: that he was trying to shag you, but that you didn't know he was married.'

'Wow, you're jumping to all kinds of conclusions there,' I say, a bit ticked off.

'Perhaps you're right. Maybe a "bit of fun" means something else in America,' Donnie says with a shrug – I can tell he doesn't think he's mistaken, though. 'Sorry, I'll mind my own business. I'll grab a drink and get out of your way.'

Who is this guy and why he is sticking his nose in my business?

I head back to... the man whose name I still don't know.

'Sorry about that,' I tell him.

'That's okay,' he replies. 'I've just checked my schedule and I've only got an hour. Plenty of time, if you fancy coming up to my room but we'd better get a move on.'

As he looks at his watch, I notice the sunlight catch on his wedding ring. His fucking wedding ring.

'You know what, sorry, I have a boyfriend,' I say.

'I have a wife,' he replies with a shrug.

'My boyfriend is here,' I counter.

'So is my wife,' he tells me, oh-so casually. 'She's in the spa. Hence me only having an hour.'

'You're not exactly twisting my arm, buddy,' I say, trying to laugh my way out of an awkward situation.

'Baby, I'll twist your arms, your legs – you won't even remember your own name,' he tells me. 'But, just, only for the next hour. Well, fifty-five minutes now.'

'My boyfriend is, like, right here,' I say, putting extra emphasis on the words. 'He's the guy who just came to talk to me. I'll have to pass,' I say. 'Sorry.'

Why am I saying sorry? I'm not sorry at all.

The man sighs.

I grab my drink and head over to where Donnie is sitting. I plonk down on the sunbed next to him, under a cabana by the pool.

'Okay, what's your deal?' I ask him. 'You're just like, what, Hawaii's friendly neighbourhood busybody?'

I'm joking, but I really want to know the answer.

Donnie laughs.

'Look, I'm here on my own, I'm bored out of my mind,' he tells me. 'I went through a bad break-up, and I thought the time away from my day-to-day life might do me some good, but being here alone, all I can really do is think – or listen. I know you're looking for a wedding date, but, come on, turning up with a guy wearing a wedding ring isn't going to impress anyone. Unless, of course, you're wearing one too.'

'Yeah, I don't think pipping my sister at the post would go down all that well,' I reply. 'And obviously, I didn't know that guy was married. We were only chatting.'

'Like I said, I'm just bored,' he replies. 'We aren't all here with side quests.'

'What do you mean?' I ask.

'You, on your mission to find a date,' he says. 'It's something to do, isn't it?'

I laugh.

'Would you like to pretend to be my impressive wedding date?' I offer up playfully.

'Oh, no, I am in no way impressive,' he replies quickly. 'But trying to find the right person must be fun?'

'Feel free to do it for me,' I reply.

'It's been said before that I make an excellent wingman,' he informs me. 'You can do a lot worse than me.'

His eyes sparkle as he flashes me a friendly smile. There's something about his face that makes me feel smiley too.

'Okay, go on then,' I say.

'What?' he replies.

'Be my wingman,' I tell him. 'I'm clearly doing a terrible job on my own, and I am going to be on my own because until I have a date sorted out, my plan is to avoid my family.'

'Totally normal,' Donnie teases me.

'Yeah, well, I've made my bed now,' I reply. 'Want to help me find someone to lie in it?'

'Okay, deal,' he says with a laugh. 'I was only going to be knocking around on the beach today anyway. Side quest accepted.'

'How about you meet me in reception in twenty minutes?' I suggest. 'I'll pop back to my suite and then see you there.'

'Ooh, she has a suite,' Donnie teases. 'Okay, sure, see you in twenty.'

Well, this is interesting. There may be a lot of men here, but it seems like I'm going to have to navigate them carefully. Ah well, at least I'm not doing it alone now.

19

As I sink my teeth into the burger, my eyes involuntarily roll into the back of my head.

'This is the best burger I've ever had,' I announce.

'Who knew pineapple in a burger worked?' Donnie replies.

'Honestly, put pineapple and cheese in everything, they're a dream pairing,' I say. 'How is your steak?'

'Really good,' he replies. 'Although that could be just because I'm not eating it alone.'

'You are brave, coming on holiday on your own,' I tell him. 'I'm not sure I could do it.'

'Well, the clue is in the title, with the bad break-up,' he explains. 'I thought it might be weird to come here with my ex.'

I burst into laughter.

'You did not just say that to me,' I tell him playfully.

'Oh, God, sorry,' he blurts. 'I wasn't taking the piss, I promise.'

'I know, that's okay,' I reply. 'Where are you from?'

'Kent, originally, but I live in London,' he says. 'You?'

'I work in London, and I live *with my parents*,' I say with a laugh. 'So that's fun.'

'There's nothing wrong with that,' he replies, seeming sincere. 'Especially with the prices in London. I do love it, though. I couldn't imagine living anywhere else now.'

'Me too,' I reply. 'I love how it's this bustling, vibrant city, but then it has all these beautiful green spaces to escape to. Hyde Park is like my oasis, in the middle of the chaos. It's where I will go and eat my lunch, to get away from work on the crazy days.'

'The Serpentine, the open spaces – I totally agree,' he says. 'Money no object, that's where I would live. And the Royal Albert Hall nearby – I might not be able to play it, but they still let me visit.'

'Don't forget the museums,' I reply. 'The British Museum, the V&A – honestly, I'll never get bored. The magic will never wear off.'

'It sounds like we go to all the same places,' he points out with a chuckle. 'Great minds think alike.'

'You know, we might have crossed paths at some point, perhaps unknowingly,' I muse. 'London can be a small world.'

'And yet, we meet for the first time in Hawaii, thousands of miles from home,' he replies.

'That's probably on me,' I tell him. 'Weird things like that are definitely built into my personality. Nothing is easy or explainable. I am somehow completely boring and totally chaotic.'

Donnie laughs.

'You mentioned work being crazy – what do you do?' he asks as he pops a chip in his mouth.

'I'm a hairstylist,' I say. 'I work in a really busy salon. It's a lot of fun, but exhausting.'

'Is it true what they say, that hairdressers are like therapists?' he asks curiously.

'We are absolutely therapists,' I reply. 'Just, you know, not paid as well. It's good though because we're not bound by any sort of code of ethics or professional standards, so when people ask us for advice, we can say whatever we want.'

'You give unethical advice?' he replies with a faux gasp.

'Oh, all the time. Say someone is having trouble with their mother-in-law. I can say push her down the stairs, go on, it will make you feel better,' I joke, laughing wildly to make sure he knows that I really am kidding.

'It must be fun, getting to hear everyone's secrets,' he replies. 'I'm a classical guitar player so, when I'm at work, all I really hear is myself – or the occasional boo.'

'Who boos classical guitar?' I reply in disbelief.

'I play in hotel lobbies, wine bars – places like that,' he explains. 'Anywhere remotely upmarket, where people have had a drink, you'll be surprised what people will say. The richer they are, the ruder they are.'

'Oh, I know, believe me,' I reply. 'Someone – who I'm pretty sure was only in two episodes of *Love Island* before they got dumped – once threatened to shit in my handbag because she didn't like the fringe one of the other stylists had cut for her, and my bag was the nearest.'

Donnie snorts.

'Oh my God, I think ketchup just went up my nose,' he replies. 'Hey, did you notice, when I asked for ketchup, they looked at me like I had lost my mind, but when you asked for some too, they couldn't get it fast enough?'

I shrug.

'What can I say? Some of us get preferential treatment,' I reply carefully. 'Speaking of which. I have this gold card that gets me into the VIP areas of the hotel, and I thought I should look in the VIP areas to try to get myself a higher-calibre date. So, I just went to reception, and asked if I could have a card for my friend too – because I figured, if you're helping me, I need you by my side – and they said yes so, here you go, your own gold card.'

'Wow, Gigi, thank you,' he replies. 'That's so cool.'

'Thank me by finding me a decent date,' I laugh.

'I'll do my best,' he replies. 'When we're done here, maybe we can scope a few places out, see where might be best.'

'Okay,' I say. Then I laugh. 'This is so weird, isn't it?'

'It is,' he replies. 'But so much fun.'

20

Donnie and I slink into the indoor VIP bar, taking point behind a large palm plant.

My eyes widen and my jaw drops at the sheer extravagance. Almost everything is gold – probably to remind the filthy rich just how filthy rich they are – and I swear to God it makes the air smell like money.

The walls are gold, the disco ball is gold, and even the bar stools are wrapped in shimmering gold upholstery. Tables, chairs, coasters – it's like someone took a regular bar and, having realised they had a buttload of gold leaf knocking around, decided to go to town on the place. Midas hasn't just touched this place, he's thrown up all over it.

I laugh to myself softly as I notice the doors to the toilets across the room. You know what I'm thinking, don't you? Surely not, though? Solid gold (or gold-coloured, at least) toilets is surely a step too far? Would that make them too nice to use, or am I really not getting the super-rich thing? Perhaps it's normal – if not, the only done thing – to exclusively pee into a bowl made of a precious metal.

'Money can't buy taste, can it?' Donnie jokes quietly. 'Bloody hell, they must have mined Fort Knox to deck this place out. I've never seen so much gold outside of a Bond villain's lair.'

I laugh quietly.

'Exactly the kind of place for me to find the wedding date of my dreams,' I reply.

'There are plenty of gold statues of buff men,' Donnie points out. 'If the worst comes to the worst, we'll stick one of those in a suit.'

'It's good to have options,' I agree with a faux seriousness. 'But, back to plan A.'

'Yes, plan A,' he replies. 'Statue dates are definitely more of a plan B – C, even.'

I laugh.

'Come on, wingman extraordinaire, who's the lucky victim?' I ask, scanning the room.

Donnie points out a man sitting alone, absorbed in his drink and the music.

'There, that one,' he tells me. 'If I were sitting solo in this literal gold bar, that's exactly what I would be doing.'

'Okay then, wish me luck,' I say, a nervous smile creeping onto my lips.

'Good luck,' Donnie replies dutifully. 'I'll stick around, just in case you need a quick escape.'

'Thanks, but if he seems normal, I'll give you a sign to bail. I know you were hitting the beach today. I can always find you there.'

'All right,' he agrees.

I approach casually, edging towards him in a way that hopefully makes it seem like I've not even noticed him yet. I'm hoping he'll spot my lime-green bikini glowing from under my clothes so that I can catch his eye. He's in his mid-thirties, with dark hair and a well-groomed beard and messy brown hair that plays off against an otherwise squeaky-clean-cut look. He has hazel eyes and the kind of outfit you only tend to see in fashion magazines. He looks effortlessly thrown together – but in that way that looks like it did actually take a tremendous amount of effort.

'Do you mind if I sit here?' I ask simply, offering a friendly smile.

'Not at all,' he replies, returning the smile. 'Cute accent.'

'Thanks,' I reply. 'It's great that I seem fancy, to Americans at least, because back home I sound just like everyone else.'

'You have a tactical advantage here,' he replies with a grin. 'Use it wisely. I'm Todd, by the way.'

'I'm Gigi,' I reply, taking a seat right next to him.

'Gigi?' he repeats back to me, cocking his head curiously. 'That's an interesting name – certainly not one you hear every day.'

'Thanks,' I reply, trying to gauge his sincerity. Was that a compliment, or was he subtly questioning my parents' naming choices?

'Can I get you a drink?' he asks, smoothly changing the subject.

'That would be great, thank you,' I say. 'Any cocktail would be lovely.'

'Coming right up,' he replies. 'I'll be right back.'

As Todd heads to the bar, I glance over at Donnie and give him a nod. He returns a supportive smile before gracefully making his exit. The last thing I want is for Todd to catch wind of my 'wing-man' observing from the other side of the bar. Let's not make any of this weird, for once, *please*.

Todd returns with two elaborate cocktails, which he places down proudly.

'It's called a Million Bucks,' he tells me, leaning in with a conspiratorial smile. 'Because it's expensive. Not quite a million bucks but it's pushing four figures, so it had better be good.'

My eyes widen involuntarily, but Todd doesn't seem bothered by the extravagant price tag. I take a sip, and it is really good – I can taste cola, vanilla, and rum, all of which I love. It's undeniably delicious, yet I can't discern any significant difference from the comparatively cheaper drink I had earlier. But, come on, cut me some slack, I've only been living the suite life for a day.

We sit together on the golden sofa, sipping our overpriced drinks, as Todd leads the conversation.

'You know, I once had this truffle-infused dish in a bistro in Paris,' he begins. 'Absolutely divine. I can still taste it. It probably cost a week's wages to some people.'

I nod, feigning interest, but not in love with the way he's telling the story.

'And then there was this dessert in Dubai,' he continues. 'It was covered in gold leaf – again, so expensive. Almost too beautiful to eat.'

'Amazing,' I say, trying to sound like I mean it.

'Come on then, Gigi.' He turns to me with an expectant look. 'What's the most expensive thing you've ever eaten?'

I take another sip of the Million Bucks cocktail – it might be expensive, but it can't work miracles.

Caught off guard, I furrow my brow, pretending to rack my brain for the answer.

'Oh, you know, it all blurs into one, doesn't it?' I reply with a casual shrug.

'I guess it does,' he replies.

Todd takes a leisurely sip of his pricey cocktail as he thinks about what to say next.

'When you're not here in Hawaii, obviously, where do you like to go on vacation? Any favourite spots?' he asks.

I feel a momentary panic as I consider my options. Blackpool and Magaluf don't exactly scream luxury, do they? I take a thoughtful pause, my mind racing to conjure up a suitable response.

'Oh, you know,' I say, trying to sound cool and casual. 'Usually Bali. It's my go-to holiday spot.'

His eyebrows raise in genuine interest.

'Bali, really? That sounds amazing. What do you enjoy doing there?'

'Just the usual, you know – exploring the beautiful beaches, relaxing...'

I've never been to Bali so I have zero idea what I'm talking about.

'Do you stay in Inagua?' he probes further, raising an eyebrow.

'Of course,' I reply.

'Inagua is in the Bahamas,' he says, suspicion building.

'I know that,' I say, laughing. 'I didn't want to embarrass you, by correcting you – obviously I've been there too, though. To be honest, my family leans more towards ski holidays than beach getaways.'

'I'm a level five,' he tells me enthusiastically, pleased to have finally found something we can talk about. 'You?'

Why did I mention skiing? What's wrong with me? Of fucking course he skis – and of fucking course I know nothing about the levels. Are there only five? Do they go up or down? Is five the best, or is it out of twenty?

'Same,' I reply simply, hoping I've given the right answer.

'We like to go to Aspen, every winter,' he tells me. 'Aspen's got this perfect blend of runs for everyone in the family. Something nice and easy for the younger members, and the more challenging ones that get my adrenaline pumping – you can't beat it. It's nice to meet someone else who appreciates it. What brand of skis do you use?'

Oh, for God's sake, always with the details. I freeze again. What brand of skis can I even name? Could I make one up? Would he be able to tell if I did? Ugh, probably.

Instead of reaching for yet another lie, I pat myself down, eventually locating my phone, which I pretend is ringing.

'Oh, I'm sorry, you'll have to excuse me, it's Geneva,' I tell him, raising my phone to my ear and walking away, pretending to engage in a conversation, taking inspiration from the married man I spoke with earlier today. As you do.

Okay, so pretending to be rich isn't going to work – I'm clearly terrible at it.

I'll go find Donnie, tell him how badly it went, and try to figure out a new approach. Next time I won't be so quick to send him away, that's for sure.

I guess it turns out I really do need a wingman.

21

Donnie's expression shifts as he spots me walking towards him, his face falling into the sand beneath his feet.

I skulk over to him, although it's hard to feel too blue when you're in Maui.

The sun-kissed sand, warm and velvety beneath my bare feet, glides effortlessly through my toes as I take each step, and it tickles like a dream. There's nothing quite like being on a warm beach, alternating between dipping your feet in the soothing ocean water and digging your toes into the soft sand. It's a very specific kind of therapy, one that can clear even the cloudiest of minds. I'm really going to put that theory to the test today.

I stroll towards him, my shoes dangling from my fingertips and my tail between my legs. The Maui breeze plays with my hair, ever so gently, making me feel like I'm in a movie. I'm half tempted to walk in slow motion, to really lean into the scene, but this is real life, and Donnie probably already thinks I'm mad enough.

'That wasn't very long,' Donnie remarks, his tone a mix of curiosity and subtle disappointment for me.

'Short and sweet,' I reply plainly. 'Like all of my efforts.'

'Let's go for a walk,' he suggests. 'We can debrief.'

'Well, we're not going to need to walk far to do that,' I tell him with a kind of pathetic laugh.

The beach sprawls before us, showing off the golden sands and bluey-green waters of Wailea. As we amble along, I look out over the Pacific. The sea stretches endlessly, meeting the horizon where one beautiful shade of blue blurs into another. A few fluffy clouds drift lazily overhead – even the sky is chilled out here.

The sun bathes everything in a warm, golden glow – even me, who could almost pass for having a tan in this lighting. It kisses my skin with a gentle heat that soothes me right through to my bones. I swear, back home, it feels like we had the longest, coldest winter this year. I was relieved when spring finally turned up, but the weather here makes spring in London seem more like the Antarctic. Okay, so maybe I'm exaggerating, but I feel like I'm drunk on the sunshine right now.

'I love this place,' I blurt, soaking in all of the beauty that surrounds us on all sides.

'It's paradise, isn't it?' he agrees. 'This time last year I was in Skegness. It was raining.'

I laugh.

'That sounds about right,' I reply. 'Still, you can't beat it, now and then, can you?'

'You're saying that as you stroll the beach in Maui,' he reminds me. 'Have a word with yourself.'

He gives me a playful nudge as he teases me.

As we walk, the sand feels like soft carpet beneath my feet, and the rhythmic crashing of the waves adds a soothing ambient white noise to our walk.

'So, what went so wrong?' Donnie asks me. 'With the guy in the bar.'

I'm glad he specified that because, honestly, where would I even start?

'I just had no idea what to say to him,' I confess, my voice carrying a mix of amusement and bewilderment. 'The conversation kicked off with him talking about the most expensive things he's ever eaten, and all of the exotic holidays he has been on throughout his life, and I just had absolutely nothing to bring to the table. And, rather than being honest with him, I stupidly tried to change the subject to skiing, to pretend that was my rich girl vibe, but of course he was an expert in that too, and I have never even seen a person ski in real life. I've probably only seen it in cartoons, where a character flies off a rock and lands in a big pile of snow, disappearing into it, leaving nothing but a print of their body and their skis on the surface – do you think that's how it goes in real life?'

'I very much doubt it,' Donnie says with a chuckle. 'So, what, you left? What did you say, did you make an excuse?'

'Of course I did,' I reply. 'The old fake phone call. It always works a charm.'

'Who did you pretend it was?' he asks curiously. 'A family emergency?'

'Geneva,' I say simply.

Donnie falls about laughing.

'It isn't that hard to pretend you're rich, you know,' he tells me. 'Anything you think sounds silly, to them, sounds completely normal. For example: I was thinking of adding a second Olympic-sized swimming pool to my yacht. What do you reckon? I think it will be a nice touch.'

I humour him, feigning a gasp.

'You only have the one Olympic-sized swimming pool?' I reply in faux disbelief. 'Darling, you're practically slumming it. Even my swan collection enjoys two Olympic-sized swimming pools. My goodness – I thought you were classy.'

Donnie raises an eyebrow and scoffs.

'Swans? How passé,' he points out. 'I've got peacocks. They're more of a statement bird. Even parks have swans.'

We both fall about laughing, unable to keep it up a second longer without cracking up.

'It's all so silly,' I say with a sigh, shaking my head.

'Don't forget, you're staying in a suite,' he reminds me. 'Here, that's practically flaunting your billionaire status.'

'Oh, I didn't book a suite,' I confess. 'They just messed up my reservation or something, and had no choice but to upgrade me. Not that I'm complaining. But I'm just a normal person.'

Donnie laughs.

'I'm a normal person too,' he replies. 'But I'm stuck in a normal person room to match.'

I laugh but then something catches my eye.

'What's that?' I ask.

We approach a traditional-looking Hawaiian beach hut, sitting there alone on the beach.

'Oh, I read about this,' Donnie tells me. 'It's part of the resort. Let's go inside.'

'Okay,' I agree, even more curious now.

As we step through the entrance I'm surprised from the get-go, as it's a regular door with a handle, absolutely not the kind of door you would expect to find on a beach hut. It's oddly out of place, and I can't help but be intrigued.

Inside, there isn't much of anything, just a simple wooden two-seater bench in the centre. I raise an eyebrow at the strange set-up.

'Okay, so, I think we just do this and...' Donnie trails off as he closes the door.

Suddenly, an almost eerie silence envelops us, and the

outside world fades into silence with the exception of one thing, the roar of the ocean, which is suddenly even louder than it was outside.

'How does it do that?' I ask. 'Is there a hidden speaker, or something?'

'I have no idea,' he replies. 'It's supposed to be relaxing. God, it really is.'

Donnie takes a seat on the bench and exhales deeply. I join him, sitting in the heart of the room, the sounds of the ocean crashing around us, as though our hut has drifted out to sea, and we're a million miles from everyone.

'Okay, so, what are you looking for in a date?' he asks me. 'Perhaps, if we can figure that out, we can find you someone that's right for you.'

I ponder the question for a moment but it's as though the tranquillity of the room has slowed down my thoughts.

'Well,' I start, taking a deep breath. 'It depends on the reason, I suppose.'

'Go on,' he prompts me curiously.

'For the wedding, I'm on the lookout for someone impressive,' I explain. 'Someone who will turn the head of everyone in the room.'

'What a normal thing to say about your sister's wedding day,' he teases.

'Yeah, I realise that sounds a little strange – not like that, obviously,' I insist. 'But someone who outshines the other guests, at least.'

'That kind of thing is important to you?' he asks, interested, but without judgement.

'Oh, no, not at all,' I insist. 'Not usually, anyway. Nathan, my ex, has brought his new girlfriend. I know you said you didn't recognise her, and I don't know if you were just being polite, but she's

Sunshine Greene, the influencer, the one who was on *Welcome to Singledom*.'

'The reality show?' Donnie checks. 'No, I don't really watch stuff like that.'

'Ah, well, needless to say, Sunshine is a big deal, and absolutely traumatising to be replaced by, because I'm never going to be able to compete with her,' I explain. 'But maybe my date could. That's the only reason I'm looking for someone to take, to save face, because the last thing I want is to seem like a tragic spinster and have everyone feel sorry for me.'

Donnie rubs his chin as he thinks for a moment.

'Okay, that makes sense,' he replies. 'I'm sure you don't need me to tell you that you don't need to do that, obviously, and that me telling you won't stop you, so I may as well help you out.'

'Thanks,' I reply. 'I know, it's tragic, and it makes me look bad. If I were looking for an actual partner, impressive would be pretty low down the list – or, at the very least, I would judge it differently.'

'You don't owe me an explanation,' he reassures me.

'I know but, even so,' I say with a smile. 'I like things to be simple. I just want to find someone who loves me for who I am, unconditionally. Someone who enjoys the simple pleasures in life too, like fun Friday nights and sleeping in on Saturday mornings. Someone to go for long walks with, to share Sunday dinners, and, you know, eventually start a family with, even if it's just the two of us. A rich, impressive person is the last thing I want, to be honest. After the ones I've met so far, I would say that kind of person is the kind of person I definitely don't want to be with, long term.'

Donnie nods thoughtfully.

'I agree,' he says. 'I want the same things.'

I smile at him.

'And if I can find someone with a big family then even better,' he continues. 'My parents are no longer around, and I didn't have any siblings or cousins growing up, so I always feel a little alone in the world.'

I feel his words in my chest.

'I'm so sorry to hear that,' I tell him sincerely.

'Ah, it's okay, I'm used to it,' he replies. 'And I have friends – great friends – of course. Friends are the family you choose, right?'

'Yep, and family are the family you're stuck with,' I point out with a smile.

God, I am lucky to have them, though.

He laughs.

'It would be nice to find a partner, one for keeps, who loves me for who I am,' he tells me. 'So we're similar, in that respect.'

The air inside the beach hut changes as our conversation shifts to more serious matters. Suddenly it feels harder to breathe and, I can't explain why, but it's not necessarily in a bad way. I find myself moving in closer to him, as he edges closer to me too, as an undefinable unspoken connection builds between us. The rhythmic crash of the waves around us almost hypnotises me, making this random little beach hut feel like the most romantic place on earth and, for a moment, Donnie seems completely irresistible.

We both seem to jolt to our senses at the same time, Donnie moving up suddenly, while I head over to the door, walking it off like nothing happened. Well, nothing did happen, but it felt like it was about to.

'We should head back towards the hotel,' I babble, my voice vaguely panicky.

'Yeah, absolutely,' he replies.

I reach for the handle but nothing happens. The door won't open. I try and I try, using more force with each attempt, but it isn't budging.

'The door won't open,' I tell him, full-blown panic in my words now.

'Don't worry,' Donnie reassures me, coming over to lend a hand. He tries once, then twice, but it resists stubbornly, almost as though it's determined to keep the two of us in here until we give it what it wants.

After a bit of fumbling, Donnie manages to jostle the door open.

'There we go,' he says proudly. 'Come on, let's head back before we get ourselves in any more trouble.'

That sounds like a good idea because, if I stay here, I really could get myself in trouble.

22

It's hard to avoid your family when you're trapped on an island with them.

It's not that I want to avoid my family, per se, more that I want to avoid the build-up to the wedding, people asking me questions about my date, and just being around Nathan and Sunshine generally.

So, here I am, reporting for dinner with Lucy, Rick, my mum and dad, Nathan and Sunshine. Three loved-up couples. And me. Fab.

I would dwell on how apparent my single status feels, sitting here with couples, but to be honest I'm sort of distracted because something is up.

I thought I was imagining it at first – everyone likes to tell themselves that they're the main character, right? It's both the reason we worry about what people are thinking about us when we're not around, and why we walk down the street listening to music through our headphones, pretending it's the soundtrack to our day.

I'm not imagining it, though, not today. Something is definitely going on. I even put on a dress that was less see-through, and it's still happening, so we can rule that out at least.

I know this is going to make me sound paranoid but, honestly, I feel like people are talking about me. I keep catching people (staff *and* guests) staring – some of them even whispering about me – and I've tested it, to make sure it's me. I went to the loo and the eyes went with me, they didn't stay with the table. Why? I have no idea.

It has its perks, though – whatever it is – because the free champagne is flowing. I swear, people keep making excuses to come to our table, to talk with us all, schmoozing us, plying us with free drinks and unlimited bread. No, I'm not complaining about unlimited bread, because who would? It's just... odd.

'They're very attentive here,' Mum says, pleasantly surprised.

'Yeah,' Dad replies. 'But is it me, or are they only this attentive with our table?'

'No one else is getting free champagne,' Rick says, glancing at the surrounding tables.

'Maybe they know we're getting married?' Lucy half-jokes.

'Maybe they know I'm here,' Sunshine adds – completely straight-faced.

'Do you know that guy?' Nathan asks me.

I follow his gaze to a man, probably in his forties, who is staring over at me. When he catches us looking, he doesn't look away – like I would, if someone caught me staring – he gives me a nod and heads over.

'Hey,' he says.

'Erm, hi,' I reply, laughing awkwardly.

'I just wondered if I could buy you a drink?' he asks.

Oh my God, what is going on?

'I'm okay, thanks,' I tell him.

'We're eating dinner, mate, do you mind?' Nathan says, dismissing him.

The man ignores him.

'You know where I am, if you change your mind,' he says with a wink.

I watch him walk off before turning my attention back to the table. Everyone is staring at me.

'What?' I blurt.

'What is going on with you?' Lucy asks with a chuckle.

'Nothing,' I practically protest.

'Something strange is happening,' Mum chimes in. 'Is this to do with your mystery date? Is he someone famous? Oh, my goodness, is he someone royal?'

It's not that I don't love how livid Sunshine looks right now, but I can at least nip that in the bud without ruining all my fun.

'No, he's no one royal, so you can put your big hat away,' I insist.

'A royal, whether senior or way down the succession line, wouldn't typically go for a girl like Gigi,' Sunshine points out – helpfully, I think? Like, she thinks she's being helpful, but really she's just being rude.

'What?' my mum shrieks, offended on my behalf. 'Any royal would be lucky to have Gigi.'

'I'm just saying, she's more of a Pippa than a Catherine,' Sunshine explains – although, again, I think she thinks she's explaining, but she's just being rude – *again*.

'Was that the one with the bum?' Dad asks. Yes, that's about as far as his interest in the royals goes.

'Okay, this is just getting weird now,' I insist, not dignifying his question with an answer. 'No one is royal, nothing is going on, you're all imagining it.'

'Ms Marsden, hello,' a man in a suit says as he appears next to me. 'My name is Trevor, I'm the restaurant manager – I trust you're all having a lovely evening?'

'Top-notch,' my dad calls out.

'Yes, really nice, thank you,' I reply.

'Our patissier was looking for someone to join him in the kitchen, to sample a few desserts so that we can whip up something truly special for your table – how does that sound?' he asks.

'Erm, yes, that sounds great,' I reply. 'Now… or…?'

'Yes, if you're ready now, please, follow me.'

'I'll be right back,' I tell a table full of my silent, frozen nearest and dearest.

I follow Trevor across the crowded restaurant, weaving in and out of tables as I try to keep up with him. I suppose he knows the layout here like the back of his hand, whereas I feel like I'm a contestant on *Total Wipeout*.

'Oh, one sec,' I call out to Trevor, as I notice Donnie sitting at a table on his own.

'Hello,' I say brightly.

'Fancy seeing you here,' he replies.

'Do you want to come with me to try some desserts?' I ask, offering no further explanation.

'Of course,' he replies in an instant.

'The more the merrier,' Trevor says.

'Gigi,' I hear a familiar Scottish accent call out. 'How are you doing?'

'But it is certainly a two-person thing,' Trevor is quick to add as he watches Gary Garrie approach us.

'Still living the dream?' Gary asks – whatever that means.

It's funny, he talks to me like we're old friends, not just fellow Brits who bumped into one another at the bar.

'You know it,' I reply politely. 'You?'

'I've really landed on my feet this time,' he tells me. 'Anyway, see you at the bar.'

'Yep,' I call after him. Then I turn to Donnie and Trevor. 'I have basically no idea who he is, but he seems to think we're old friends.'

'You and Jack Daniels,' Trevor dares to joke. 'Shall we?'

We follow Trevor to the kitchen where a small table is laid out with what I'm going to guess is every dessert on the menu.

'We thought you might like to sample a bit of everything, undisturbed,' Trevor says. 'I'll leave the two of you to enjoy.'

'Do I want to know why you're getting a private table, with every dessert on the menu?' Donnie asks. 'Not that I'm complaining, if I get to join you.'

'Honestly, I have no idea, but just go with it,' I suggest as I pull a plate of profiteroles closer to me.

'Do you think this will work at the bar?' Donnie asks curiously.

'We could try one after dinner, to find out, if you like?' I suggest with a shrug. 'There's no way, after I put away this lot, that I can have dessert with my family too.'

'Sounds good,' he says with a laugh. 'Oh, wow, is that a lemon tart?'

'Have at it,' I say generously – because I'm so generous with my free desserts when I have fourteen of them.

'You have to try this,' he says, offering me a mouthful on his fork.

I laugh as I lean over to take a bite.

Oh, boy, that's good. The bursts of citrus, the crunch of caramel, and the smoothness of the velvety custard. I've never had a lemon tart like it.

'Mmm, that's great,' I tell him, my eye scanning the table for our next victim. 'Ooh, try this.'

I grab two small deep-fried dough balls, popping one in my mouth, before passing one over to Donnie. They're covered in chocolate sauce so, rather than take it in his hand, he opens his mouth for me to pop it straight in there.

'Amazing,' he says through a mouthful.

I suck the chocolate from my fingertips.

'Honestly, I'm in heaven,' I announce. 'I don't think there is anything you can say, to convince me I'm not dead.'

'It doesn't get any better than this, does it?' Donnie replies. 'Unless we had a cuppa.'

'Oh, my God, imagine having a cup of tea to wash it all down,' I say, fantasising.

'It's worth a try, right?' Donnie says with a wink.

I watch as he gives Trevor a wave, beckoning him over.

'How are the desserts?' Trevor asks.

'Just... phenomenal,' I tell him.

'Yeah, they're really good,' Donnie agrees. 'We were just wondering if it might be possible to get two cups of tea.'

'Of course,' Trevor replies. 'We have honey orchid oolong, ginger spice chai, Egyptian Chamomile...'

Trevor's voice trails off.

'English breakfast tea?' Trevor says, already knowing that the answer is yes.

'That would be amazing, cheers,' Donnie says.

'I'll be right back,' Trevor tells us.

I notice some kind of pineapple and meringue dessert in a bowl so I place it between us.

'This one next, I reckon,' I say to Donnie as I pile my spoon high.

'Let me at it,' he replies, swooping in with his cutlery. 'Did they let you do this with the starters and the mains too?'

'I wish,' I reply. 'Maybe tomorrow.'

Donnie laughs.

'Well, you always know where I am, if you need any help eating,' he says.

'It's the one thing I've never had any issues with,' I point out. 'But it's fun to have a partner in crime.'

Trevor soon returns with two cups of tea.

Yep, something strange is definitely going on. But, whatever it is, I'm into it.

23

'Does everyone always stare at you, wherever you go, or is it a Hawaii thing?' Donnie jokes.

'It's very much a Hawaii thing,' I reply with a laugh. 'But I'm glad you see it too – I was starting to think I was imagining it.'

'Oh, no, it's definitely happening,' Donnie says, whipping his head around just in time to catch a group of men staring over at me. They avert their gazes, in different directions, trying to pretend that they weren't just looking over here.

We're back in the golden VIP bar, and I'm definitely attracting an audience, I just have no idea why.

'Honestly, you'd think they'd never seen a thirty-something spinster chain-drinking cocktails before,' I joke, raising my eyebrows playfully. 'Do I have something on my face?'

'Not that I see,' Donnie replies.

'And we don't have an Emperor's New Clothes-type situation, where I'm actually naked, but think I'm fully clothed?' I check.

'Only if I can see the clothes too,' he says with a laugh, his eyes meeting mine.

'Then, honestly, I'm stumped,' I confess, leaning back in my chair. 'And frustrated that, whatever it is, it doesn't seem to be translating into wedding dates.'

'I don't know, I think you might be in luck,' Donnie tells me, his gaze scanning the room. 'I definitely keep seeing people giving you the eye.'

'No one ever gives me the eye,' I state firmly. 'Unless "the eye" is what we're calling strange, judgemental looks now.'

'Compliments from the bar,' a waiter says as he places two more cocktails down in front of us. As he sets my drink in front of me, he winks with a mischievous twinkle in his eye, leaving me as puzzled as I am amused.

'Okay, so this is either like something out of a romantic comedy, or a horror movie, and I can't quite be certain,' I tell Donnie through a forced smile, keeping my lips still, like a ventriloquist, because you never know who is watching.

'Which would you prefer?' Donnie asks with a chuckle.

'To watch or be in?' I laugh. 'Actually, it's probably horror either way. I love horror movies, I watch them all the time, so I reckon I would be better equipped for dealing with one. If this were a romcom, and all these guys were lusting after me, then if I knew what I was doing, I'd be rolling around in the sand with one, not sitting here glaring back at them.'

Donnie snorts with laughter.

'Fair enough,' he says. 'That's another thing we have in common. I love horror movies.'

'Really?' I reply.

'Really,' he confirms with a grin.

'*The Shining* is my comfort movie,' I tell him – for most people it's usually something light, or something from their childhood, but not me, oh no.

'And to probably every other man on the planet, that would be the biggest red flag,' Donnie replies with a laugh. 'But I'm so into it.'

Butterflies find their way into my stomach, fluttering with a mixture of surprise and delight.

'Oh, really?' I say, matching his playfully flirtatious tone, feeling my cheeks start to warm.

'Really,' he replies, leaning in slightly, his voice a breathy whisper. '*Black Christmas* is my favourite Christmas movie.'

'The original, or one of the remakes?' I ask, lowering my voice too.

'That's not a serious question,' Donnie says through a smile.

I quickly sit back in my seat again, having found myself once again leaning into Donnie, but he was definitely meeting me in the middle.

'So, if this were a horror movie, how would I get a date for the wedding, do you think?' I ask.

Donnie chuckles, his eyes narrowing playfully.

'Well, in the classics, the lead always lures someone in with their charm, maybe a shared interest in scary movies. Then, just when they think they're safe—'

Donnie barks like a rabid dog and lunges for me playfully. I jump out of my skin and I love it.

'Well, it would be classic me, to take a dog to the wedding,' I point out.

'He's a ten, but he's secretly a werewolf,' Donnie jokes. 'Or what about a vampire? You should have known he was sus, when you found him on Matcher and he didn't have any photos, just ominous descriptions like "Night owl who enjoys moonlit walks and being invited over".'

'Brilliant,' I reply, caught up in the playful banter. 'Or – it might seem like I'm at the wedding alone – but I do have a date, it's just that he's a ghost so, you know, you can't actually see him.'

'Oh, but he's a gentleman ghost, so he holds the door for you and pulls out your chair – terrifies all the guests,' Donnie continues.

'Chivalry isn't dead, not even in the afterlife,' I say with a smile.

There's a playful ease in our conversation, a shared sense of humour that makes the evening feel like a fun escape from my tragic reality, even if we are joking about the shitty situation I've found myself in.

I can't help but smile to myself. It's nice, seeing more of Donnie's personality, beyond him just being a really kind (if slightly nosy) guy. I like what I see.

I stretch as I let out a yawn.

'Gosh, I'd best go to bed,' I announce with a casual smile.

'Lucky you,' Donnie replies, a hint of mock envy in his voice. 'Back to your lovely suite. My room is next to the hotel club – the twenty-four-hour club.'

My lips part sightly at the thought.

'Oh, wow, that sucks,' I say sincerely. 'I'd heard there were cheap rooms here but... yeah, wow.'

A playful grin crosses Donnie's face.

'It's okay, if I can't sleep for the noise, I just go for a dance,' he says with a shrug. 'Do you want to give me your number? We can make a plan, for tomorrow, to try to find you a date?'

'Okay, sure,' I reply with a smile, weirdly looking forward to it.

We exchange phones, tapping in our respective numbers, which isn't really a big deal, but I don't know, it feels like a thing.

We say our goodbyes and I head for my suite, looking forward to getting in my bed after what feels like one hell of a long day.

It feels late. The dimly lit reception area is quiet, deserted even

– yeah, I've definitely got horror movies on my brain now. I navigate through the open space, the only audible sound being the soft echo of my footsteps against the polished floor.

As I pass the front desk, a young man looks up from his station, breaking the stillness of the night.

'Ms Marsden,' he calls out, his voice carrying a touch of urgency. 'Ms Marsden, do you have a moment?'

He rushes over, holding a pile of newspapers.

'Your business papers, for the morning,' he says breathlessly. 'I was going to drop them later but, if you're here now...'

I offer a grateful smile, taking the stack of papers from him.

'Oh, thanks,' I reply as he hands them over.

I did notice that on a morning there are these huge newspapers left for me in my suite, but nothing fun or gossipy or anything I would be remotely interested in. Just business – although I suppose that's for the sort of person who usually stays in a room like this. Still, I politely take them with me. I don't have the heart to tell him that I don't want them, not when he went out of his way to get them to me.

The hotel corridor stretches ahead, the subdued lighting casting shadows that seem to dance alongside my steps. As I navigate towards my suite, I can't shake off the nagging feeling that something is off. I've definitely creeped myself out.

The papers briefly slip from my grasp so I grab hold of them and, as I do, I spot something that sends a genuine shiver down my spine. I close my eyes briefly, as if attempting to erase the words that have appeared on the page. But when I open them again, the headline is still there:

Where is G. G. Marsden?

I hurriedly read the article, trying to take it all in.

As far as I can tell, it turns out that when Martin Savage – the head of huge media corporation Mediworldwide – passed away earlier in the year, his two kids were set to inherit everything. That is until it came to light that he had a secret third child, who never even knew they were related to the tycoon until he passed away. Obviously the business world is going mad, trying to track this person down, and all of the rumours are saying that they reckon the unknown Savage child is checking into somewhere private, to hide out. Not only is the Grand Palm Resort floated as one of the most exclusive resorts on the planet, but at some point a name, from an unnamed source, has been thrown into the mix of rumours, and that name is G. G. Marsden.

Shit. So that's why I've been getting special treatment, and a suite, and why so many eyes are on me. Hotel staff, who have been told to look out for someone called G. G. Marsden, heard me give my name and just decided that I'm the elusive heir to the Mediworldwide empire. Yeah, right. Do I look like I'm rich? I mean, okay, obviously I do right now, but they've made me this way. Then again, I suppose that's the point. The newly minted G. G. Marsden could be anyone, from any walk of life. I'm as much a contender as anyone.

I can't believe they think it's me. None of this is my fault, right? I didn't pretend to be anyone, or suggest I was anyone, I simply gave my name when I checked in, and the rest was down to them. If the hotel, and everyone in it, is jumping to the conclusion that I am G. G. Marsden then that's on them, not me.

Still, I suppose I could come clean, and tell them their mistake, but if I do that then I can kiss goodbye not only to my suite life here, but to everyone in the wedding party thinking that I have some mysterious sugar daddy wedding date who is keeping me in my new lifestyle.

I should sleep on it – I'm too tired to make any big decisions now. I need to think long and hard about what to do and I can't do that with a clear head now, not at this time. I'll decide it in the morning, after a good night's sleep, in my glorious super-king bed, in my wonderful, beautiful suite.

I'm not coming clean, am I? Not a chance.

24

The Hawaiian morning sun is something that I could seriously get used to. How does anyone ever have a bad day, when they kick things off bathed in such a warm, glorious glow? I could actually be a morning person, for weather like this, which is something I never thought I would say, because I've always considered myself to be a night owl.

I'm making my way through the hotel, to the outdoor restaurant where breakfast is served, alone, because I'm still desperately trying to avoid anyone from the wedding party, lest I have to explain myself.

It's not that I don't want to spend time with them – of course I do – but it's getting harder and harder to dodge the awkward questions. It was hard enough when I was dodging questions about this (non-existent) super-date I'm supposedly bringing to the wedding, but now that I know why I'm getting such special treatment here at the resort, I feel like I need to dodge their prying questions about that too, at least until I figure out what I'm supposed to do about it.

Oh, and I do still need to find a date, which is not only time-consuming (who knew?) but also isn't something I can do in front of my family, for obvious reasons.

I just need to work out how to play this, because right now I seem cool, and interesting, and desirable, and I can tell that my family and friends think something exciting is going on for me. Just imagine, if they found out that not only am I pretending to have a date when I don't have so much as a sniff of one, and that my super-special resort treatment, and my fancy suite, were down to nothing more than a classic case of mistaken identity. It would take this whole thing from absolute magic to totally tragic. Honestly, I didn't think it was possible for me to look like more of a loser in this whole 'ex at the wedding' situation – which is why I've been trying so hard to find a date – but if people found out about all of this, I really would look like an extra-special sad sack – and a sociopathic one at that.

The hotel lobby is a scene of pure luxury and tranquillity, as always. The scent of fresh flowers lingers in the air pretty much everywhere you go here, which isn't something anyone can claim about London, and the combination of the warming morning light and the gentle cool breeze drifting in through the open bifold doors is the best cocktail to start the day with.

As I step outside, getting closer to the outdoor restaurant, the peaceful ambience is almost meditative. The rustle of palm leaves and the distant murmur of the ocean sound suspiciously perfect, like this whole place is a simulation designed for relaxation. It's hard to believe somewhere could be so flawlessly soothing on the senses.

It's a jarring change, and a burst of life back home, when my Zen moment is abruptly shattered as a man's body collides with mine. It's not just any man, it's Gary Garrie, and he is almost certainly drunk.

'Whoa, sorry about that.' Gary slurs his words, offering a

sheepish smile that his confused eyes can't seem to get on board with as they dart nervously from side to side.

'No worries,' I tell him, picking up the key card that he just dropped. 'I think this is yours.'

I hold the card out for him to take.

'Which one?' he asks, puzzled.

I laugh as I take him by the hand and press his key card into his grip.

'This one,' I say. 'Are you on your way to bed, or is the day just starting for you?'

Gary squints, as if trying to decipher that one for himself too.

'I'm not sure, really. Just going with the flow,' he mumbles before meandering off – bumping into someone else almost immediately, dropping his key card again.

I can't help but chuckle to myself.

Gary Garrie, such a party animal that they probably only named him twice so that he only had one name to remember, is having the time of his life. I don't know what kind of competition he won to bring him here, but he's certainly making the most of it. Good on him, I suppose. It's not a million miles different from what I'm doing. Making the most of my freebies while I can.

With a shake of my head and a lingering smile, I continue towards the restaurant, reminding myself why I'm here.

The breakfast bar is a real treat for the senses, a vibrant array of colours and tempting aromas that practically pull me towards it. Trays of fresh tropical fruit, platters of golden pastries, and the tempting aroma of Kona coffee mingle in the air, making my mouth water. I'm not here for breakfast – well, I am, obviously, I'm not crazy, but I have something I need to get off my chest first, to someone very specific.

As I stroll past the food, my eyes eagerly scan the restaurant, looking for Donnie. I'm relieved when I spot him, at a table tucked away in a corner. I join him, plonking down with an ungraceful thud.

'Mind if I join you?' I ask him. 'Also, good morning.'

I get that in there sharpish, realising how abrupt my tone is, but I'm itching to tell him what's going on.

'Good morning – of course not,' Donnie replies, the skin around his eyes wrinkling as he smiles warmly.

I stop in my tracks as I notice two plates on the table, piled high with a mouth-watering and incredibly varied assortment of foods from the breakfast buffet. There are stacks of fluffy macadamia nut pancakes drizzled with coconut syrup, fresh slices of pineapple and mango glistening under the light of the morning sun, and an assortment of pastries that look almost too pretty to eat. I feel like I am eating them already, just by smell and sight, and I have never been hungrier. The colours are so vibrant – the deep greens of avocado, the golden hues of fresh honey, and the burst of red from the ripe strawberries. Donnie has a bit of everything here, and I want it all, but I suddenly realise I might be intruding on something. Well, it's easy to forget I'm not the main character here, when I'm seemingly making everything all about me. I think I might be interrupting some kind of breakfast date.

'Oh my gosh, I'm so sorry, do you have company?' I ask, embarrassed, pushing my chair out. 'I can leave you to it. My story will keep until later, don't worry.'

'No, no, I'm here alone,' Donnie insists. 'Please, stay. Have breakfast with me.'

I look down at the two plates again and then back up at Donnie.

'There are two plates,' I point out. 'Did you guess I would be joining you?'

'Erm, yes,' Donnie says with a charmingly awkward laugh. 'Sure. We'll say that's the reason.'

I smile. It is suddenly so obvious he has loaded two plates for himself – a man after my own heart.

Donnie's brow furrows with concern as he seemingly notices the tension in my shoulders.

'Are you okay, Gigi?' he asks. 'You seem a bit tense.'

I let out a deep sigh, glancing around to ensure no one is eavesdropping on our conversation.

'I need to tell you something,' I confess. 'I'll go mad if I don't tell someone.'

'Go on,' Donnie says, leaning in so that I don't have to talk as loudly.

'I've worked out why I'm getting so much special treatment here at the resort, and why I'm getting so much male attention – it's because they all think I'm someone else,' I blurt.

Donnie looks confused.

'Who do they think you are?' he asks, puzzled.

'When I checked in, I gave my real name, which is Gigi Marsden, but they've all mistaken me for someone who has been in the news recently, called G. G. Marsden – have you heard about them?' I ask.

For a moment, Donnie just stares at me blankly.

'So... sorry, I'm just... I don't understand what's happening,' he tells me.

'I barely understand it myself, so I can only give you the simple version, but basically when Martin Savage died – the head of Mediworldwide – it turned out he had a mystery child from an old relationship, and the press has worked out that their name is G. G. Marsden, and that they were probably coming here, but they don't know anything else about them. So I've turned up here, given my name, and they've assumed that I'm *the* G. G. Marsden! Martin Savage basically chose our current prime minister, and he's a billionaire, and people think I'm one of his heirs, that I'm this influential, powerful woman. So that's why there's all this buzz around me, and why I have an amazing suite – it's all a big misunderstanding.'

'Wow,' Donnie says simply. 'That's... wow.'

I nod, taking a moment to breathe before grabbing his orange juice and chugging it down. Eventually, I come up for air.

'It's okay, Gigi, calm down,' Donnie says, his voice soothing. 'Have you told anyone else about this?'

I shake my head.

'No, just you,' I tell him. 'I only found out late last night. Do you think I need to do something about it? Do I need to tell anyone? Oh my God, they won't bill me, will they? I could never even begin to afford it.'

'You have nothing to worry about,' Donnie says as he leans back, considering the situation for a second or two. 'Keep it to yourself, Gigi. It's their mistake, and you deserve to enjoy all this. Plus, it might just be the stroke of luck you need to find a date for the wedding. Call it karma balancing things out for making you attend an event with your ex and his new flame.'

I can't help but laugh at the absurdity of it all.

'So, you're saying it's not unethical to let them believe I'm this heiress?' I reply.

'Not for the girl who tells people to push their mother-in-law down the stairs because it will make them feel better,' Donnie jokes, a mischievous twinkle in his eyes.

I snort a laugh, grateful for his light-hearted way of looking at things. Then I take a deep breath, allowing Donnie's reassuring words to sink in.

'Okay, if you co-sign this scheme, I won't spill the secret,' I say. 'Thanks for letting me vent to you.'

'No problem,' he says with a smile. 'Anytime you need to share a secret, I'm your guy. I don't know anyone else here, so I've no one to tell. Have you told your family about this whole mix-up?'

I shake my head and smile nervously.

'I'm avoiding them like the plague at the moment, so it's not exactly come up,' I confess.

'You know, you shouldn't be avoiding them, Gigi,' he tells me, serious for a moment, but still softly. 'You should cherish every moment with your family. Some people would give anything to have them around. My mum – who is no longer with us – would have absolutely loved it here.'

His words tug at my heartstrings. I can tell that he isn't saying any of this to guilt-trip me, just to remind me how important family is.

'You're right,' I admit, genuine gratitude in my voice. 'I'll make more of an effort to spend time with them. And I wish I'd never started this whole charade about having a date, but now I'm knee-deep in it.'

Donnie offers a sympathetic smile.

'I understand why you did it,' he says. 'You thought you were doing what was best to keep things moving smoothly. But your family loves you no matter what. And the right date will come along when you least expect it, or maybe even when you stop actually looking for one.'

I nod, appreciating his wisdom.

'You're probably right,' I say with a heavy sigh. 'I'll go and get you another drink, seeing as though I drank yours, and it's the least I can do for you hearing me out.'

Donnie grins, lifting his empty glass.

'Yeah, okay, but I don't want the regular orange juice, I want whatever super-special hand-squeezed, sun-sweetened extra-special vintage orange juice they save for the heirs and heiresses,' he jokes.

'Coming right up,' I say with a laugh, before heading towards the breakfast buffet to see what I can find.

As I stroll over to the breakfast buffet, my flip-flops make a subtle slap against the tiled floor. There is no way I could sneak up on anyone in these bad boys.

As I fill two glasses with freshly squeezed orange juice – the normal kind, because no one has popped out to offer me an extra-special version for heiresses – I'm interrupted by a voice behind me.

'Excuse me, do I know you?' he asks.

I turn to find a man in his late twenties or early thirties. He's tall and slender, with a physique that knows its way around a gym. As my eyes lock with his, I notice him eyeball me curiously.

'Hmm, I don't think so,' I say with a smile. 'Should I know you?'

He grins, revealing a perfect set of pearly whites.

'Maybe through work?' he says. 'I play for Liverpool City.'

I just about manage to stop my eyes from widening as I realise I am chatting with a Premier League footballer. I know that Liverpool City is a football team, because who doesn't? But otherwise I am totally clueless about football. I am not clueless enough, however, not to realise that a footballer would make an impressive date for a wedding though.

I play it cool, feigning nonchalance.

'Oh, I'm not really into football,' I tell him. 'But who knows, our paths might have crossed somewhere.'

He extends a hand, introducing himself.

'I'm Olly Jones,' he tells me. 'And what's your name?'

'Gigi,' I say with a smile.

As the words leave my lips, I notice his eyebrows raise ever so slightly.

'Do you want to grab a drink later?' he asks. 'We can figure out if we know each other, and if not, we can get to know each other.'

I smile as I think about his offer. Is it possible that he's heard about G. G. Marsden? I can't help but wonder. Still, if he's only interested in me because he thinks I'm rich, then maybe I don't need to feel bad about taking him to a wedding, just because he's got a good job.

'Okay, sounds good,' I say, allowing my excitement to lightly bubble above the surface.

Maybe Olly likes me, or maybe he's drawn to the allure of G. G. Either way, he could be the answer to all of my problems.

Donnie was right – perhaps the perfect wedding date does just pop up when you least expect it. Olly might not be *the one*, but he could be the someone I've been looking for.

25

As soon as I learned that the resort had its own clothing boutique, I knew that I needed to visit. Don't get me wrong, I love shopping at the best of times, but tonight I've got a date with a footballer, and I definitely didn't pack anything to wear that screamed: WAG.

I stroll into the resort shop, a casual air about me – because the last thing I want is to get *Pretty Woman*ed – and begin to browse the rails. I just need to act like I own the place, like I can afford anything in here – while secretly praying that I can actually afford *something* in here.

It's a fashion lover's dream. Rails upon rails of dresses, each one more exquisite than the last, are just waiting to be tried on, and then taken out somewhere fancy. The fabrics range from delicate silk to bold sequins, in every colour, length and style I can think of.

Oh, and then there is the wall of shoes. High heels, sandals, and boots in every imaginable style and colour are neatly displayed like a work of art. I honestly don't know where to begin – but if there was a way to sort them priced from low to high, that would be super helpful.

The woman behind the counter glances up and, as if hit by a

bolt of lightning, her eyes widen. She hurries over, all smiles and excitement.

'Hello there!' she greets, practically beaming. 'Ms Marsden?'

'Uh, yeah, that's me,' I reply, bewildered.

'Fantastic,' she replies with a clap of her hands. 'We did wonder if you were going to stop by.'

'You did?' I say.

'Of course – did no one tell you that our VIP guests can borrow anything they want while they are a guest here?' she says.

No, they did fucking not. Oh my God, why am I wearing a single item of my own clothes?

'I didn't know that,' I say with a smile.

'Well, in that case, we've got some catching up to do,' she replies. 'My name is Corin, I'll be your fairy godmother today.'

Corin barks orders at different members of staff, calling them all to action.

Different staff members emerge, each bearing an armful of garments, all looking like they're ready to transform me into a goddess. Someone else materialises with a tray of champagne. Okay, now I really do feel like I'm in *Pretty Woman*, but the nice bit, where they let her shop.

'Oh, thank you,' I say, accepting a glass.

I think I've had more champagne on this holiday than I'd had to date before I arrived.

'We're so thrilled to have you here!' another woman chimes in, already holding a silky dress towards me. 'This is a must-try!'

'Erm, okay,' I say, a little taken aback by it all.

'So, are you doing anything special later?' Corin asks.

'Just a date,' I reply, taking a sip of the champagne.

'A date, you say?' she replies with a smile. 'Well, we must dress you for the occasion. Do you want to charm, seduce, or destroy?'

I burst out laughing.

'A bit of all three, if that's an option,' I suggest.

'Darling, we've got just the dress for you,' she declares confidently. 'Here, take this into the fitting room, see what you think.'

I don't dare not do as I'm told, even though the dress in question isn't my usual style, material or colour.

But as I try on the long, white slinky dress in the luxurious changing room, I can't help but smile. I never thought it would suit me, but, damn, it looks good. I twirl in front of the mirror excitedly.

'Wow, you look incredible!' Corin exclaims as I step out from behind the curtain to show them. 'Now, we need to find you some killer shoes.'

A male employee, appearing from nowhere, takes this as his cue.

'I've never known a man not propose if a woman walked on his back in these,' he informs me as he shows me a bright red pair of ridiculously high heels.

'I'm not planning on walking on anyone's back,' I say with a laugh. 'But sure, why not? I'll try them on.'

'I'm sure you could have your pick of any man here in that dress,' Corin says, obviously just kissing my arse. 'I'll bet you're having to fight them off with a stick.'

I laugh politely until it hits me. Oh, no. No, no, no. Suddenly it all makes sense.

It did occur to me that, not only does there seem to be a high volume of single (or willing, at least) men at this resort, but that for some reason a disproportionate number of them seem to be interested in me. It's not that I thought it was because I was a hottie, I just assumed it was the sea air making everyone holiday-horny. No one is interested in me, not really. It's because they think I'm G. G. Marsden. I guess good news travels fast, around the hotel, and with loads of business types, I'm not surprised other people are making the same mistake. I guess I'm lucky that my lot are distracted by the wedding, and uninterested in business news – I'm sure I would have heard by now, if any of them had heard the rumours.

Well, do you know what, that suits me just fine. If people are only interested in me because they think I've got money, then I have no problems being interested in them for their potential to be an impressive date to the wedding. Don't get me wrong, I'll give people the benefit of the doubt, but I'll be keeping it in the back of my mind.

'Oh, honey, you're going to turn heads tonight!' he says, handing me the shoes.

'Here's hoping,' I reply.

Everyone bustling around, fetching shoes and accessories, dressing me up like a doll – it's definitely something I could get used to. It's nice having a team of people help me get ready. It's a shame they're only kissing my arse because they think I'm someone else.

26

Tonight is a perfect night for a date. The weather is spot on, now that the sun has gone down, leaving us with a temperature that is just right. The stars are twinkling above us, the atmosphere at the poolside bar is great, and the cocktails are delicious.

The only thing that isn't perfect about this date is the date himself.

Olly and I are not getting on at all. As though it isn't bad enough that he isn't laughing at any of my jokes, we're yet to find a single thing we have in common.

'So, what sort of movies do you like?' he asks as he swigs his beer. He sounds frustrated, obviously realising that this isn't going all that well either.

'I enjoy everything really,' I tell him, trying to be agreeable and friendly. 'Horror movies are definitely my favourite, though.'

Olly narrows his eyes.

'Really?' he says in disbelief.

'Yep,' I reply – what else can I say?

'Don't you think they're kind of pointless?' he replies. 'And harmful – I'd ban them, me.'

'You would ban them?' I blurt, struggling to keep a lid on my feelings on the matter. 'Why would you ban them? They're fun, they're imaginative, and they can be really meaningful – look at something like *The Babadook*—'

'I've never even heard of that,' Olly interrupts me. 'But you can't convince me it's anything more than just a bunch of creepy stuff and blood and things that will traumatise you.'

'Life can be traumatic,' I point out.

'Not really,' he replies. 'Not actually traumatic.'

Is he not on the same date as me? Because this is starting to feel like it's up there.

'What do you like to do for fun?' I ask, changing the subject.

'Well, I like to play football, obviously,' he tells me – which isn't going to be something we can talk about.

Bloody hell, there is more life in the cocktail I'm drinking – which, ironically, is a Zombie. This tall glass of bright red deliciousness is genuinely the highlight of my night. I wonder how many of them I would need to drink, for Olly to suddenly seem interested, charming or even nice. I know all of my drinks are paid for here but, damn, they would probably run out of mixers, if I were to give it a go.

'I never would have guessed,' I joke.

Olly doesn't laugh.

'All right, footballers are sharper than you think, you know,' he ticks me off. 'I'm sick of people thinking that footballers are thick, and that football is only enjoyed by thick people. It's not true.'

'I'm sure it isn't,' I say sincerely, feeling bad that he mistook my crap joke for passive-aggressive sarcasm.

'You have to be smart, to be a footballer,' he continues. 'Not like those folks doing menial jobs.'

'Menial jobs?' I repeat back to him for clarification.

'The ones you don't need to be smart for, like cleaning or hairdressing,' he replies.

Not only is that deeply offensive but it's entirely wrong. Speaking as a hairdresser, I can assure you, you have to be smart to do a good job. If I was thick, would people trust me with scissors and chemicals?

Olly hasn't even asked me what I do for a living (which makes me think that he might have assumed I'm G. G. Marsden), and maybe he wouldn't have said it, if I had told him what my job was, but even so, it's not a good look, and it's made me kind of angry. He's more of a miss than a match.

Olly, seemingly oblivious to my irritation, changes the subject.

'So, Gigi, what's your dating history like? Must be a line of suitors, huh?' he says as he drains the last of his beer.

I take a large gulp of my drink, willing it to go down faster, maintaining a diplomatic smile.

'Oh, you know, just the usual,' I say. 'Nothing notable to report. I've always believed in quality over quantity, though.'

He smirks, thinking he's getting somewhere.

'Well, I've had my fair share,' he informs me. 'Being a footballer, you know, every girl dreams of being a WAG. Can't blame them. It's always quality, though.'

I fight the urge to roll my eyes.

'Really? I don't think I've known that many women, who would describe that as their dream,' I point out.

I don't think I've known *any*.

'Well, it might not be what every woman strives for. But let's be honest,' he continues, seemingly proud of himself. 'Who wouldn't want to be with a footballer?'

I somehow maintain my diplomatic smile, not willing to burst his bubble. I wish I had it in me, to put him in his place, but being rude doesn't come all that naturally to me. I'd rather we just called it a night.

'Well, charm and kindness go a long way, regardless of the profession,' I say.

'Thanks,' he replies, taking that as a compliment.

As he continues to boast about the number of women he's dated, I find myself less and less willing to politely stick this one out for a moment longer. His arrogance, lack of curiosity about me, and the casual way he belittles certain professions don't sit well with me. I'm done.

With my glass now empty, I glance at my watch, feigning surprise.

'Oh, look at the time,' I say as genuinely as I can. 'I've got an early morning tomorrow. Thanks for the company, Olly, but I better head back.'

'Oh, okay,' he says.

Relieved at the thought of escaping this cringeworthy date, I stand up, and make a move.

'I'll walk you,' he tells me.

Oh, so he is capable of being a gentleman – not that it's enough.

'That's okay,' I tell him. 'I'll be fine on my own. Goodnight.'

'Yeah, goodnight,' he says.

He seems genuinely surprised that I'm not falling at his feet and this only makes me even more convinced that he isn't the man for me in any way, not even for a wedding date.

The Maui night air is cool and refreshing as I walk away from the bar, seeking solace in the garden area where the fountains are. The only sounds I can hear are the rhythmic roar of the ocean, the gentle flow of the fountains and the distant hum of activity from the bar. I'm relieved to be away from Olly, who seems determined to turn this evening into a horror movie of its own, which is kind of ironic.

I stop for a moment, admiring the fountain, enjoying the feeling of the cool breeze on my warm cheeks.

'I knew you'd change your mind,' Olly says, appearing suddenly, wrapping his arms around my waist from behind me.

'Just having a breather, before I head to bed,' I tell him.

'Want some company?' he asks me.

I try to pull myself from his arms but he doesn't let go, so I turn around in his grip.

'Come on,' he insists. 'Let me show you what you've been missing out on all these years. I've got quality and quantity, if you know what I mean.'

Olly leans in to kiss me. I try to pull away but he persists.

He's so casual, like he doesn't even realise he's forcing himself on me, I just don't think he's ever experienced anyone saying no.

'Olly, come on,' I tell him.

'You come on,' he says, flirtatiously, trying to persuade me.

His lips are almost touching mine when he pulls away suddenly. Wait, no, he isn't pulling away, he's being pulled away, by someone else.

I'm half expecting it to be Donnie, swooping in to save the day, but it isn't.

A mysterious stranger pushes Olly away from me.

'Why don't you get lost,' my knight in shining armour tells him – well, he's not actually wearing a suit of armour, just a regular (but very expensive-looking) suit, but you take my point. 'Come on, get out of here.'

Olly hovers, practically snarling at us both, so the stranger shoves him again.

My mysterious hero is a tall and well-built man – probably in his late thirties. His features are chiselled, and he sports a neatly trimmed beard that adds a rugged charm to his otherwise clean-cut appearance. His stylish suit accentuates his physique – so does his easy confidence, as he manhandles Olly. His dark hair is styled with a subtle tousle, not only adding to his overall charismatic and approachable demeanour, but it's giving Clark Kent vibes too. I'm trying to place his accent – Canadian, I think.

'You want to watch your back, pal,' Olly sneers, his bravado unyielding even in the face of rejection.

But despite his threats, Olly walks away, and the relief I feel is immeasurable. So much so that I feel compelled to hug my hero. The man doesn't take his eyes off him until he's gone.

'Thank you so much,' I tell him. 'I'm scared to even think about how that could have escalated if you hadn't stepped in.'

'Are you okay?' the mystery man asks, his attention fully on me now, concern evident in his eyes.

'Yes, I'm fine, just a bit freaked out,' I say.

'Do you know him?' he asks.

'I just had a drink with him but it wasn't going well,' I confess. 'I guess he thought otherwise. Needless to say, I won't be going near him again. You're my hero...'

'Jeff,' the man says, offering up his name.

I never in a million years thought my hero would be called Jeff.

'And I'm not a hero, just a guy who can't stand seeing pushy men make women uncomfortable, never mind putting their hands on them,' he tells me, his nostrils still flaring. 'Okay, you're distractingly beautiful, but that doesn't mean he can put his hands on you.'

His compliment takes me aback.

'Sometimes I wish I could apologise, on behalf of all men, for the seriously shitty behaviour my gender seems to love so much,' he continues.

'It's okay, I know you're not all bad,' I reply. 'You really are my hero. How can I ever thank you?' I ask as I rack my brain for something, anything I can do, to show him how much I appreciate him stepping in. If there's one thing I've learned about this resort and the people who stay here, it's that they pretty much always get what they want.

'Can I buy you a drink or something?' I suggest – as though that even comes close to making it up to him.

'How about I buy you dinner, tomorrow evening, show you that we're not all bad?' he suggests with a friendly smile. 'You would actually be doing me a favour. I'm here for business and I'm sick of eating alone. Plus, we can watch each other's backs. That guy did threaten he would return…'

I laugh at what is obviously a joke – the last part, anyway. I pause for a moment, considering his offer. Do I really want to go on another 'date' with another guy? Olly has definitely put me off the idea of finding a date. Genuinely, I hadn't even considered the fact that things could go wrong, that the people I meet might not be genuine, or might even have bad intentions. It's either the reason why I should give up, or it's a reason for me to give Jeff a chance. He saved me – surely he's a good guy? But, regardless, hanging out with him might be best because if I don't, I'm worried I'll get the fear, and stop trusting men altogether.

'How do you know that I'm not the weird one?' I ask with a smile. 'I might ruin your life.'

'I think I would let you,' he says flirtatiously.

'Okay, well, worse than that, we might not have anything in common,' I persist. 'Olly, the guy you just manhandled, and I didn't have anything in common. He made fun of me for liking horror movies, and he thought he was so amazing, because he was a footballer, and all he wanted to talk about was football, and how everyone loves footballers.'

'Oh, well, there you go,' Jeff says with a clap of his hands, as though he's cracked the case. 'I actually love horror movies – and everyone knows footballers aren't the sharpest knives in the drawer.'

I laugh. That's music to my ears right now.

'Look, I get that you're probably freaked out, and I shouldn't even be asking, but there's just something about you... Let me take you out, let me spoil you, let me help you forget about Olly the Premier League loser. Have you done much exploring here in Wailea? Have you seen much of Maui?'

I shake my head.

'I haven't left the resort since I got here,' I tell him.

'Okay then, how about I take you out, and I show you something cool – something exciting?' he suggests. 'No pressure, no getting handsy. My driver can take us, and he can be our chaperone, so you know you'll be safe.'

I chew my lip thoughtfully.

'I can't think of anything else to sweeten the deal, other than offering to pay you, but that's a whole other ball game,' he jokes.

'Okay, okay, put your wallet away, you've twisted my arm,' I tell him with a laugh. 'Tomorrow evening it is. Yes, to all of the above.'

I feel as nervous as I do excited, as I make plans with Jeff, but this is the right thing to do, to not let creeps like Olly put me off living my life.

Jeff walks me the rest of the way through the hotel garden until I'm back in the safety of the lobby.

'See you tomorrow,' he says.

'Yeah, see you then,' I reply. 'Good night.'

As I navigate through the lobby, I notice a few people sitting in the lobby bar, where a man is playing piano. It's only as I look closer that I spot Donnie, sitting on one of the sofas, all on his own.

Now that I think about it, he doesn't look too happy. I should check on him, before I go to bed. I feel like if the roles were reversed, that's exactly what he would do.

'Hey, Donnie,' I greet him, snapping him from whatever deep thought he was stuck in. 'Are you okay?'

He nods with a sigh.

'Hi, yeah, I'm okay,' he reassures me. 'Just tired. It turns out sleeping in a room next to a twenty-four-hour club is impossible. It's like trying to sleep in the middle of a party.'

'I don't know what I'm more surprised about: that there is a twenty-four-hour nightclub, or that they put rooms next to it,' I say.

'Yeah, and I'm certain it isn't what I paid for, but they're fully booked,' he replies. 'So I came here, for some peace and quiet. The pianist says, if I tip him, he'll stop playing so I can have a nap.'

I laugh. Whether he's joking or not, that's kind of funny.

'Hmm, if only you had a friend with a suite here, with a perfectly comfortable sofa, who wouldn't mind you sleeping on it, if it meant that you could get some rest. Plus, now that you know my secret, I kind of feel like I need to bribe you to keep it, so consider us even.'

Donnie laughs.

'Thanks, Gigi,' he says with a smile. 'I really don't want to impose on you but it's good to know that, if I get desperate, I can give you a call.'

'It's honestly no trouble,' I tell him. 'It's a big suite, for one person.'

'I'll keep that in mind,' he says with a laugh. 'You on your way to bed?'

'Yes – not to rub it in,' I admit guiltily. 'Hey, are you doing anything tomorrow morning?'

'What do you think?' he asks, chuckling as he makes a funny face.

'How would you like to join me, at the spa – the one for gold card holders only?' I suggest. 'That might be just what you need, to de-stress, and relax yourself back into holiday mode.'

Donnie's eyes light up.

'Okay, thanks,' he replies. 'I'd really like that.'

'I'll drop you a message with the details,' I say through a yawn. 'Are you sure you don't want to sleep on my sofa?'

'I'll give it one more night,' he says. My yawn must be contagious, because now he's yawning too. 'See you in the morning.'

'Yeah, sweet...' My voice tapers off as I playfully wince. He's not going to have sweet dreams, is he?

I do feel bad, heading back to my suite, when Donnie is trying to nap in the lobby, but I did offer. Perhaps, if he's still having trouble sleeping tomorrow, he'll accept my offer, and I'm sure a trip to the spa will do him the world of good.

And then there's my dinner date with Jeff, tomorrow night, to look forward to.

I think I might actually be looking forward to it, you know...

27

I've never met a spa I didn't like. I've also only ever been to comparatively cheap ones in the UK, it turns out, because I thought I knew what to expect today, but I was wrong.

This spa makes every other spa I've ever visited seem like a local swimming pool. Of course, this is the gold card spa, not the regular spa for the regular guests.

Everything here is so pristine and white – from the walls to the robes – but then there are these vibrant pops of colour everywhere in the form of these elaborate displays of fresh flowers, the kind that look too perfect to be real but, here, I know that they are.

When Donnie and I rocked up earlier we were first taken off in different directions. This place is unreal, with fountain walls along the corridors, and the most peaceful music playing ever so quietly, following you around wherever you go, like your own personal relaxation soundtrack.

I was given the softest, whitest robe to put on, and then I was led into a room for my massage. I genuinely feel like a new woman. At first it was painful, as she gave me a deep-tissue massage, but as she worked the tension from my muscles and the stress from my body, suddenly, all at once, it all just melted away.

I practically floated from the room, heading to the pool area where I eventually met up with Donnie, who looked almost drunk from his session. We looked over the list of other treatments – most of which we didn't even know what they were – before deciding that chilling out and making the most of feeling so relaxed was exactly what we wanted.

We're in the steam room, which is currently engulfing us in a cloud of warmth, the air thick with moisture. I'm wearing a bikini, while Donnie, who I'm sure must have trunks on, sits with a towel casually wrapped around his waist. As the steam swirls around us, I can't help but notice the droplets forming on his forehead, trickling down his chiselled jawline.

A bead of sweat lingers on his chin. I notice him smile, causing the droplet to land on his toned torso, and run down his abs towards his towel. I catch myself staring, suddenly looking at Donnie through a different lens, I realise that he's looking back at me so I quickly avert my gaze, trying to pretend I wasn't staring in the first place, probably doing a terrible job as I examine the ceiling.

'It's hot in here,' I blurt, as though that might explain why I was perving over him – it definitely doesn't.

Donnie chuckles, the sound resonating in the steamy enclosure.

'Well, it is a steam room, Gigi,' he teases me, rubbing his face with his hands, probably unaware of the unexplained effect it has on me.

'Har-har,' I reply.

'Maybe we should take a break,' he suggests. 'Grab a drink or something?'

'Good idea,' I say. 'I could do with cooling off.'

The pool area is half indoors, and half outdoors – you can even swim back and forth between the two. Inside is sleek and minimal whereas outside is a tropical oasis, surrounded by lush greenery and flowers. I need to cool down so we opt to sit indoors, where daybeds are laid out, draped with soft, inviting towels. Donnie and I find a pair, settling in, our bums only just touching the seats before a hotel employee appears with two large glasses of cucumber water.

'Here you go,' she says, her tone somehow bright but calming – just like everything else here. 'Is there anything else I can get for you two?'

I glance at Donnie, mischief in my eyes, before looking back to the staff member.

'Hmm,' I begin, as though I'm deliberating something, but my mind is made up. 'I really fancy a mai tai.'

I look back to Donnie as his eyes light up in agreement.

'I would love one too,' he adds.

'Coming right up,' she tells us with a smile.

'Do people usually booze in spas?' I ask Donnie when we're alone again.

Donnie laughs, shaking his head.

'I'm not sure, but, seriously, is there anything this hotel won't do for you?' he asks.

I playfully shrug.

'It's the G. G. Marsden effect,' I reply in hushed tones. 'They're convinced I'm this rich, influential VIP, and that catering to my every whim is beneficial to them. But, hey, I'm not complaining. I haven't heard a single "no" yet.'

'You should make some ridiculous requests,' Donnie jokes. 'See how far you can get them to go.'

I think for a moment, a grin spreading across my face.

'I want to swim with dolphins – but I want it to be extra magical, so someone needs to follow alongside us, in a boat, playing music,' I suggest – obviously joking.

'Or you could ask for the most elaborate dishes, but insist they swap ingredients for pineapple, even if it doesn't make sense,' Donnie suggests, joining in.

'I want my bed sheets ironing every morning, and once in the middle of the night, because I hate sleeping on wrinkled sheets – do not wake me, though,' I continue, fully in character now.

'What you really need is a member of staff who follows you around, and their entire job is to simply push your sunglasses back up your nose, when they slip down,' Donnie suggests.

I laugh.

'Do you know what though, jokes aside, I'll bet there are people who do make ridiculous requests,' I point out. 'I'm all for making the most of my time here, but I would never take the piss, or make anyone do anything so pointless for me. I don't iron my own bed sheets at home, so I certainly don't expect anyone to do it for me here. I'm a simple woman, with simple needs. Right now, if I could have anything – absolutely anything – it would be a plate of nachos. Not just any plate, though, the biggest plate of nachos I have ever seen in my life, with absolutely everything on top of it. Oh, and pineapple, because I kind of like your idea about having it with everything. The pineapple here just hits differently.'

'I couldn't agree more,' Donnie says, laughing softly.

The spa employee returns with two mai tais, and they look like liquid sunshine in a glass – bright, tropical, and I can smell them from here. Pineapple wedges adorn the rim, and a sprig of mint is delicately placed on the surface. There's even a flash of blue through the drink, giving it this sort of tie-dye effect. It's a work of art, it really is.

'Here you go, enjoy!' the employee beams, presenting them with a flourish.

She has a look in her eye, like she knows she's in tune with exactly what we want.

I heap her with praise because it must be a thankless task, running around after rich people all day. I mean, it can't be fun running around after anyone, but the super-rich seem to have this level of entitlement that would drive me mad.

Alone again, Donnie and I clink our glasses together in a silent toast before taking a sip. Damn, it tastes even better than it looks.

I lie back on my lounger again, making myself comfortable as I wonder when might be a nice time for a dip in the Jacuzzi.

'Did they say the different Jacuzzis are different temperatures?' I ask Donnie.

'Yeah,' he replies. 'Did you know the different levels of the swimming pools are all different temperatures? They get warmer, as you go down.'

'I didn't know that,' I reply. 'I haven't tried the pool – have you?'

'Yeah, it's amazing,' he replies. 'There are multiple water slides, and a lazy river, you can leisurely float down to a bar, in the pool, it's amazing.'

'Okay, that I have to try,' I say. 'Maybe not the water slides, but a lazy river to a bar sounds like a dream.'

'We could go later, if you fancy it?' he suggests. 'I'll even get you those nachos you've been dreaming of, if you fancy dinner later?'

I smile, the mention of nachos triggering a craving again, and that does sound like an absolute dream of a day. But then my smile drops, as I remember that I already have plans – my dinner date with Jeff.

'Oh, actually,' I start, trying to find the right words. I notice Donnie raise an eyebrow. 'I think I have a date later.'

Probably best I just blurt it out, right?

Donnie looks genuinely surprised.

'Oh? A date?' he repeats back to me. 'That was quick.'

'Yeah, I met him last night. His name is Jeff,' I share, watching for Donnie's reaction.

Donnie smirks, a playful glint in his eyes.

'Well, it's not every day you meet a young Jeff,' he points out, lightly roasting him.

I'm taken aback, noticing a hint of something in Donnie's tone.

'Oi, there is nothing wrong with the name Jeff,' I retort, laughing it off.

'Not if you're seventy, listen to the radio and hide from your wife in your shed,' Donnie jokes.

'It's not like you hear the name Donnie every day, is it?' I counter, a teasing smile playing on my lips.

Donnie laughs at me, shaking his head.

'I do,' he reminds me, and I can't help but laugh too.

Duh. Because that's *his* name.

This is what I love about hanging out with Donnie, it's so easy, everything is so much fun, and the gaps between bursts of laughter only ever seem to get shorter.

'So where is Jeff taking you?' Donnie inquires, his tone a curious blend of casual and interested.

'It's a surprise, apparently,' I reply. 'Something outside the resort – I'm excited to see more of the island.'

But as I glance at Donnie, I catch some peculiar shifts in his mannerisms. If I didn't know any better, I'd say there's a hint of jealousy in his eyes.

'He could be the answer to my wedding date problem,' I remind him softly, hoping to ease any tension I might have unintentionally created.

Donnie opens his mouth, as if he's about to say something, but nothing comes out. Before he gets a chance to say anything, the spa employee reappears and, oh my God, she must have heard my one wish, while she was delivering our drinks.

She presents us with the biggest plate of nachos I have ever seen – a genuine mountain. Layers of crispy tortilla chips, generously coated in gooey melted cheese, adorned with jalapeños, tomatoes, salsa, guacamole – it even has the pineapple. I want to plunge my face into them and scoff them down.

You've got to hand it to them; they are seriously on the ball with this stuff. If I were actually G. G. Marsden, I would be well and truly schmoozed.

Donnie and I dive into the nachos, our crunching briefly silencing any lingering tension. We don't speak – but that could just be because we're hoovering the food, or maybe it's something else. Whatever is going on, I can't quite put my finger on it. I guess I'll have to try to work it out.

28

I smile at the view as I watch the sun begin to set from my bedroom window. Bursts of orange and bright pink interrupt the blue sky, slowly taking it over as the evening draws in.

I've done something similar myself, swapping my yellow sundress for a navy-blue wrap dress ahead of my dinner date with Jeff tonight. I've washed my hair and applied date-levels of make-up, finishing everything off with silver jewellery and a generous spritz of perfume. I'm going for elegant and polished, but hoping that it doesn't look like I'm trying too hard at the same time.

I switch from admiring the sunset to checking myself out in the full-length bedroom mirror, doing one last sweep, making sure that I am the best version of myself that I can possibly be – whatever that is. I don't know, I guess I'm nervous, not just because this is a date, and I'm not ideal at those, but because Jeff might be my best shot at a date for this wedding.

Just as I'm about to grab my clutch, I hear a knock at the door. I head downstairs and open it to see Lucy standing there, her face like a tropical storm.

'So you are still here then,' Lucy says sarcastically, smiling just enough to take the edge off.

'Still here,' I reply. 'As though I'd go anywhere else right now.'

'Yes, because you're not acting out of character at all,' she replies. 'Are you going to invite me in?'

I laugh, stepping to one side so that she can come in.

'What's up, Lucy?' I cut to the chase. 'You're being weird.'

'I'm being weird?' she replies. 'Gigi, we're on holiday together, and we're barely seeing you. Catching a glimpse of you is like spotting a rare Hawaiian bird.'

I laugh.

'Sorry, I've just been busy, making the most of the resort and stuff – this is my one holiday this year,' I remind her.

'And my wedding,' she points out.

Fair enough.

'You're right, sorry, I've just been getting a bit carried away,' I tell her. 'Let's make some plans to do some things together.'

'Are you joining us for dinner tonight?' she asks, looking my outfit up and down.

'I'm busy tonight,' I tell her, practically wincing, because I'm only proving her point.

'Busy?' Lucy scoffs.

'I'm seeing a friend,' I reply.

'We're on holiday, Gigi, and we've been here a matter of days,' she says in disbelief. 'How do you have friends here already?'

'I make friends fast,' I say with a smile and a shrug.

'No, you don't,' she replies.

You can always count on your sister for a dose of reality.

Lucy chuckles, her eyes scanning me as though I really were some kind of rare bird she had never seen before, that she wasn't sure if she needed to fear or not.

'Seriously, Gigi, who are you, and what have you done with my sister?' she asks me.

I playfully roll my eyes.

'I'm just... cracking on with things,' I say simply. 'You're all always telling me I need to get my life back on track after, you know, everything that has happened.'

'Is this your break-up just properly hitting you?' she asks. 'Do you need help?'

'I need to go to meet my friend for dinner,' I tell her with a laugh.

'Okay, okay, fine. Look, I'm not saying it's a bad change, it's just unexpected,' she explains. 'I'll leave you to it, just promise me you're all right.'

'I promise I'm still me and I'm all good,' I reassure her. 'Let's catch up tomorrow, yeah? We can all do something fun, together.'

Lucy nods, giving me a half-hug.

'Tomorrow it is,' she says. 'Message me a plan. And tonight, don't do anything I wouldn't do.'

'You're getting married, that doesn't leave much,' I point out with a laugh.

Lucy glances around the suite with wide eyes, moving on now that she's sure I'm okay. She stands in the open doorway in the lounge and, for a few seconds, she just enjoys the cool breeze.

It makes me feel all warm and fuzzy, to see Lucy looking so content. Her hair and her sundress blow lightly in the breeze, making her look a little like a Hollywood starlet standing in front of a wind machine.

I know it sounds strange, but getting married really suits her. There's this undeniable glow, a mix of happiness and excitement, that lights up her eyes. The dress, the setting, and her beaming expression all come together to create this picture of pure happiness. It's one of those moments where you look at someone and you can't help but think: 'Yep, she's exactly where she's meant to be,' and, in the nicest possible way, I am so envious. I really want what she has and, stupidly, right now, I'm looking for anything but. Imagine if I put the same effort into finding love as I did trying to find a wedding date – I would probably be going to the wedding with someone who did actually care about me.

'Okay, this place is unreal,' she blurts. 'Like something out of a movie. Seriously, Gigi, how did you swing this?'

I shrug my shoulders as I smirk ever so slightly.

She nudges me with her elbow.

'Your mystery date?' she asks.

I shake my head, playing it coy.

'Maybe we could all come to you, tomorrow,' Lucy suggests. 'Seeing as though you basically have your own place here.'

'Don't you dare,' I practically cackle. 'This is the only place I'm safe from Nathan and Sunshine – this place is my sun cream.'

Lucy rolls her eyes as she laughs off my comments.

'Sunshine isn't that bad, is she? I know, she's a bit full of it sometimes, and I'll never forgive Nathan for dropping you like he did, but we've all moved on, right?'

The look in her eyes suggests that suddenly she isn't so sure.

'Don't worry, I'm just messing around,' I insist. 'It's nice in here, isn't it?'

Lucy walks over to the bifold doors that look out over the private pool area.

'It's more than nice,' she says. 'It's fit for royalty. Are you sure your date isn't...?'

Her voice trails off. It's like she knows it's a ridiculous question, but she can't quite rule it out.

'Just wait and see,' I insist with a laugh.

'You know this is weird, right?' she checks, raising an eyebrow. 'And that you could tell me, if something was wrong.'

Lucy knows me better than anyone in the world, and this situation is undeniably sketchy. I wonder if even Lucy is beginning to doubt my version of events now. This is her wedding week, she's supposed to be happy and enjoying herself, not worrying about me.

'Sis, I'm fine, I promise you,' I tell her, placing my hands on her shoulders, giving her a squeeze. 'And I'm so, so excited for your wedding.'

She allows herself to sigh with relief.

'Well, I'll let you get to your dinner, and I'll see you tomorrow,' she says.

'Yeah, see you tomorrow,' I reply as I see her out.

I'm almost certain that, if I were to come clean to Lucy, and tell her that I don't have a date for her wedding, that she wouldn't judge me at all. She would be kind, understanding, and tell me that it didn't matter. However, that's the last thing I want to be putting on her, in the run-up to her big day. I don't want her worrying about me or how I might be feeling.

All the more reason for me to turn up tonight and wow Jeff – but for good reasons, I hasten to add. I've managed to get the bad 'wow' down to a fine art.

29

Let me start by saying that, when Jeff pitched this 'date' to me, and really went the extra mile to reassure me that I would be safe, and that it wouldn't be weird, the last thing I expected was for him to kick things off by blindfolding me.

And yet here I am, wearing a blindfold, with a man I hardly know. Truthfully, if I get murdered right now, I deserve it. I really don't want to stop trusting people, or lose all the excitement from my life – I also don't want to get murdered, though, so here's hoping it's a nice surprise he has waiting for me.

It's a good job I'm excited because, were it not for that distracting me, I'm not sure travelling in a car with a blindfold on feels all that great.

The steady hum of the engine, the rhythmic vibrations beneath me, and the not-so-subtle sway with every turn that jolts me around. It's disorientating and it's making me feel ever so slightly carsick.

All I know so far is that Jeff has taken me on a mysterious adventure, but I have absolutely no clue about our destination. We hopped into a car, leaving the Grand Palm Resort behind, but Jeff only let me enjoy the scenic drive for a few minutes before it was time to be blindfolded. As you do.

Perhaps it's something about being blindfolded that has made all of my other senses stronger, but everything feels heightened right now. I fell in love with the scent of Jeff's after-shave, and it made my skin tingle, when he would give my shoulder a reassuring squeeze. Not only that but we've been chatting through the short journey, and we're getting on really well. This is, so far, the makings of a dream date. I'm seriously impressed.

Potentially the only thing I need to worry about is that I don't ruin it. I mean, come on, I've got previous.

We arrive at our destination and, after a short walk with Jeff carefully guiding me, it is finally time for me to take my blindfold off.

'Here we are,' he announces, a note of excitement in his voice.

I can hardly contain my curiosity as I remove the blindfold, squinting against the daylight. Slowly, the surroundings come into focus, but I have absolutely no idea where we are, or what we are inside. We're standing inside a strange wooden stairwell.

'Where are we?' I ask, taking in my surroundings.

Jeff grins, a mischievous glint in his eyes.

'Follow me and find out,' he suggests as he heads up the stairs.

Intrigued, I follow Jeff up the winding staircase, trying to hide how tragically out of breath I am – who knew I was so unfit?

I'm so, so excited. I'll say one thing about Jeff: Donnie may have thought he had an old man's name, but Jeff sure knows how to set up one hell of an exciting date.

My imagination races ahead of me, envisioning a fancy and exclusive restaurant with a scenic view, or something equally unique. The thought of something special and romantic sends my mind into overdrive. In fact, I can feel my legs moving faster, despite my muscles feeling absolutely knackered, because I suppose I never really walk up more than a few steps.

'You strike me as the kind of woman who likes to have fun,' Jeff says, very much like it's a compliment, as we reach the top of the stairs.

My smile drops and my breath catches in my throat as I realise what lies ahead of me. I'm not really sure what it is, exactly, I suppose it's some kind of double zip line where people go two at a time, stepping off the platform before whizzing down together at an alarming speed and, oh my God, we are so, so high up. Panic sets in; obviously I'm terrified of heights, which Jeff doesn't know, and he's absolutely wrong in saying that I seem like the kind of woman who likes to have fun – it turns out I don't. I'm the kind of woman who prefers a nice beige cardigan and a cup of tea, and having both feet planted firmly on solid ground. I am absolutely not the kind of woman who gets excited at the prospect of wilfully dangling from elevated podiums attached to glorified string.

I mean, come on, how safe is this anyway? Surely zip-lining is the kind of thrill-seeking activity that is exclusively for very brave, very experienced adrenaline junkies?

Right on cue, a child pushes past me, and it's almost as though he senses my fear, because he laughs at me. Then he and his dad step to the edge and – poof – they're gone.

Okay, so I am terrified, but there's a part of me that appreciates Jeff's effort to make this date unique and exciting. Maybe it's a chance to confront my fears, or perhaps it's a test of just how far I'm willing to go to find a date for this wedding. Am I really willing to face my biggest fear, just to impress a man?

'Okay, guys, you're up next,' the instructor declares, and I swear I can feel the nachos I had earlier zip-lining from my stomach to my throat. My heart starts pounding as I desperately search for an escape route, but, nope, we're handed helmets and harnesses faster than you can say 'wheeeee'.

As Jeff and I shuffle toward the platform's edge, the instructor leans in close.

'Couples usually go for the hand-holding option,' he tells us.

I shoot a glance at Jeff, and we exchange a look that screams: Are we really doing this? But from the look on his face, I can tell that he's not only planning to do it, he's excited.

I glance out ahead of me. It isn't just one zip line, it's two that run side by side, and it isn't just one stretch. This line takes you to another platform, which takes you to another, and then another, getting a little lower each time. I couldn't be higher from the ground right now unless I was in a helicopter, which I wouldn't love, but it feels like a safer option than dangling from wires.

'Ready? Here we go...'

The instructor's words hang in the air, but when it comes time to take the plunge, I decide that I would much rather be a spectator than a participant.

And so Jeff sails off solo, leaving me on the platform, hanging on to the staff member for dear life.

'Sorry,' I tell the instructor, feeling a tinge of embarrassment as I peel myself off him, and slip out of my harness.

'It happens more often than you would think,' the instructor tells me. 'Although it's usually kids.'

Smooth, Gigi. So smooth.

I awkwardly trail back down the stairs – lacking the energy I found on the way up – my cheeks burning with a combination of the awareness that comes from seeing the judgemental looks from very, very brave men (women and children) on their way up, and, let's face it, the most physical exercise I have done since school.

Finally back on solid ground, I resist the urge to plant a dramatic kiss on the earth beneath my feet. Instead, I hop into the waiting car, informing the driver that Jeff will be back shortly, and then I sink into my chair and think about what I've done. In years to come, when I'm an old woman, tucked up in bed, I will allow my mind to wander back to this day and I will run it through my head, again and again, thinking about what I should have done.

Jeff eventually returns to the car, triumphantly carrying two plates piled high with food.

'I hope you're hungry,' he says with a smile.

There are saucy chicken wings, balls of rice, and then a small container full of shrimp.

'I don't like seafood,' I blurt, getting it out of the way. 'Or heights. Sorry about all that, up there.'

'I know that now,' he says with a chuckle. 'But I didn't even consider that, when I arranged it. That was silly of me and I'm sorry so... peace offering?'

He hands me a plate before lifting the container of shrimp off it, dumping it on his plate instead.

'It's okay,' I reassure him, waving off the concern. 'Did you enjoy it at least?'

'I've done it before,' he says, with a shrug. 'Anyway, forget that, here we have Huli Huli chicken, which is super sweet and delicious – if you haven't had it before. I thought we could eat in the car, maybe take a scenic ride around the island, watch the sunset. There's a great route, along the Hana Highway, with some amazing views. Oh, and I know a great shave ice place, when you're ready for dessert.'

I smile as I nod enthusiastically. Food, with a view, and my feet on firm ground. Now this is my idea of a dream date.

'And maybe we could get to know one another a bit better,' he suggests. 'Just so I don't put you face to face with any more of your fears.'

'Good idea,' I reply. 'I'm terrified you've got a boot full of spiders.'

'So, Gigi, let's take it from the top: what was little you like?' he asks curiously.

'Barbie crazy,' I confess. 'I had a collection of dolls that could rival a toyshop, and I always loved to do their hair, which is ultimately what led to me wanting to train to be a hairdresser.'

'Well, they sound like the ideal test subjects,' he says with a laugh.

I know it sounds silly but I feel relieved when he doesn't react negatively to the mention of my job.

'What about you?' I ask. 'What was it like growing up in... Canada?'

'Good ear,' he points out, leaning back in his seat. 'Well, I grew up in a small town where everyone knew everyone – and everyone else's business. Hockey was practically a religion – I played on the local team, which I know sounds like a cliché, but I was a typical Canadian kid, dreaming of being the next Wayne Gretzky. But... I sucked.'

I smile at the mental image.

'I mean, I have no idea who that is, but that's cute,' I reply. 'You kept playing though?'

Jeff nods.

'Oh, you bet,' he replies. 'My parents practically had a second mortgage, to fund my equipment. I had everything I could need – still sucked.'

I laugh.

'You're laughing but, you know, what I really wanted was to be an astronaut,' he tells me. 'I was fascinated by space, stars, and the great unknown.'

'Wow,' I blurt. 'So, do you work in...'

Jeff shakes his head.

'I work in finance,' he tells me. 'Which isn't like hockey – although I suppose it is brutal – but working in mergers and acquisitions is nowhere near as interesting as space travel. But, hey, it pays well, and I can still look at the stars, right?'

'That's a nice way of looking at it,' I reply with a smile. 'My soon-to-be brother-in-law works in finance. My sister, Lucy, says it's the cure for insomnia. All jobs keep the world turning, though, right?'

'They sure do,' Jeff responds with a knowing smirk. 'It takes a strong... everything.'

I laugh as I glance out of the window. On one side of the car there is lush rainforest, on the other, beyond the roadside, the ocean stretches endlessly towards the horizon. The sun bathes everything in a warm, golden glow as it threatens to set. I wonder what this road is like in the dark, because of course I do, because nothing can be just nice with me, can it? With single-lane roads – and bridges over water – I imagine it can be scary, if you're not used to the drive. Still, for the views, it's worth it.

'So, when's the big day?' Jeff asks, pulling my attention back to him.

'Hmm?' I reply.

'You said "soon-to-be brother-in-law",' he reminds me. 'When is the big day?'

'Oh, it's this week,' I tell him. 'At the resort. The whole family is here for it.'

Jeff raises his eyebrows.

'Oh, is that why you're here?' he replies. 'I didn't realise you had family with you. I thought you were here alone.'

'Sorry if that ruins your plans to murder me and dump my body in the Pacific,' I joke – even the driver laughs at that one, which is either reassuring, or deeply menacing. 'I haven't been spending much time with them, to be honest, but I promised I'd hang out with them tomorrow, so I'll make it up to them.'

'Ah,' he says simply.

I glance at him curiously.

'Oh, it's not a big deal,' he insists. 'I was a bit presumptuous and booked the resort cinema, for just the two of us. I thought we could watch horror movies. You know what, though, if you're wanting to spend the day with your family, it's not a big deal, bring them along. In a cinema you won't even have to talk to them.'

I laugh at his joke, but I'm taken aback by his gesture. It's either incredibly generous or a little intense. It's nice that he's willing to include my family, but there is an obvious problem with him meeting them – what if Jeff could be my wedding date? It would be weird, to invite him to the wedding, right now, which means that if he did meet my family tomorrow, and seemingly didn't know he was my wedding date, but later turned out to be... oh my God, even I'm confused.

'Wow, that's really kind of you,' I reply, trying to keep my tone light. 'But we've got plans for tomorrow and there will be hell to pay if I don't stick to them. How about we grab dinner together after?'

Jeff looks a tad disappointed but quickly recovers.

'Sure, I've got a meeting tomorrow evening anyway,' he tells me. 'But if you're up for a late dinner, count me in.'

'Perfect!' I reply.

As we drive along the scenic Hana Highway, I breathe a sigh of relief, glad that I haven't put him off. I glance over at Jeff, whose eyes are fixed on the breathtaking views outside the car window. He must have seen it all before, as he seems to know what he's doing on this island, but it's nice to see that he still appreciates it... unless he is annoyed at me.

'Are you sure that's okay?' I ask him. 'I would have loved a cinema day but, seeing as though I haven't been spending much time with my family, I'm on thin ice.'

'It's absolutely fine,' he reassures me, squeezing my knee. 'You're worth the wait.'

My mouth twitches into a smile as I steal a glance at Jeff, and for a moment, it feels like something could actually blossom between us, if I open my heart to it.

I do feel bad, not accepting his wonderful offer, but things need to happen in a particular order, if it's all going to work out.

Bottom line: Jeff cannot meet my family tomorrow if he could be my date for the wedding, and I'm really starting to think he could be.

30

I practically float back towards my suite, on little clouds, after a dream of a date with Jeff.

I can't fault him in any way. He was charming, attentive, chatty and an absolute gentleman from start to finish. I may have been too scared to zip-line but, if I'm being honest, everything else made my heart race.

I take my phone from my bag, looking at it for the first time since our date started (which is another sign that it went really well) and see that I have a message from Donnie.

He says that, despite his attempts to get an early night, the noise outside his room is unbearable, and could he please take me up on my offer of sleeping on my sofa.

I really feel for him – mostly because I'm pretty sure that, were it not for the mix-up, I would be right next to him in the cheap rooms.

I tap a message back to him saying that he is more than welcome, and that I'm heading back there now, if he wants to head over.

The resort is so lovely and peaceful on an evening – well, it is here in the most expensive part. You could hear a pin drop. I love it, because it really heightens your other senses, like the dreamy scent of the greenery around you, with just a hint of the ocean beyond it. It's like having the world's nicest diffuser in every room.

I smile as I hit send. Is it weird that I'm looking forward to having some company in my suite? It's certainly big enough for at least two.

I let myself in and prep the sofa for Donnie. There are extra cushions and a blanket in a cupboard under the stairs so I grab them and make a bed up for him.

It's warm tonight – more so indoors than it is outside – so I open the bifold doors that look out over the pool. The second the doors open, I feel cool air creeping in, and warm air sneaking out. That's much better.

I'm just about finished when I hear a knock at the door, so I head over to open it.

'Is this the sleepover?' Donnie asks with a playful grin.

I feel myself light up when I see him standing there, with an overnight bag waiting to come in. I'm pleased to see him, and to have some company here too. Well, it's a big suite, and it feels quite empty with just me in it. Plus, left to amuse myself, I seem to wind up flashing poor unsuspecting members of staff, so at least having Donnie here will nip that in the bud.

'It is, and we're just about to tell ghost stories,' I reply with a chuckle. 'Come on in.'

'Thanks again for letting me do this,' Donnie says. I can hear the gratitude in his voice.

'You are welcome,' I reply sincerely. 'What's the point of having all of this space if I can't sublet?'

'A holiday from my holiday,' he jokes.

'Exactly,' I reply. 'Holidays can be hard work.'

And, boy, am I insisting on making this one that way.

Donnie smiles appreciatively, taking in the opulent surroundings.

'Oh, wow, it's even more luxurious than I imagined,' he blurts, twirling around like a kid in the snow.

'It's a five-star sofa-sleeping experience,' I inform him.

Donnie plonks himself down on the sofa.

'Wow, it really is,' he says, wiggling his bum to make himself comfortable. 'Actually, wait, no – no chocolates on the pillows?'

'Best I can do is an open bag of crisps,' I reply. 'They're really nice, though.'

Donnie chews his lip thoughtfully.

'Hmm, maybe four stars then, but I suppose it is free,' he continues.

'And beggars can't be choosers,' I remind him.

Donnie laughs.

'So, what's on the agenda for our sleepover?' he asks.

'Pillow fights and swapping secrets?' I tease.

He looks around the room, his eyes eventually landing on the large wall-mounted TV.

'Wow, that is a TV,' he says. 'It must be at least 75 inches.'

'Oh, of course, I expect no less,' I joke. 'Apparently, there are thousands of movies and TV shows on there. I've not even turned it on yet.'

'That's a crime against big TVs,' he tells me. 'Do you want to watch something? I'm wide awake now.'

It may not be a private cinema, but I'm not as fancy as this suite makes me seem.

'Yeah, okay,' I agree, settling onto the sofa beside him. The softness of the seat causes a gentle shift, and suddenly we're sitting shoulder to shoulder.

Donnie leans in slowly.

'What is your favourite horror movie?' he asks in a creepy voice. 'It looks like they've got everything – oh, here it is, *The Shining*, your favourite. Shall I stick it on?'

My eyes light up with excitement.

'Go for it,' I say, always happy to watch it. 'It's not even that late – not by my standards, anyway. I'm a night owl.'

'Sounds good to me,' he replies as he hits play. 'I'm definitely a night owl too. Love late nights, hate early mornings.'

I smile as I grab the remote and turn down the lights.

The room is bathed in the eerie glow of the TV screen as *The Shining* begins to play. The suspenseful music echoes through the suite, and even though I've seen this movie a thousand times, I still feel nerves and anticipation building inside me.

Donnie and I sit side by side, our shoulders touching, as we watch the movie in the silence it deserves.

As the camera pans across the vast, snow-covered landscape of the Overlook Hotel, I steal a glance at Donnie. It's strange, considering we only met a matter of days ago, but things between us just feel so natural. I'm so comfortable next to him, so at ease, and whatever we find ourselves doing, it always seems to be fun.

He said it was a bad break-up that brought him here, alone, to clear his head. It's hard to imagine anyone breaking up with him, if he's always this fun and easy-going. I'm not sure I would have let Nathan go so easily, if he was such a catch. Okay, so Donnie isn't flashy, or as romantically theatrical as Jeff, but relationships are about more than that. He isn't only a lot of fun, he's pretty good-looking too, he always smells nice, he's kind – I don't know if there's a label on his back somewhere but, if there is, it almost certainly says: 'boyfriend material'.

As the movie progresses, I can't help but inch a bit closer to Donnie. I guess that's what you do, when you're watching a horror flick, but I don't know. Something about doing so just feels right. His closeness is comforting, and as Jack Torrance descends into madness, I feel like, on the flip side, things are becoming clearer for me.

What am I doing? Why does this feel romantic? *The Shining* is not a romantic movie. I think I'm just being bewitched, by the soft lighting, and the fact we're sitting so closely together, and because I'm thinking about what a great guy he is.

Is he moving closer to me? I feel like he is? I feel like he's going to...

The sudden appearance of a shadowy male figure outside the bifold doors, at the exact same time Danny first sees the creepy twins in the movie, startles us both. With a collective jump, we cling to each other, like Scooby-Doo and Shaggy when they see a ghost.

The intruder isn't a crazed murderer or a man in a mask, oh no, it's much worse than that. It's Nathan.

'What the hell are you doing here?' I ask, my surprise (and annoyance) evident in my voice.

'I was on my way to see you and I thought I could hear screaming,' Nathan explains, his gaze drifting between Donnie and me.

'It's just the TV,' I tell him.

'Hello,' Nathan says directly to Donnie.

'Hi,' Donnie replies.

The air is thick with an unspoken tension as Nathan turns his attention back to me.

'What's going on?' he asks, furrowing his brow.

'Nothing,' I reply nonchalantly. 'We're just watching a movie – what's up?'

The casual atmosphere only seems to further baffle Nathan. I can't say I'm not enjoying the look on his face right now.

'Can we talk, Gigi?' he asks me, his eyes still darting back and forth between Donnie and me.

I glance at Donnie, who nods with an understanding smile.

'I'll keep it paused,' he tells me.

'Thanks,' I say to Donnie before turning to Nathan. 'Let's step outside.'

The Hawaiian night air is warm and fragrant, perfect for a stroll – the company could be better, though. Nathan and I walk along the edge of the pool, the distant sounds of the waves just about audible in the silence.

It's so nice out here at night – a totally different vibe to the daytime. Soft lights scattered around give everything this warm, cosy vibe. The pool itself is perfectly still and flat, like a giant mirror, reflecting the moon above.

Palm trees cast these cool shadows on the ground, and you can smell a hint of salt in the air, thanks to the sea nearby. The loungers and cabanas are empty, it's just so peaceful out here. It's so quiet that you'd think you're in a different world, miles away from the resort.

All that's missing is the right person to share it with – this would be a lovely romantic stroll, were I with someone I didn't want to push in the pool, before holding his head under the water. It's not that I'm a violent person, more just that Nathan probably deserves it.

'What's up?' I ask, attempting to cut to the chase.

'What's going on with you?' he asks. 'You're staying in this suite, which we both know you can't afford. You're bringing a mystery date to the wedding – that guy in your suite, he's the guy I thought worked here, right? Is he the date?'

I raise an eyebrow, unbothered by Nathan's directness.

'Not that it's any of your business, but that's Donnie,' I say. 'He's my friend, and I've said he can sleep here because his room is a nightmare.'

For a moment, Nathan looks almost angry.

'He's sleeping with you?' he replies, his tone almost accusatory.

'Under me,' I correct him, but then I realise that doesn't sound much better. 'As in, downstairs, on the sofa.'

'I think he likes you,' Nathan points out, a hint of jealousy lacing his words. 'He looked... suspiciously close. It seems like lots of the men here like you, actually. The waiters, the guy who wanted to buy you a drink... Did you get this much male attention when we were together?'

I can't help but drop my jaw in disbelief. I was definitely lacking in male attention when I was with Nathan, mostly from him, though.

'Come on, what are you doing here?' I ask again.

Nathan hesitates, his jaw tightening as his eyes shift from side to side. I narrow my eyes at him, sensing there's more to this surprise visit than he's letting on. Is he jealous?

'Just... checking on you,' he says vaguely. 'Lucy has been worried.'

The tension in the air is palpable.

'Well, as you can see, I'm absolutely fine,' I point out, my tone hinting at the absurdity of his sudden concern – where was this when he dumped me, huh? 'I'm going back in there to finish watching the movie. Try not to peep on anyone else on your way back.'

With that, I turn on my heel and head back into the suite, leaving Nathan standing by the pool on his own.

I can't help but smile to myself, as something occurs to me: I'm finally over him. If I'm being completely honest, I'm not all that sure that I was, or that I was ready to move on, and I think a tiny part of me still entertained the idea of me wanting him back. But seeing him here, all jealous and possessive, has given me the ick. I don't miss him, I just miss having someone to spend time with, someone to love me – someone to watch movies with. But there are plenty of other people out there who want to watch movies with me.

Suddenly I'm excited about what the future holds, and I haven't felt this way in a long time.

31

I stretch out in bed, my limbs extending into all four corners, as I come to. God, I sleep so well in this bed.

I rub my sleepy eyes before slowly opening them, allowing them to adjust to the light slowly, until I notice someone standing at the end of my bed.

I'm relieved to see that it is Lucy, and that she hasn't written 'redrum' on the wall, but it's still a surprise.

'What are you doing in here?' I mumble, my voice croaky with sleep.

'A random man let me in,' she replies.

'That's just Donnie,' I say through a yawn. 'He's a friend. He's sleeping on my sofa.'

'Because that's not weird at all,' she says, raising an eyebrow. 'Anyway, he's making us coffee. Throw some clothes on and meet me downstairs. In the meantime, I'll find out more about this mysterious Donnie.'

She leaves the room, and as I rub the sleep from my eyes, I can't help but wonder if I'm dreaming. Shaking off the confusion, I stumble towards the bathroom to face the day, starting with my reflection. Grabbing my make-up bag, I go through the motions, slapping on the basics. I would never bother for Lucy, who has seen me in various states of disarray plenty of times. I guess it's for Donnie, technically, because I'm not ready for him to see the unfiltered version of me. Why? I don't know, years of conditioning by women's magazines and the unrealistic beauty standards set by the likes of Sunshine Greene on Instagram could have something to do with it. Sunshine once claimed her 'no-make-up' make-up routine took a whopping forty-five minutes. When I do the works, it doesn't take me that long, but I suppose Sunshine always looks stunning, whereas sometimes the best I can pull off is a potato rolled in glitter.

Finally semi-presentable, I head downstairs, my heart racing with a mix of curiosity and sleep-induced delirium. Donnie and Lucy are already sitting at the table, deep in conversation, laughing together like they've been friends forever.

'Gigi, I am in love with Donnie,' Lucy declares, her eyes sparkling in a way that makes it seem like she really means it.

'Okay,' I say with a bemused laugh, because I can't have been more than fifteen minutes. 'I don't know how Rick is going to feel about that.'

'I think he's going to be in love with him too,' she replies. 'He's saved the wedding.'

'Did I fall back asleep?' I ask in disbelief. 'What happened?'

'The guitarist for the wedding ceremony broke his wrist,' Lucy explains. 'I was on my way here to share the crisis, and it turns out Donnie's a professional guitar player. He says he'll step in, so crisis averted – before I even got the chance to tell you about it.'

'That's great,' I say with a smile. 'Good old Donnie.'

'You're invited to the wedding too,' Lucy informs him. 'It's the least we can do, to say thank you. If you want to come, that is.'

'I'd love to,' Donnie replies. 'I've heard a lot about it from Gigi.'

'Amazing,' Lucy says. 'Honestly, I thought I was going to have to walk down the aisle in silence – imagine that.'

'I'm glad I brought my guitar with me,' Donnie says. 'It's amazing how often it comes in handy.'

'Back in a sec,' Lucy says. 'I'm going to call Rick, tell him to come here so we can tell him the good news together.'

'Well, you're coming to the wedding,' I tell Donnie once we're alone.

'I'm coming to the wedding,' he replies with a grin.

Is it weird that I'm glad that Donnie is coming? Somehow it feels like we're in this together. And if things don't work out with Jeff, well, at least I won't be at the wedding alone. I'll have a friend.

32

Now that the wedding crisis has been averted, this morning, as promised, is family time.

I have my second date with Jeff, relatively late tonight, and I've made plans to meet up and hang out with Donnie after lunch, which leaves me alone with the wedding party and, for better or worse, I've invited them all to my private pool area to hang out for a bit.

My parents, Lucy and Rick, and Nathan and Sunshine have all taken me up on my offer and, honestly, watching them all approaching at once is an almost terrifying sight – made no less scary by the fact that my dad is carrying a giant inflatable unicorn rubber ring.

'Hello,' I say, welcoming them as warmly as I can – something you think would be easy under the hot sun but, eesh, I can already tell this isn't going to go well. I can just feel it.

'Fucking hell, Gigi,' Rick announces – there goes the neighbourhood. 'This is unreal.'

'Wow, Gigi, this is where you're staying?' my mum says, leaning in to kiss me on the cheek. 'This is like a resort all of its own.'

'Well, I never thought I'd be invited to sip cocktails by a private pool, Gigi,' my dad says proudly. 'Have you won the lottery and not told us?'

I laugh because, while that isn't true, that's not completely unlike the situation I've found myself in – or the situation hotel staff think I'm in, anyway.

'It's incredible, Gigi,' Lucy adds.

'Yeah, you've been holding out on us,' Sunshine adds, with just a hint of snippiness.

Is it weird that I feel embarrassed? I mean, I know I'm not rich, and that I have no right to be here but, still, it feels oddly shameful to have something so nice, all to myself.

'Anyway, let's get comfortable by the pool,' I say, moving things along. 'There's waiter service here if anyone wants drinks.'

'Screw that,' Rick announces. 'I'm getting in!'

Rick charges towards Nathan, grabbing him on his way to the pool, flinging the both of them into the water at the same time.

'*Water* you doing,' Dad jokes with an amused laugh, following them, an inflatable unicorn in hand – oh, great, it is his. 'I suppose I'll play lifeguard – someone has to be the mature adult around here.'

Says the man with the inflatable unicorn.

'Well, why don't us girls get set up on the sunloungers,' Lucy suggests. 'I love to warm up my skin in the sun, before getting in a cool pool.'

'Girls just wanna have sun,' Dad calls back as he heads for the pool steps, getting one last dad gag in there – he's on top form today.

'And yes to the drinks,' Mum enthuses. 'Do you get better cocktails here?'

She's joking but I actually think we do.

We take our seats on the sunloungers outside my suite. If it were just my mum and Lucy, I would invite them in, and show them around, but Sunshine's presence is – ironically – a black cloud. I just know she'll find some way to ruin it for me, because it's almost as though she can't stand to see people have something she doesn't. That's actually a trait that she and Nathan have in common.

The morning sun bathes the private pool area in a warm golden glow, casting long shadows across the beautifully manicured surroundings. That gentle Hawaiian breeze that I've come to love dances through the air, carrying with it the subtle fragrance of scenery around us. The temperature is just right, neither too hot nor too cool, making it a perfect day for hanging out by the pool.

'Mother Marsden, cover your ears,' Sunshine commands jokily. 'Lucy, I've got a little something for your wedding night.'

'Oh, really?' Lucy replies, one of her eyebrows raised with curiosity.

'Yes, I got the most stunning lingerie, for a sponsored post, and now I've got my shots, there are a few items going spare – they would be perfect for your wedding night,' she explains.

'Oh, thank you,' Lucy says with an awkward laugh. 'I hadn't really thought about… that part of the wedding.'

'Well, why not?' Mum muses. 'You've planned every other part of it in great detail. You can't start slacking on the wedding night – start as you mean to go on.'

I snort with laughter. Lucy covers her eyes with her hands.

'Your mum is right,' Sunshine tells her. 'Nathan honestly loves it when I dress up for him – literally obsessed – in fact, these days, I swear, he would rather I was wearing something spicy, than have me completely naked. I don't think he's had much sexual stimulation, in previous relationships, it's all been so vanil…'

Sunshine's voice tapers off about, oh, I don't know, ten minutes too late.

'Awkward,' she blurts, avoiding eye contact with me.

Wow. I mean, if that wasn't an intentional dig, then I don't know what is.

I don't think I'm vanilla – I was certainly more adventurous than Nathan who, frankly, never wanted to do anything that wasn't strictly horizontal. Honestly, the man probably thought foreplay was the name of Channel 4's streaming service, and to him sixty-nine was nothing other than the number that comes before seventy.

If Sunshine dressing up in the freebies she has been given to flog on Instagram does it for him then good for him – good for both of them. I'm not going to let her make me feel embarrassed. Instead, I'm going to double down, and hit her where it actually hurts.

'So, you like the suite, huh?' I prompt, mostly in Mum and Lucy's direction.

'It's all so amazing,' Lucy says. 'I still can't believe it.'

'What can I say? My mystery wedding date is well and truly hooked,' I brag. 'I can get anything I want.'

'No way,' Sunshine blurts. 'I mean, this is all nice and all, but don't exaggerate.'

'Okay then, tell me something you want?' I suggest.

'What?' she blurts back.

'Tell me something you want,' I say again. I turn to Lucy. 'Lucy, it's your special week, tell me something you would love to have here right now.'

Lucy laughs as she racks her brains for a moment.

'Oh, I don't know – a grilled cheese sandwich and a massage,' she says.

'Back in a sec,' I say simply, heading inside.

I peep out of the window, to see their reaction. Mum and Lucy are excited but Sunshine is currently morphing into her alter ego – Thunder.

I head back outside and plonk myself on my sunlounger.

'And now we wait,' I say.

'Yeah, okay, we'll see,' Sunshine says.

'What's going on?' Dad calls out from the water, looking quite the picture of relaxation on his inflatable unicorn.

'Gigi is getting us massages and sandwiches,' Mum calls back. 'She can get us anything we want. Is there anything you want?'

'More inflatables,' he calls out. 'They're my reason for living – they're keeping my head above water.'

I smile to myself smugly. I already guessed that he would say that.

'Well, this is exciting,' Mum says. 'And it's so nice, to spend time together – I feel like I've hardly seen you, Gigi – although maybe I'm just used to seeing more of you, because you've been living with us since, oh... er... Anyway, it doesn't matter, it's going to be great, to spend the day together. Let's just focus on now, and all have a lovely day together, yes?'

I think about what Donnie said, about how important it is to make time for family, and I feel bad that I have plans for the rest of the day. Although I suppose, now that Lucy has met Donnie, and that he's going to be at the wedding, there's no reason I can't invite the family to join us. We're only planning on going for a drink anyway.

'I'm supposed to be meeting a friend this afternoon – Donnie, the one who is going to be playing the guitar at the wedding,' I explain.

'He's a bit of all right, isn't he?' Lucy points out in hushed tones – well, she is soon to be a married woman, after all. 'I was gutted when I realised he wasn't your wedding date. The two of you look great together.'

'Oh, really?' Mum sings curiously, a knowing smirk on her face. 'I look forward to meeting this Donnie then.'

I avert my gaze, so that she can't see me, because my mum has always had this way of reading me like a book. I'm not giving her anything – not yet.

'So, what are the two of you doing?' Mum asks. 'Anything nice?'

'Will I be jealous?' Lucy chimes in.

I don't know about that, but Sunshine looks so angry, you could almost mistake her rabid jealousy for sunburn.

'We're going to the gold bar, for a drink – you guys should come and join us?'

'Really?' Lucy squeaks. 'I didn't think we were allowed in there?'

I shrug with a seriously cool level of casualness.

'I'm sure it will be fine,' I say simply. 'When we're done here, if you want to go back to your rooms and get changed, we can all meet there. If you fancy it, that is. It's just a bar.'

'Just a *gold* bar,' Lucy corrects me.

We chat about the weather, the wedding – little bits here and there, until eventually my 'order' arrives.

'Oh my God,' Dad blurts as a pile of pool toys approaches him. I assume there's a person under there, carrying them all, but you would never know.

Next come the waiters, with silver platters piled high with enough grilled cheese sandwiches for all of us – oh, and they look so good. They are maybe the fanciest grilled cheese sandwiches I have ever seen in my life, and I am not exaggerating.

And finally the staff from the spa arrive, armed with bottles of oils and various massage tools, ready to make us feel like a million bucks.

With everything finally here, I turn to Sunshine and look at her over my sunglasses.

'If you can think of anything else you want, just shout,' I tell her with a smirk.

And with that I push my sunglasses back up my nose, lie back on my sunlounger, and bask in my own smugness.

You have no idea how long I've fantasised about being able to do that.

33

'Wow,' Donnie blurts. 'I wish I could have been there, to see the look on her face.'

He finally sips his mai tai, after being on the edge of his seat through my story, about how I used my suite life powers to wipe the smirk off Sunshine's face.

I lean back in my chair, sipping my own cocktail as I revel in smug satisfaction, and let out a long, contented sigh.

We're hanging out in the gold bar, which is actually quite busy today. We've got our mai tais in hands – our new favourite drink. Yes, we have a drink now, which has really cemented our friendship. It's serious, once you have a drink – like a loved-up couple having a song.

'I might have got a little bit carried away, though,' I confess. 'I invited them all to join us here, because they were all asking about the infamous gold bar, but none of them have shown up so we might be off the hook there. I can't imagine it being anything but stressful, having that lot here.'

The gold bar really is a sight to behold. It's just so, so gold. I've never seen so much gold in one place. I don't imagine it's real because not only would that cost a fortune – even by Grand Palm Resort standards – but because you would have to be crazy, to make a room so valuable, and then decide that its main use will be to house drunk people.

Donnie laughs, clinking his glass against mine.

'You can take the girl out of the suite, but you can't take the suite out of the girl,' he jokes.

'Oi, it's not like that,' I insist. 'I mean, like with Sunshine, she is so hostile, and Lucy's other bridesmaid isn't exactly a bag of laughs, and Nathan is Nathan.'

'I'm just teasing, you don't have to explain yourself to me,' he insists.

'You, of all people, should feel relieved that they haven't turned up,' I point out. 'Lucy is lovely, and my parents are great – although my dad does tell too many dad jokes, so brace yourself for that on the wedding day,' I warn him. 'But I can't imagine Sunshine coming in peace, seeing as though you're a friend of mine.'

'I'm resilient,' he tells me. 'Factor 50 – Sunshine can't touch me.'

I laugh. I like that a lot. I need to slather myself in some of that attitude.

My eyes dart across the room. I keep being distracted by a group of men over at the booth in the corner, who are clearly having a wild time. They're being so loud and lairy. Not to sound like a gold card snob, but this certainly isn't what I've come to expect, from these exclusive areas. I suppose I'd forgotten what it felt like, to experience something that you would absolutely not class as luxury.

As one of them screams, slamming his hands down on the table, it makes me jump. They're like a tropical storm that is growing closer by the minute.

I shoot Donnie a wide-eyed look.

'Geez, I thought I was paying for peace and quiet?' I say with a faux snobbery. 'I didn't realise I would need to bring my earplugs to the bar, to enjoy a quiet drink.'

I say this quietly enough so that the men don't hear me, obviously, because as annoying as they are, I'm only joking.

He smirks, appreciating the bit.

We're interrupted by the cough of someone wearing a 'manager' badge next to us. He's wearing a three-piece suit and a mortified look on his face.

Awkward! I wasn't really complaining, just pretending to, although to explain that to this guy would be to confess that I'm way above my pay grade here. Were I on the *Titanic*, I wouldn't have had a window, which is probably the best way to explain it to the elite here. I'm Jack Dawson in his suit right now, and I intend to keep it that way.

'I was on my way to talk to you, Ms Marsden, and I couldn't help but overhear,' the manager says, his apologetic face mirroring his sincere tone. 'First of all, let me apologise for the noise – I will have the men removed immediately.'

'Oh, God, no, don't do that,' I quickly insist, because I don't actually mind that much, and I don't want to ruin anyone's day or embarrass them – I'm not Sunshine Greene. 'We were just after a quiet few drinks – do you have anywhere else we could hang out? Like a private bar or function room or something?'

I'm channelling my inner G. G. Marsden right now, putting the theory to the test, to see whether staff here at the hotel really will say yes to anything I ask for.

'Now that you mention it, our yacht is free today,' the manager tells us, and it takes every facial muscle I have to keep my face neutral. 'It's fully staffed. You could take in the scenery – we have some beautiful views that can only be enjoyed from the water – you can have a meal, enjoy some more drinks from the on-board bar, and best of all you can get some peace and quiet, away from the resort for a few hours – all on us, of course, to say sorry for the disturbance today.'

I blink at him, momentarily taken aback by the grand gesture for what was barely a mild inconvenience.

'That would be wonderful,' I say, unintentionally slipping further into my G. G. Marsden persona.

He looks relieved that I've taken it so well, to the point where I wonder if the actually wealthy guests usually kick off at him.

'Would you like your party to join you?' he enquires.

In my mind, I translate that to: Would you like Donnie to join you? What an incredibly fancy way to ask a simple question.

'I would love for my party to join me,' I reply, stifling a laugh, in my best la-di-da voice, flashing a playful smile at Donnie.

He looks thrilled, and I can't blame him. The idea of being on a yacht is as surreal as it is exciting. I can't imagine Donnie has ever been on one either – because, come on, how many people actually have? – so it's going to be a fun first time for both of us.

'Fabulous,' the manager replies. 'I will go make the arrangements, you two finish your drinks, and I will be back for you when it's time to board.'

Time to board! Incredible. Although I don't think I will actually believe it is happening until my feet are firmly on the deck – look at me, already knowing the lingo (I think?). It's like I was born for this life, and this whole name mix-up is just karma, putting things right, ushering me into the lifestyle I so clearly deserve.

I take a big gulp of my mai tai and immediately hiccup loudly, practically projecting it at the poor hotel manager, making him jump. Okay, maybe not, but I'm here for a good time, not a long time, so I'll take my yacht while I can.

'Splendid,' I say, cringing at my choice of words. Maybe I did slip a little too far into character there.

The manager heads off to 'make the arrangements', leaving me and Donnie alone again. We exchange bemused glances, our jaws fully dropped.

'We're going on a yacht,' he says simply.

'We're going on a yacht,' I repeat back to him.

'Look at us,' he jokes.

'Look at us,' I reply with a laugh. 'Going on a yacht!'

'Well, I can't think of a better way to spend the day,' he says.

'And neither can I,' I tell him.

And I mean it. Just me and Donnie, on a yacht. It's going to be absolutely perfect and, best of all, there's going to be no one else around to ruin it.

Bon voyage!

34

When the hotel manager told me that they had a yacht, I imagined, well, a yacht. A boat-type thing, with a cabin below deck, maybe consisting of a few small rooms, and maybe a nice comfortable spot to sit above deck.

This – this thing in front of me – isn't a boat. It's more like a bloody cruise liner.

'This is just so much bigger than I imagined,' I blurt, unable to keep a lid on it.

'It's a superyacht,' a crew member wearing navy-blue trousers and a crisp white shirt informs us as he escorts us on board.

'It really is,' Donnie replies. 'It's more than super, in fact, it's incredible.'

'My name is Ron, I'll be at your service today,' Ron tells us with a smile. 'There are various crew members on board but it's my job to liaise with guests, so it will be my job to make sure you have everything you need – if there is anything you want, just ask.'

As we walk on board, I stare at the superyacht before me, savouring the moment, taking it all in. The sun bounces off its polished surfaces, making it sparkle like a diamond – very appropriate, given how monstrously expensive everything looks.

Ron seems like a really accommodating guy, and I'm used to hotel staff trying to give me whatever I could possibly want, but Ron's powers must be limited, when he's out at sea – not that I'm planning on testing the theory. I'm on a frigging yacht! I have everything I want and need.

Ron begins by taking us on a tour of the yacht, showing off its various decks and rooms – it has more bathrooms than any house I have ever been in, it turns out. He explains that people usually hire the yacht for several days, which is why there are bedrooms on board – and not just any bedrooms, but ones that are probably bigger and have better views than the flat I used to live in with Nathan.

'Usually, guests make the most of every amenity – and they want for nothing,' Ron explains. 'From the bridge deck, where you can dine al fresco, to the cosy cabins for a peaceful night's sleep – it's all here for your enjoyment. Seeing as though you will only be joining us for a few hours, we thought you might appreciate a nice meal – although do feel free to make use of the cabins, if you wish.'

I almost blush as I wonder what on earth short-stay guests could possibly use a cabin for, before the answer hits me like a ton of bricks. Duh, that one should have been obvious. I guess it's been a while – it's no wonder I've forgotten about the concept. I should've got in on that fourgie while I had the chance.

I can't help but think about how beyond stunning this yacht is – just unreal – and now, more than ever, I really wish that I actually was *the* G. G. Marsden, because I could certainly get used to this, and the more I experience, the harder it's going to be to give it all up.

Ron leads Donnie and me up the stairs, to the bridge deck, where he says guests tend to do most of their hanging out on nice days. I can't control my grin as I follow him. This is perfect. So, so perfect. Everything here is like a dream come true, except...

'Oh my God,' I blurt out as we arrive at the top of the steps.

'Erm...' is all Donnie manages, laughter breaking up the word.

I take back everything about perfection because, as it turns out, there's something that is far from ideal: the bridge deck. Not that there's anything wrong with it, necessarily, other than the fact that the seats are already taken. Taken by my mum, dad, Lucy, Rick, Nina (who, until now, I've been successfully avoiding), Rick's brother Alfie, and – of course – Nathan and Sunshine.

'Bloody hell, Gigi,' Lucy exclaims, jumping to her feet, rushing over to give me a big squeeze. 'This is phenomenal, thank you. Thank you so much. Honestly, I doubt people have unmemorable weddings, but I really, truly am never going to forget how special you made this one.'

'Your only one,' Rick quickly adds. 'But, yeah, Gigi, thanks a bunch. This is seriously cool.'

'You guys made it,' I say, as I wonder how the heck they got here.

'We turned up at the gold bar, like you said,' Mum explains. 'A manager stopped us, as we didn't have gold cards, so we told him to come and find you. The next thing we knew, he was back, telling us we were all going on a yacht!'

Ah, so that's why the manager was hunting me down – to talk, and that's what he meant when he asked if my party could join me. Not just Donnie, every last one of them.

Crap. I was so, so looking forward to spending some alone time with Donnie, enjoying the yacht, and soaking up some peace and quiet. With this lot here, it's going to be anything but.

And is that... yep. The yacht's moving, we're off, out to sea, and there's no turning back now.

As I look around everyone, I notice Sunshine is too busy with her camera to even realise I'm here. She's snapping away – this must be like a content-creating gold mine for her. She hands her phone to Nathan, so that he can take some shots of her. I never thought Nathan would be the guy dutifully taking photos for someone's social media – I mean, he used to kick off when I snapped the occasional photo of my food.

'This is going to be an unforgettable day,' Nathan tells Sunshine, as he snaps photos of her with the sea behind her.

'So, is this the famous Donnie?' Mum asks, interrupting my thoughts, which I'm grateful for. I appreciate being dragged back to the present.

'It is,' I reply with a smile. 'Donnie, to formally introduce you to this yacht full of characters, that's my mum, my dad, Lucy, who you already know, her fiancé Rick, her friend Nina, Rick's brother Alfie, and over there, doing the impromptu photo shoot, we have Nathan, who you've encountered, and his girlfriend, Sunshine.'

'Wow, okay, I think I've got everyone,' Donnie says, giving the group a friendly nod. 'Great to meet you all.'

'It's great to finally meet you,' Mum says, flashing a warm smile.

'We hear you're saving the wedding,' Dad adds.

'Oh, I don't know about that,' Donnie says, almost shyly. 'I'm happy to help, though.'

Sunshine drags herself away from her photo shoot and heads over to us, looking Donnie up and down.

'Hi,' she eventually says. 'You are not what I was expecting.'

'Hi,' he replies, ignoring whatever that means. 'Sorry, you're... I'm terrible with names.'

'Sunshine,' she says, stressing each syllable.

It's like she can't quite believe that he doesn't know her name, and it's amazing.

'We're going to explore the yacht, and to take some more photos,' Sunshine says. 'Nathan, come.'

'You're welcome,' I say quietly – and sarcastically – once they're out of earshot.

'There's a bloody bar on this thing, can you believe it?' Dad says. 'Do you two want a drink?'

'Another mai tai?' I suggest to Donnie, who, with a nod, takes a seat next to my mum.

As soon as we settle in, the grilling begins. My mum and Lucy are on him like a pair of detectives – really excitable ones, who like boys.

'So, Donnie, tell us about yourself,' Mum says, leaning in.

Donnie, ever the charmer, replies with a grin.

'Well, where do I start?' he says.

'How did you become a guitarist?' Lucy asks. 'Are you in a band?'

'I've been playing since I was a kid,' Donnie explains. 'I was in bands when I was younger but, these days, I play classical guitar. It's a different vibe, that's for sure.'

'And how did you meet Gigi?' Mum asks – oh, I'll bet she's been itching to ask that one.

'Oh, just here, at the resort,' Donnie explains simply. 'We just bumped into one another, hit it off, and here we are.'

'Here we are,' Lucy says. 'I bet you never thought you would be invited to a wedding.'

'Stranger things have happened,' Donnie jokes. 'But, no, I really didn't. Thanks again for inviting me.'

Nina catches my eye and waves me over, a genuine smile on her face, which is low-key suspicious. I make my way over to her, feeling slightly guilty about potentially leaving Donnie alone with the inquisition, but I'm sure he can handle himself.

'Thanks, Gigi,' she says, sincerity evident in her tone which… I'm pretty sure seems genuine. 'I really appreciate you inviting me along. I've been working from my room all week, because I couldn't get the full week off work, and this is exactly what I needed to let off some steam.'

Alfie, Rick's brother, joins in, giving me a grateful nod.

'Same here,' he says. 'I've been running the show at work, making sure Rick didn't have to lift a finger this week, and I'm knackered. This yacht escapade is just the ticket. Thanks, Gigi.'

I smile at them both.

'You're welcome,' I tell them. 'Enjoy yourselves.'

Back with Donnie, I find him in the midst of a laughter fit, courtesy of my dad's infamous dad jokes. I don't know which one it was, and I don't want to know. It's probably for the best I keep it that way.

'One more, I'll give you one more,' Dad tells him, grinning like he's lost his mind. 'Why did the scarecrow win an award?'

Donnie, God bless his heart, plays along.

'I don't know, why did the scarecrow win an award?' he replies.

'Because he was outstanding in his field!'

Dad bursts into laughter, and Donnie joins in, genuinely amused – or doing an amazing job of pretending he is, at least.

'You know, you ought to try some new material, dear,' Mum, ever the voice of reason, points out.

Dad winks at Donnie.

'I'd sooner try a new wife,' he jokes. Then he turns to me. 'So, Gigi, what's the plan now that we have the world at our fingertips, or rather, a yacht menu at least? What are you having?'

'I haven't even looked yet,' I say, smiling to myself, because it's so Dad, to ask what I'm having.

'Apparently, we can have anything to eat that we want,' he replies. 'Anything!'

'And yet you'll have your usual – steak and chips,' Mum points out.

'Yeah, well, imagine the steak they will have on here,' Dad replies.

'Okay, well, let's all just make the most of it, before it's time to order,' I tell them. 'We're going to have a walk around, and explore the yacht a little.'

'Be good,' Mum teases playfully.

Donnie and I head upstairs, to another deck, the wind tousling our hair as we glance back at Maui. The view is nothing short of spectacular – lush greenery, golden beaches, and the turquoise sea stretching out endlessly. The manager was right, some of the views of Maui, you really can only appreciate from the ocean.

'Wow, look at this,' I say with a sigh. 'Who knew Maui is even more stunning from out here?'

Donnie joins me at the railing as he takes in the view.

'It's breathtaking,' he replies. 'I can see why people fall in love with this place.'

'I really can't believe we're here,' I say. 'Honestly, when I imagined being on a yacht, I didn't picture all this. I expected it to be more... like a little sailboat.'

Donnie laughs.

'A pineapple has more in common with a sailboat,' he jokes.

'I see that now,' I reply. 'You know, you pretending not to know Sunshine's name is nothing short of a stroke of genius. It makes her livid, when she thinks people haven't heard of her.'

He shrugs with a playful smirk.

'Sometimes, the little victories are the sweetest,' he tells me.

'Can you believe she's already using this yacht for her content?' I say. 'And she probably won't even thank us.'

'Do you think she's posted anything yet?' he asks curiously.

'Let's see,' I suggest.

I fire up the InTheMo app, the social network for real-time life updates. Sunshine's profile reveals a stream of photos and videos –

already – each carefully curated to make it seem like this is her yacht, or that she has paid for it, at least. I roll my eyes.

'Just typical,' I say with a sigh. 'We're on this yacht together, on holiday together, and she's turning it into her own personal photo shoot.'

I'm just about to close it when I notice something else in there, with the yacht photos – it's a video of me, one that she has taken in secret. What the hell?

'Oh my God,' I blurt, feeling the heat rise in my cheeks.

Donnie, ever the calm presence, leans over to get a glimpse.

'Who is that?' he asks.

'That's from days ago – one of my failed dates,' I explain. 'He was some footballer, and an idiot. Why has Sunshine filmed me with him?'

Donnie thinks for a moment.

'I don't know, but she must have posted it by mistake,' he points out.

The gears in my head start turning.

'Do you think she's been saving it, to use against me in some way?' I suggest.

'I can't think of any other reason,' Donnie replies. 'I guess, if you don't bring him to the wedding, she could show people?'

'Yeah, to try to make me look bad.' I sigh. Why is she like this?

'Quick, take a screenshot,' Donnie insists.

I do, quickly, before she can realise her mistake.

'What are you going to do?' he asks.

'I'm going to show Lucy,' I tell him. 'Not right now, but later, when it's quiet, and I can get her alone. I don't want to stress her out or anything, but I can tell her it's nothing, and that Sunshine is being crazy – maybe she can talk to Rick, and he can talk to Nathan, and then Nathan can ask her to chill.'

'Good thinking,' Donnie replies, offering a reassuring smile.

God, this is the last thing I need right now. And I can't believe this lot are here, on board with us, and that Sunshine is causing trouble already.

'Come on, it will be fine, we'll find a way to have fun,' he assures me, reading my mind. 'Plus, there are so many other rooms here, we can always go and find our own space to be alone – well, you know what I mean, just to drink mai tais and chill.'

'I know what you mean,' I reply, grateful for his understanding.

Spending time alone with Donnie is what I really want, if I'm being truthful, but that's a thought for later. Right now, I'm in shark-infested waters, I need to keep my wits about me. Sunshine is clearly up to something. Here's hoping I can nip it in the bud, before it gets out of hand.

35

After a big meal – of, genuinely, whatever anyone wanted – we're spread out around the yacht, which suits me just fine – it means there is plenty of room to breathe (and to avoid people).

I have, however, managed to lose my phone, in a move that is just so unbelievably me.

Donnie's phone isn't compatible with mine, so I can't use his to locate it, but I can probably use Lucy's. There's no way she hasn't brought her phone. If not, God, I might even have to ask Sunshine if I can use hers – I would probably rather just buy a new one than ask her for a favour.

'Lucy, can I borrow your phone to try to track mine, please?' I ask. 'I've managed to lose it.'

'Of course you have,' she says with a laugh. 'Here, take it – it is dead, though. Reckon they've got a charger on board?'

'They have live lobsters and a machine that dries you when you get out of the shower – if they don't have a charger, I'll be shocked,' I joke.

'Gigi, do you and Donnie fancy playing a game?' Mum calls out. 'They've got Monopoly, Cluedo – everything.'

'Sounds good,' I agree. 'I just need to find a charger but see who else wants to play and find us a space.'

'Okay,' she calls back.

Ron, of course, has a charger for an iPhone, so Donnie and I take a seat in a small lounge, as we wait for it to fire up.

'What if I dropped it in the ocean?' I wonder out loud.

'I doubt it,' Donnie replies. 'You haven't been near enough to the edge.'

'True,' I reply. 'Unless… wait a minute… do you think InTheMo sends notifications when you screenshot? Sunshine might have nabbed my phone to erase that screenshot I took. You said it yourself, she probably posted it by accident, she was probably saving it for leverage.'

Donnie looks sceptical.

'Stealing a phone, though,' he says. 'That seems a bit much, even for Sunshine, don't you think?'

'Well, let's wait for this phone to come back to life, and we'll have our answers,' I say.

I'm sure I'm right, though.

After what feels like an age, Lucy's phone fires up and I log in to locate my phone.

'Good news – it's still on the yacht,' I tell Donnie. 'And I can practically pinpoint the room. Let's go – if someone has got it, we're about to catch them red-handed.'

'Okay, let's do it,' he says with a bemused laugh.

As we near a door, it seems like the phone is right behind it.

'I definitely haven't been this way,' I tell him. 'So someone must have it.'

The doors swing open dramatically, and I make a grand entrance into the room, where it turns out absolutely everyone is gathered around the table, as my mum sets up a game of Cluedo.

'Here you are,' Mum chirps, 'just in time to play. Donnie, come over here, we saved you a seat.'

Donnie obediently takes his place, but I linger in the doorway.

'I'll sit down in a minute, Mum. First, I need to find my missing phone,' I announce confidently.

'Oh, did you locate it?' Lucy asks, bemused.

'Yep,' I reply. 'It's somewhere in this room – someone has it. Someone at this very table.'

Dad, ever the joker, snorts.

'What's with the dramatics? You're acting like you're Poirot,' he teases.

'I basically am,' I reply.

Sunshine places her hands on Donnie's shoulders and gives them a playful rub.

'I promise you, we're not usually this dramatic,' she tells him. 'It seems like Gigi has had too many cocktails – as usual.'

A fictitious drinking problem. Amazing.

I roll my eyes, unfazed, as I find my own name in Lucy's phone.

'And the person who has my phone is...'

We all follow the sound of my ringing phone, tension building. Donnie's face falls as he pats his pocket, and everyone here realises that the sound is coming from him. He takes out the phone, eyeballing it suspiciously.

'I didn't take this,' he insists. 'Gigi, I was helping you look for it.'

'I know,' I reassure him. 'Let's see?'

Donnie hands me the phone, before turning round, eyeballing Sunshine suspiciously.

'Are you having money troubles?' Sunshine asks Donnie with faux sympathy.

I open my camera roll, and the evidence is clear – the screenshot has vanished. It was definitely Sunshine.

'You think I stole it?' Donnie replies in disbelief.

Sunshine winces, avoiding a direct answer, but making her feelings clear.

'It's okay, I know you didn't,' I reassure him.

'Maybe you picked it up by mistake, it happens,' Mum reasons, attempting to defuse the tension.

'Yeah, no harm done, no one thinks you stole it, lad,' Dad reassures him. 'Now, are we playing, or not?'

'I'm just going to get some air,' Donnie says.

'Yeah, I'll join you,' I reply, following him out.

As we walk along the corridor, I spot a door to one of the suites and suggest we step in there to chat.

'I take back what I said,' Donnie starts. 'Stealing is exactly the sort of thing she would do.'

'Yeah, it must have been her,' I tell him. 'The screenshot is gone.'

Donnie sits down on the bed, his back against the headboard. I join him, taking a seat next to him.

'You get used to it,' I joke. 'To her, I mean. Honestly, don't worry about it. No one thinks you stole anything. Shall we just stay here for the rest of the trip? They probably have movies on this TV.'

'Yeah, okay,' Donnie says with a sigh. 'I can't believe you have to put up with her.'

'Neither can I,' I say with a laugh. 'But I don't know, now that you're around, for some reason, it's not bothering me as much.'

'That's because you have me to hide in here with,' he replies, as I intertwine one of my hands with his.

'Sorry you got dragged into this,' I tell him.

'Do you know what?' he says, smiling and looking at our hands together. 'Suddenly, I don't mind all that much either.'

36

As Jeff and I stroll along the moonlit beach, honestly, it's like something out of a movie. The rhythmic crashing of the waves against the shore, the moonlight shining down on us, the cool sand beneath our feet, the beautiful ocean sparkling, the stars in the sky shining bright. It's like being in a landscape painting.

We just had our second date and it couldn't have been more perfect on paper. We ate at the chef's table in the VIP restaurant – where thankfully they served more than just seafood – and we ate, drank and chatted all evening. Again, Jeff has been nothing but a gentleman so, when he suggested we go for a night walk, I said yes.

Jeff is great. He's nice, he can be quite funny, and of course he's handsome, and his accent is easy on the ears. I wouldn't exactly say that sparks were flying between us, but that's not really how these things go, is it? Plus, not to sound like a jaded old cynic, but my plan was never to find love, just someone to take to the wedding. I'm wondering, tonight, whether or not I should ask him. Jeff is perfect on paper, and he has a good job, and a nice smile, and okay, he may not be a celebrity chef or in a metal band, but a date like that would seem like a gimmick, and no one would take it seriously, would they? But Jeff, he seems like the real deal, and the real deal is what I need, if I'm going to convince them all I've moved on and that I'm happy and that I'm not unhinged which, I realise, I do seem right now.

We're chatting about travel, although this time I haven't made any bold claims about places I haven't really been, I've been nothing but honest, and it turns out it makes conversations so much easier when you're not constantly trying to keep up with your lies – who knew?

'I love LA,' Jeff says with a sigh.

'We flew via LAX, but I've never been otherwise,' I say truthfully. 'I don't think spending time in the airport really counts, does it?'

Jeff laughs, letting me down gently with a pat on the arm.

'There are some great places in the US,' he continues. 'Have you been to Florida?'

I shake my head.

'No, but my sister and her soon-to-be husband are going there on honeymoon,' I reply. 'She's been making so many plans, booking so much fun stuff. I'm jealous.'

'I love that they're getting married here,' Jeff says with a sigh. 'Starting as they're meaning to go on, huh?'

'Something like that,' I reply.

'If you don't mind me saying, you don't seem all that excited about the wedding,' Jeff points out. 'Forgive me, if it's not my place to say.'

'Oh, no, it's fine, and it's nothing,' I insist. 'It's silly really, but I had a date for the wedding, and now I don't, so it's just a bit awkward. I think everyone is still expecting me to turn up with someone.'

There it is, I've said it, and I feel better for my honesty... until I realise that Jeff has gone quiet. Shit.

'Oh, okay,' he eventually says. 'Well, add Florida to your bucket list. There are so many places I haven't been that I would love to visit. The pyramids, for example. I really want to see them in real life.'

'Wow,' I reply, leaning into the subject change – I would probably rather whizz down the zip line than experience that rejection again. 'There isn't much on my list yet. I figure I'll start small, with the Eiffel Tower perhaps.'

'The Eiffel Tower is taller than the pyramids, you know,' he teases.

'You know what I mean,' I reply with a smile. 'Somewhere closer to home.'

'Jokes aside, the Eiffel Tower is really something,' he tells me. 'It wasn't what I expected at all – I'm not sure if it was bigger or smaller than I thought it would be – but I took the most amazing night shots of it. Would you like to see?'

'I'd love to,' I tell him.

Jeff stops in his tracks and takes his phone from his pocket. He places one hand on the small of my back, holding me close, while he messes with his phone with the other.

'Oh, I can't access the cloud off Wi-Fi,' he tells me. 'But I can show you on my laptop.'

'Ooh, the suspense,' I tease, still reeling from his weird shutdown of my wedding date dilemma, but even more eager to put it behind us with every second that goes by. 'I'm expecting big things from these photos – I can't wait to see them.'

'You're mocking me,' Jeff says with a smile. 'Right, I'll show you.'

Jeff steers me back towards the hotel. Once we're in the lobby, he directs me to the lift. Oh, wow, he's showing me now? In his room? Gentleman Jeff has been nothing but perfectly behaved so far so, if he says he's taking me up there to show me photos, then I believe him. And if he's got something else in his mind – which I doubt – then we'll cross that bridge when we come to it.

'This is me,' Jeff says as we arrive at the door to his room. 'Prepare to eat your words.'

'I am so full after dinner, I don't think I could eat my words if I wanted to,' I chuckle.

The moment the door of Jeff's room closes behind us, I can't help but feel a sudden jolt of uncertainty. I am a firm believer in going with my gut, and right now my stomach is in knots. His room is nice – it's made up of at least two rooms, because there isn't a bed in this one – but nowhere near as nice as mine, obviously.

'Okay, you sit at the desk,' he tells me, pulling out the chair.

Jeff takes his laptop in his hands, holding it in the air as he finds what he wants to show me, before placing it back down in front of me.

A beautiful photo of the Eiffel Tower at night fills the screen. The moon is in just the right place, the tower is illuminated, and there isn't a tourist in sight. Okay, I have to admit, this really is great.

'Just tap the arrows to flick through them,' he tells me. 'Paris might be the most romantic place I've ever visited.'

I sigh.

'It looks like it,' I reply. 'And now I want to go more than I did before – so thanks for that.'

Jeff moves behind me, lightly rubbing my shoulders. His fingers, light and rhythmic, trace a comforting pattern, but it doesn't seem to do much to relax me.

'It's definitely more of a fourth date thing,' he muses. 'But our third could be your sister's wedding, if you're still looking for a plus-one.'

Before I have the chance to say a single word, Jeff leans forwards and starts kissing my neck. Slow, sensual kisses, his tongue lightly flicking against my skin. All I can do is freeze. But this is what I wanted, right? A handsome, charming, seemingly perfect guy to be my impressive date for the wedding. More than that, though, I want to move on from Nathan, and this is my chance. I'm bound to be nervous, right? He's my first since Nathan, so of course it's going to be weird, being with someone new for the first time in a long time.

I wriggle involuntarily as he gets nearer my ear.

'I'll get us champagne,' he says.

'Yeah, okay,' I reply, definitely in need of a drink.

'In fact, give me five minutes, there's a comfortable sofa in the bedroom, we can sit in there, I'll be right back.'

'Okay,' I say again, sounding less sure this time.

Jeff dashes off, oblivious to my hesitation, to pop the cork in the other room.

I go back to flipping through the Paris pics on his laptop. They're all so dreamy and romantic, and I really would love to go, and I feel like he just invited me, and said he'd be my date for the wedding, and I should be so smugly happy right now, but...

A pop-up about updates springs onto the screen, snapping me from my thoughts, minimising Jeff's Paris pictures. I open my mouth to call him, to ask what he wants me to click, but before I get the chance, I notice another window open – Jeff's messages. I don't mean to look but an open message from 'Eleanor' catches my eye.

Sorry for the things I said, I'm just missing you. You know I don't care about money, only about you, so hurry home to marry me. I love you Geoff.

I stare at the screen as I search my brain for an explanation – other than the obvious one, of course. Sure, I've been imagining

Geoff's name with a J in my head, but it's probably pretty safe to assume that this message was sent to him, not some other guy called Geoff who he just happens to share a laptop with – oh, and that he's definitely engaged, so that's nice. Honestly, what is wrong with some men?

I can't help but wonder what Eleanor was talking about when she mentioned money. The only thing worse than Geoff just being your standard-issue arsehole who is happy to cheat on his fiancée while he's away on business would be if that was all a grift, a way to get money out of 'G. G. Marsden' and the thought of him sleeping with me, to try to get his hands on the money he thinks I have, turns my stomach.

There's nothing to say, is there? There is no way he can talk himself out of this one, and I'm sure it goes without saying that I would take absolutely any of the other men I've met recently to Lucy's wedding before I would go with him – I would sooner rock up as part of the fourgie I turned down.

I'm not up for a confrontation, I just need to get out of here. I glance at the notepad lying on the desk. With a deep breath, I grab a pen and scribble a concise 'no thank you' message. I also leave his laptop open, so that he knows I've seen his message from Eleanor. I'm sure Geoff can put the pieces of this puzzle together on his own. If he's got an ounce of decency, he'll get the message, and he won't try to find me. It's my cue for a hasty exit, leaving the tangled situation behind.

I slip out of Geoff's room like a burglar – I would say I was leaving with less than what I arrived with, but knowledge is power, and I'm definitely leaving smarter. I tiptoe a few steps before picking up the pace. Soon, I'm practically sprinting toward the lift, my heart pounding like I'm being chased by a lion. The elevator doors close behind me, and I release the breath I've been holding as if I've just finished a marathon. Pathetic really, because he's not scary at all, he's just a Geoff with a G – and a GF.

I laugh to myself, now that I'm safe. I was so close. I almost had a wedding date. If I hadn't ventured into his room, I'd be oblivious to the fact that he wasn't single, and I would have taken him to the wedding. I'm a real mix of emotions – relief, disappointment, and a splash of disbelief.

For some reason, the first person I want to tell about this whole ordeal is Donnie, so I head back to the suite. It's only as I'm approaching that I spot Nathan lingering outside.

Wow, I didn't realise it was National Dickhead Day today. Can't believe I missed that in the calendar.

'Gigi, there you are,' Nathan calls out as he sees me approaching.

'Here I am,' I say, sighing at the sight of him. 'What's up?'

'Sunshine and I had a row,' he confesses.

'Well, you can't sleep on my sofa, it's taken,' I point out as I try to walk past him.

'Gigi, wait,' he insists, putting his hand on my arm to stop me. 'Don't you want to know what we've been arguing about?'

'Not really,' I tell him with a laugh, smiling to myself. It's nice to know that I actually really don't care.

'We were arguing about you,' Nathan blurts to the back of my head. 'She doesn't think I'm over you.'

I stop in my tracks.

'I don't think I'm over you,' he adds.

I exhale deeply as I turn to face him.

'Nathan, you don't want me,' I insist. 'I know you better than you know yourself, and if you think other people want something, you want it too, and if you think you can't have it, then you want it even more.'

'It's not that,' he insists. 'You seem... different.'

'No, I don't,' I reply. 'And neither do you. We weren't happy, but I probably never would have pulled the trigger, so I owe you a thank you.'

'You seem happy,' he points out, seeming horrified at the thought.

'I am,' I tell him. 'And so are you, so you go back to Sunshine, and I will go in here, and we'll pretend this conversation never happened.'

'I can't,' he replies. 'When we were together, we were happy, right? Things were good. Life was normal. With Sunshine, nothing is ours. Every single thing she does is for social media. I'm sick of my life being plastered all over the internet, where every tool with a smartphone or a laptop can unload exactly what they think of me in the comments. Not only that but, with Sunshine too, I never know what's real, and what's for her Instagram. Even her gestures seem empty, when she uses them for content. You never did that. You just loved me.'

'That's right, *loved*,' I reply. 'Past tense. Nathan, come on, we weren't happy – plus, you left me, remember? You definitely thought it was worth doing at the time. Your issue isn't with me, it's with Sunshine, caring more about her followers – and ultimately herself – than anything else. So go and take it up with her, like an adult, or do what you usually do and dump her to go off in search of something better like you did with me – I really do not care. Your happiness isn't my problem any more, okay?'

Oof, that felt good.

'Gigi—'

'Okay,' I cut him off. 'Have a good night.'

I walk into my suite with my head held high, certain now more than ever that not only am I completely over Nathan, but, so much so, that I'm not actually that bothered about competing with Sunshine any more. If they're happy, then good for them. That's what I want – to be happy too. I would rather spend my time looking for someone to love than some silly date for a wedding.

I realise Donnie is fast asleep on the sofa, so I decide not to wake him. Instead, I watch him for a second and smile to myself.

If I'm being honest, I would rather hang out with him at the wedding.

Perhaps I don't need that plus-one after all.

37

'I know what you're thinking,' Lucy says, narrowing her eyes at me. 'You're thinking about how crappy my luxury hotel room seems, in comparison to your suite.'

I laugh, because she's obviously joking.

Lucy's hotel room, while by no means shabby, is obviously smaller than my suite – it would be weird if it weren't. It is, however, a beautiful room. The walls are painted in a soothing shade of blue, the decor is tasteful – and she's certainly kept the bedroom area a lot tidier than I have in my suite. Jokes aside, though, I can't help but feel a pang of guilt, knowing that this is Lucy's special week, and I'm the one with the luxurious room. Then again, Rick is well off (a combination of his inheritance and his work running the family business – something to do with finance, that I'll probably never be wealthy enough to need to understand) so I'm sure she has a lifetime of luxury holidays ahead of her, whereas for me, this is probably my one shot to experience how the other half live.

'Lucy, darling, I don't know how you survive in such humble

surroundings,' I tease, giving her a playful nudge as I lean into the joke. She rolls her eyes, a smile tugging at her lips.

'You're lucky I'm excited about tonight – and that I need you here, to curl my hair – or I would boot you out of my humble room,' she jokes before turning her attention to our mum. 'Are you sure you don't want to join us?'

Mum waves a hand dismissively.

'Oh, no, definitely not,' she insists. 'A nightclub – whether it be an outdoor one or an indoor one – is absolutely not our scene. You young ones have fun, your dad and I are going to enjoy a quiet, romantic evening – and if he had heard me say that he would probably joke that I'll be enjoying it, but that he will just be there.'

I laugh. We all love Dad's jokes.

'You don't want us oldies cramping your style,' she adds.

'I know that we're not exactly old,' I point out to Lucy, 'but have you been referred to as a "young one" recently?'

'I have not,' she replies. 'I must be getting on, though, because I like it.'

'You two were always keen to pretend you were older, when you were teens,' Mum reminds us.

'And now we're older, trying to pretend we're young,' Lucy jokes back. 'I'm going to jump in the shower while Gigi works her magic on your hair, Mum. Don't leave before I get a chance to say bye, will you?'

'Of course not,' Mum says. 'It might be my last chance to see you, as a technically single woman, before your wedding day.'

'Don't freak me out,' Lucy replies as she disappears into the bathroom.

I plug in my straighteners in front of the dressing table, ready to work my magic on my mum. She usually wears her hair straight but, when she's going out, she loves me to curl it for her.

'Come on then, let's show your dad I'm not totally past it,' she says with a playful sigh.

My mum takes a seat, and I begin curling her hair, adding a touch of glamour to her already elegant look. She always looks great – certainly not past it. The level Mum will dress up to, even just to go to the supermarket, is beyond the effort I would put in on most nights out these days. Age doesn't come into it at all – in anything, I think my generation is lazier about how they look. Honestly, at work people reckon balayage is trendier than a full head of highlights now, and maybe it is, but I reckon it's mostly just because you don't have to keep on top of the regrowth like you do with highlights, you can just leave it to grow out, and it looks no different. It's a lazy person's dye job, that's for sure – that's why I have it.

Mum is wearing a chic, knee-length floral dress that perfectly complements her vibrant personality. Her make-up, which Lucy did before she headed for the shower, matches it too.

'Mum, you look stunning,' I tell her as I allow another curl to fall down at the side of her head.

She smiles back at me through the mirror.

'Why, thank you, my dear,' she says. 'It's been a while since your dad and I had a romantic meal out together. I thought I'd give your father a pleasant surprise, by showing him I can still dress up.'

'So, what's the plan for you and Dad tonight?' I ask, making conversation as I focus on the task at hand – it's a reflex, it really is.

'Oh, a nice quiet dinner, just the two of us,' she says. 'Maybe a stroll on the beach after…'

'That sounds perfect,' I reply.

Perfect and, to be honest, more my scene than an outdoor nightclub. Maybe I am getting older, because I would much rather eat, and then take a stroll under the stars.

'I wonder if your dad will put in as much effort,' she thinks out loud.

'If you're lucky, he might even use shampoo tonight, instead of just using his usual shower gel from head to toe,' I joke.

'You tease but you're not wrong,' she replies with a smile.

It's cute, that she still finds his little quirks charming, after all these years.

As I continue styling, my mum glances at me through the mirror.

'Are you okay, Gigi?' she asks me. 'You seem a bit off tonight.'

'Oh, I'm fine,' I insist. 'Just, you know, the chaos of the wedding and stuff.'

'Ahh,' she says, with an all-knowing look on her face. 'Your date...'

I shake my head. Well, she can read my mind, no one needs to say anything out loud.

She doesn't press me further on the details, which I appreciate.

'Are you okay with that, darling?' she asks.

'I am,' I reply, surprisingly at peace with the decision. 'And, you know, Donnie is coming to the wedding, so it's not like I'll be knocking around on my own.'

Her eyes light up at the mention of Donnie.

'Well, I think that's wonderful,' she says. 'Donnie seems like a great man. I'm sure you'll have a fantastic time with him, even without a formal date.'

I agree wholeheartedly.

'You know what, Mum, I think you're right,' I reply. 'I'll probably enjoy myself more with Donnie than with a date. He's kind, funny, and we have a lot in common. And we already know how to have a laugh together, so I can't imagine anything being boring, with him by my side.'

'It sounds as though you may have found your perfect wedding date after all then,' she points out, flashing me a smile that speaks volumes.

'Yeah,' I admit, a smile spreading across my face too as the realisation hits me head-on.

Donnie really is the perfect wedding date for me. Everything is so much fun when he's around. He's a good person, he really makes me laugh, and most of all he seems to really care about me.

Now that I think about it, he might not just be the perfect wedding date for me, he might be the one for me.

I can't believe it has taken me this long to realise it.

38

Outdoor nightclubs are better than indoor nightclubs in so many ways. Even the nicest indoor clubs get warm, have sticky floors, and stink of sweat and booze. Outdoor clubs, on the other hand, not only get to breathe, and are cooled by the sea air, but the gorgeous Maui backdrop only adds to the atmosphere.

Coloured lights are flashing all around us, and thumping music reverberates through the night air. I can feel the bass in my chest, rumbling through the furniture, making my entire body tingle.

The VIP area is all ours tonight – because of course it is, people still think I'm G. G. Marsden, so the special treatment is coming in thick and fast.

Champagne flutes clink as a waiter materialises, presenting us with another bottle of bubbly. It's nice being able to share this with Lucy and our friends. If hotel staff thinking I'm more of a big deal than I am means that Lucy and Rick get an absolute dream of a night out, then I'm all for it. Nathan and Sunshine are here, along with Nina and her boyfriend Calvin, who has finally joined us. Alfie's wife has arrived for the wedding, but neither of them are party animals, so they've headed to bed already. Donnie is here too, now that he's basically part of the wedding, and even Gary Garrie has popped under the red rope after spotting us (I told the bouncers he could) to raise a few glasses with us, like we're old friends, not just fellow Brits at the same resort.

The party is in full swing. Lucy and Rick, the newly-weds-to-be, are tearing up the dance floor together. Nina's boyfriend has had far too much to drink, far too quickly, so she's taking him to bed. Oh, and Nathan and Sunshine have clearly reconciled, the two of them are sitting in the corner, trapped in a PDA, her serpent-like arms and legs wrapped around him possessively. But do I care? No, I don't, because I've been hanging out with Donnie all night.

We're tucked away in our own little corner, in our own little world.

Donnie is just so easy to get on with. The conversation is effort-less, and he makes me laugh – the kind of laughter that makes your stomach ache and your cheeks hurt.

I catch him stealing glances at me, and every time our eyes meet, we burst into laughter again.

'You're being so goofy,' he tells me. 'It's cute.'

I feel my cheeks warming.

What I'm actually being is awkward, in the most ridiculous way, because now that I've realised I like-like him, I feel so giggly and girly and silly, and I can't help but flirt with him – but it's been a minute.

I chuckle nervously, twirling a strand of hair around my finger.

'I'm just having a nice time,' I tell him, feeling the champagne all of a sudden.

'Well, I'm glad to hear it,' he says as he grins, taking a sip of his drink. 'I'm having a nice time too. I really like hanging out with you.'

I blush, feeling the warmth creep up my cheeks even further.

'Thanks,' I say, trying to play it cool.

Donnie laughs – God, I love his laugh.

'Are you sure you're okay?' he says, still smiling. 'You seem lighter. Did you find out Michael B. Jordan has checked into the hotel, track him down, and get him to agree to be your plus-one to the wedding?'

'Michael B. Jordan is here?' I reply, whipping my head from side to side as I pretend to look for him.

'Maybe,' he replies. 'Perhaps it's safest for him, if I don't confirm or deny.'

I playfully nudged him.

'He's safe, either way,' I insist. 'I'm not bothering with a plus-one now. I know, I wanted an impressive date to prove a point but now... I don't know. I'm not bothered.'

Donnie gives me a knowing smile.

'You know, you don't need a date to prove anything,' he tells me. 'You're impressive enough on your own, Gigi.'

His words catch me off guard, and I feel a flutter in my stomach.

'Oof, someone is full of compliments tonight,' I joke awkwardly, because I clearly don't know how to take a compliment.

'I'm pretty generous with compliments when they're true,' he replies, locking eyes with mine.

I grab my drink, like a security blanket, and take a big drink.

I notice Lucy and Rick weave through the crowd, laughing together as they fall into the seat next to us.

'I am starving,' Lucy announces. 'Is anyone else hungry?'

'I don't think Nathan and Sunshine are,' Rick jokes. 'They've been eating each other all night.'

'They need to get a room,' Lucy jokes.

'They have one – they need to go to it,' Rick replies. 'I don't know what's up with them today. Did you see that proper cringe she put on Instagram about him? Mortifying.'

'Really?' Lucy replies. 'I haven't been on.'

'Let's see it,' Donnie suggests.

'I'll find it,' I say, shaking my head with amusement as I take my phone from my clutch.

I search for Sunshine's profile and find the saccharine post in question. I barely get to read a word of the caption before my face drops.

'Let's see,' Lucy says quickly, noticing my reaction.

I turn the phone to face her.

'What?' Lucy blurts out, her eyes darting between the screen and me.

'What?' Rick adds.

'It says their first date was on Halloween,' I tell him. 'It was November when he broke up with me.'

'Let's see properly,' Lucy says, taking my phone from me to read the whole caption.

'Did you know?' I ask.

'Of course we didn't,' Lucy insists, glancing at Rick. 'Did we, Rick?'

Rick's expression betrays him. He definitely knew something.

'Rick?' Lucy presses, sensing there's more to the story.

'Luce, it's none of our business,' he says quietly, attempting to defuse the tension.

'She's my sister, of course it's my business,' Lucy retorts with fire in her eyes. 'You knew?'

'Look, let's just go for a walk, talk about this,' Rick suggests, attempting damage control.

'It's okay, Lucy,' I reassure her, trying to downplay the situation, but she's having none of it.

'No, it's not,' Lucy replies as Rick tries to take her hand in his. 'I can't do this right now.'

She abruptly stands up, snatching her hand away from Rick again, before walking off down the beach. Rick, in a blind panic now, runs after her.

I watch them disappear into the night, their silhouettes blurring with the neon glow of the resort. Then I sigh every bit of air from my lungs.

Donnie glances at me, giving me a sympathetic look, but I can tell he doesn't know what to say. I shake my head. I don't know what to say either.

I look over at Nathan and Sunshine. They're looking over, concerned looks etched on their faces, having witnessed what just happened from a distance, but clearly having no idea what caused it. As my gaze locks with Nathan's, I notice his eyes narrow suspiciously.

'Shit,' I mutter quietly to myself as the two of them march over.

'What's going on?' Sunshine asks angrily. 'Have you upset them?'

My eyebrows shoot up in incredulity.

'Have *I* upset them?' I repeat back to her. 'No, I haven't upset them.'

Nathan looks at Donnie accusingly.

'Was it you?' he demands.

'No, it was you, you tosser,' Donnie claps back, unable to stifle a bemused laugh. The absurdity of the situation isn't lost on either of us.

'Me?' Nathan's eyes widen in disbelief.

'Let's not do this here,' I say, trying to calm things down.

'No, we're doing it here,' Nathan insists, his curiosity unwavering. 'Come on, what have I done?'

Donnie, recognising the delicate nature of the situation, defers to me with a supportive look.

'Lucy basically found out that Rick knew that you cheated on me,' I tell him. Then I turn to Sunshine. 'With you.'

Sunshine's eyes widen as she realises I know. She looks at Nathan, a mixture of betrayal and heartbreak etched across her face. She looks like her world just ended. Okay, so maybe she didn't know either.

'Wait, I can explain,' Nathan pleads, reaching for Sunshine's hands.

'Go away,' she demands firmly. 'I'm serious, right now, get out of here.'

Nathan looks genuinely terrified. Without a word, he does as she asks and hastily flees the scene.

Sunshine collapses into a chair with a dramatic sigh and starts sobbing.

I don't know what to do other than sit down next to her and rub her shoulder.

'Sunshine, it's okay,' I tell her, trying to comfort her as she sniffles and wipes her snotty nose with the back of her hand.

'Gigi, listen to me,' she just about manages to say between sobs. 'I had no idea that he was still with you when we got together. I never would have done that to you – to anyone.'

'You were single, he wasn't – you have nothing to apologise for,' I assure her. Obviously it's not great, to facilitate someone cheating, but at the end of the day it's always down to the taken person to resist.

She wails, flailing her arms around dramatically.

'I really, really like him – I love him,' she says.

'Go after him,' I suggest gently. 'Talk it through, sort it out.'

'No,' she replies firmly. 'I'm a girls' girl. We don't do that to each other, it's not girl code.'

I smile softly at her.

'Listen to me, okay?' I start, squeezing her shoulder a little more firmly. 'Nathan and I were not happy together. We were going to break up sooner or later. It really wasn't your fault. But I'm over him, and he's over me, and you two actually stand a chance of being happy together. So, if you love him, go after him, hear him out, and see how you feel then. But don't lose out on a shot at love because of the way he treated me. I promise you, I'm okay.'

Sunshine sniffs hard, contemplating my words.

'Are you sure?' she checks.

'I'm certain,' I reply, offering her a reassuring smile. 'And Lucy and Rick will figure it out too. It's all going to be okay.'

Sunshine grabs me, pulling me into a tight hug.

'Thank you,' she says. 'I'll go find him now.'

Sunshine springs to her feet and heads off in the direction Nathan left in. As the bouncer moves the red rope to let her out, Gary Garrie joins us again.

'Are you going to drink that?' he asks me, nodding towards an open bottle of champagne.

'I'm pretty tired, I'm going to bed,' I tell him. 'It's all yours.'

'I just keep landing on my feet,' he says to himself, jumping up and down giddily on the spot.

'Back to the suite?' Donnie suggests.

'I think that's a good idea,' I reply. 'Quick – before anything else happens.'

As Donnie and I stroll, he gently takes my hand in his.

'Are you okay?' he asks softly.

'I've had worse nights out,' I say with a half-hearted laugh.

'You know what I really love about you?' Donnie begins. 'The fact that even though you just found out your boyfriend cheated on you, you still found it in your heart to comfort the person he cheated with.'

I give his hand a squeeze.

'To be honest, she was way more upset than I was,' I admit. 'Obviously, being cheated on doesn't feel very nice, and I imagine I wouldn't have taken it as well if I had found out at the time, but now, I don't know, I'm just not bothered any more. I don't feel anything for him, good or bad.'

'I think that's how you know you've moved on,' he replies. 'It's good that you're through it and above it. You don't give yourself enough credit, you really don't. When most people go through a break-up, they don't have to keep seeing their ex all the time – they definitely don't have to be in a wedding party with them. But you're doing this for your sister, and, boy, was she ready to go to war for you too.'

'I know,' I say with a smile as I unlock the suite door. 'I know her, and she knows me, and she and Rick will talk it through, and they'll be fine. And hopefully, Nathan and Sunshine will figure it out, and the wedding will go ahead as planned – well, as planned, but with a significantly better guitarist.'

Donnie smiles.

'Well, I'm assuming you're better,' I joke. 'I've just realised we've never heard you play.'

'I did a rehearsal yesterday with Lucy,' he tells me. 'While you were on your date.'

'He was engaged, you know,' I confess. 'He took me to his room, left his computer open, and I saw messages from his fiancée.'

Donnie shakes his head.

'Would you believe me if I said we weren't all bad?' he asks.

'Yes,' I reply simply.

We're standing in the living room together, next to Donnie's makeshift bed, still in relative darkness as we look into each other's eyes. I feel my heartbeat speed up, my breathing quicken, and my thoughts racing at a million miles an hour, but they're all in agreement: I should kiss him.

I open my mouth, hoping the right words will come out. Instead, there is nothing so I just laugh. I smile at him, staring into his eyes, begging him to read my mind. He moves closer to me slowly – so slowly I wonder if it's just wishful thinking at first, that I might be imagining it but, no, he's definitely stepping closer.

He cocks his head curiously and smiles. Can he read my mind?

He reaches out and takes my hands in his, locking our fingers together. We swing our arms gently in the small remaining space between us for a second, almost dancing on the spot.

Kiss me. Kiss me, I am begging you.

'Okay,' Donnie says, catching me by surprise.

He lets go of my hands, but only to wrap them around me, pulling me close, placing his lips on mine.

God, I have been waiting for this moment – probably since before I even realised I was waiting for this moment.

Now isn't the time to be goofy, or shy, or whatever it is I have been. Now is the time to be confident, to go for what I want, to move on. Now it feels right.

I jump into Donnie's arms, wrapping my legs around his waist and my arms around his neck.

'I think you can probably sleep upstairs tonight,' I whisper into his ear.

'I don't think I'm going to get much sleep,' he replies.

39

I wake up in bed with the cool breeze drifting in through the open windows, the sunlight casting a warm glow through the net curtains, and Donnie's arms wrapped around me.

For a moment, I'm scared to move. This moment is perfect – too perfect, perhaps, almost like any little thing could ruin it. I feel like I'm in a dream, like all my senses are satisfied. I feel so safe in Donnie's arms, and the world seems like such a soft, gentle place. It's so soothing.

I lie still, savouring the tranquillity of the moment. The room just smells like Hawaii, there's no other way to define it, and the gentle rustle of the curtains practically tickles my ears. Donnie's sleepy breathing is calm, and I can feel his heartbeat against my back, and the sheets are cool against my skin, a stark contrast to the warmth coming from his body. Everything just feels so good.

I steal a glance at the clock, and I know that we'll have to move eventually. But right now, in this moment, everything feels still, like the world outside has paused just for us.

Of course, in typical Gigi fashion, my mind is racing ahead, asking a million questions, none of which I can answer right now.

What does last night mean? Does it mean anything? Could I have a future with Donnie? I don't want to seem like the kind of girl who sleeps with a guy on holiday and then seemingly falls head over heels in love with him, but I wouldn't have done it if I didn't think there could be something more.

I'm still scared to move, although I know I'll have to soon – it's Lucy and Rick's wedding day, after all.

Suddenly, a loud banging noise interrupts *everything*. It sounds like it's coming from the suite door, so I jump up, inadvertently waking Donnie with a start.

'Is everything okay?' he asks, rubbing the sleep from his eyes.

'Yeah, I think so, it's just someone at the door,' I tell him as I throw on a white hotel robe.

Donnie frowns as the banging continues. There's definitely something urgent about it.

I hurry downstairs and open the door to find Nathan standing there. I can see the worry on his face as he invites himself in, stepping through the door.

'What?' I ask Nathan, my mind still foggy from sleep. 'What's wrong?'

I notice Nathan's gaze shifting beyond me. I turn to follow his line of sight to see Donnie, making his way down the stairs in nothing but his boxers.

'It's Lucy and Rick,' Nathan explains, bringing his attention back to me. 'We can't find them anywhere.'

'What?' I blurt out in disbelief. 'Have you asked my parents?'

'I checked for them there, although I didn't tell them they were missing – I didn't want to worry them,' Nathan explains. 'I did manage to check their room – Sunshine had Lucy's key card in her bag – but it doesn't seem like they've been back there. Their passports and things are still there. It doesn't seem like anyone has seen them since they walked off last night.'

'Shit,' I mutter softly, anxiety tightening in my chest.

I feel Donnie's arms wrap around me, comforting me when I need it most.

'Don't worry,' Donnie reassures me. 'Let's get dressed and go look for them – they will be here somewhere.'

Nathan, who seems hyper-focused on finding the happy couple, glances at Donnie's arms before seemingly letting any thoughts he has on the matter go.

'Yeah,' I reply optimistically. 'Perhaps they just lost track of time somewhere, or they're having a pre-wedding spa, or... something.'

'I'll keep looking too,' Nathan says. 'I'll call you if I find them.'

'Yeah, I'll do the same,' I reply, trying to get my thoughts in order.

'The wedding is in a few hours,' he reminds me.

'Yeah, okay, I know,' I say, my mind racing. 'Don't worry, we'll sort it.'

As Nathan heads out again, I turn around in Donnie's arms and he hugs me tightly for a few seconds.

'You don't think something bad has happened to them, do you?' I mumble into his chest.

'No, come on, it's all going to be okay,' he reassures me. 'I'll help you find them. Let's throw some clothes on and get searching.'

'Thanks,' I tell him sincerely. 'I couldn't imagine doing this on my own.'

I worried that something might ruin my perfect morning. I never thought it would be this.

40

Lucy and Rick are nowhere to be seen.

Donnie and I have looked everywhere, in all the public areas of the hotel – even the VIP ones, just in case they managed to blag their way into a fancy bar by telling people they were getting married the next day, but there's no sign of them.

We're standing in the deserted VIP area of the outdoor night-club we were in last night, retracing our steps, like TV detectives. In the harsh light of day, it looks almost alien – the empty dance floor, the abandoned VIP booths, and with the darkness that encased it last night gone, it feels so open and vulnerable.

Credit to the hotel staff, they're on the ball with the cleaning and tidying, because there isn't so much as a trace of last night's revelry. Unfortunately this means that there are no clues to be found – but realistically we were never going to find any hot leads, were we? Lucy and Rick left here before we did.

I anxiously run a hand through my hair. Whenever I'm stressed, it's almost as though I revert to being a teenager, sweeping away my centre parting. My hair piles up on one side of my head, a habit from my younger days – something one of the Gen Z trainees in the salon recently called an 'ick' they had about millennials.

'It's just hard to think where they could have gone,' I say, my voice echoing in the deserted VIP area of the outdoor nightclub.

I steal a glance at Donnie. He's quiet, his gaze fixed on the floor below him. I can't help but wonder if all he wants to do is run a mile from all of this. I wouldn't blame him if he did.

All at once, his expression changes, like he's just had an epiphany. His eyes light up as he slaps his leg excitedly.

'I've got it,' he declares triumphantly. 'I know where they are – come on, quick.'

With new-found determination, Donnie dashes off in the direction Lucy and Rick disappeared in last night. I hurry to keep pace with him, navigating the sand slipping beneath my feet. Determination, mixed with a bit of luck, keeps me upright, and I can't help but think the balance gods are smiling down on me today – because I have no right to be this vertical, in these conditions.

As I catch up with Donnie – only because he's slowing down – I know where we are and, suddenly, everything falls into place.

'Do you really think...' I begin.

'Come on, let's see,' Donnie replies.

We're outside the beach hut, the same one we nearly got stuck in a few days ago when we couldn't get the door open. Donnie attempts to open it, but it won't budge. Then he tries the same lift and twist motion that he used to free us the other day and, thankfully, it works.

I smile with relief as we look inside the hut and see Lucy and Rick, sprawled on the floor, fast asleep in each other's arms.

'Lucy,' I whisper. 'Lucy, wake up.'

Lucy stirs, her eyes fluttering open. A smile graces her face when she spots me, but as her gaze shifts to Donnie, she suddenly remembers where she is.

'Oh my God,' she exclaims, nudging Rick. 'Rick, quick, wake up.'

Lucy leaps to her feet and rushes over to hug me.

'Oh my God, we thought no one would ever find us,' she confesses. 'We came in here to talk, and the door got stuck. We didn't have our phones or anything, so couldn't call for help.'

'What time is it?' Rick mumbles. 'The wedding...'

'You're all good; we've got time to get you guys ready,' I reassure them. 'It was Donnie who figured out that you would be in here.'

Rick extends his hand for a handshake but decides on a bear hug at the last moment.

'Thanks, pal, you're a hero,' Rick tells him.

'Donnie saves the day again,' Lucy cheers. 'Oh my God, there's so much to do; I need to get ready and...'

I usher Lucy outside, to get her some air, because she's starting to flap.

'Go, go,' I insist. 'I'll catch you up. I'll just let Nathan know everything is okay – I promised I would call him. You guys are okay, right?'

Lucy nods.

'He should have told me,' she says. 'But he didn't want anyone getting hurt unnecessarily. I suppose it makes sense but... Are you okay?'

Rick and Donnie are still inside the hut, so I lean in closer and lower my voice.

'I'm great,' I tell her. 'Something happened between me and Donnie. I like him, I really do.'

'That's great. He seems like such a nice guy,' Lucy says, pulling me in for another hug. 'Right, I can't even imagine how bad I must look. Tell Nathan crisis averted, and catch me up.'

I take my phone from my pocket and call Nathan, letting him know that we've located Lucy and Rick and the show can go on. Relief floods through his voice. Whatever issues Nathan and I have had, there is no denying that he and Rick love each other – they've been friends since they were kids – and I wouldn't ever want to come between that. Since our break-up, I've always done my best to be around him, for Lucy and for Rick, but it hasn't been easy. But that's what you do, for the people you care about. I imagine things will be much easier, now that I know I'm over him, that I'm happy to move on – who knows, I might even get to enjoy the wedding, something I didn't think was remotely possible.

Rick walks out of the beach hut, offering me a wave before dashing off towards the resort to get ready. Part of me is scared to let them wander off again, in case we lose them, but I know last night was just one of those things. Ahh, I bet they can't wait to tie the knot.

After assuring Nathan that we'll all be there soon – he had a similar thought to me, that we shouldn't let them out of our sight – I head back towards the beach hut where I left Donnie.

'...of course I haven't told her,' I overhear Donnie saying into his phone. 'No, and I don't want her to find out. I'm going to her sister's wedding today – can we talk about it later?'

I back away from the door, recoiling in horror like I've just stumbled upon a body, retreating to the safety of the beach. It's only a matter of seconds before Donnie joins me.

'Sorry, I just had to take a work call,' he says as he steps outside. 'All good?'

'Yep, all good,' I reply – but it's not all good, is it? 'I'll see you at the wedding – I've got to go help Lucy get ready.'

'Okay, see you there,' Donnie calls after me.

As I make my way to the resort, I can't help but shake my head.

He was definitely talking about me, and he's definitely hiding something.

They really are all the same, aren't they?

41

I was worried, for a hot minute, that it wouldn't happen, but it's official: Rick and Lucy are husband and wife.

They tied the knot in a beach ceremony, which is something I always thought might be one of those things that looked good in the movies, but wasn't practical in real life, but the moment I step onto the beach for Lucy and Rick's wedding ceremony, I couldn't get over how perfect it all looked.

Lucy looked so beautiful in her wedding gown – you would never know what a panic we had on, trying to sort her hair and make-up, after the strange start to the day.

The sun was shining, the breeze was just right, and everything went down without a hitch. Lucy and Rick swapped vows, surrounded by the natural beauty of the beach, and everyone who loves them. I am so relieved because, after the night of worry they must have had, they really deserve it.

And then there was Donnie, whose beautiful guitar playing gently accompanied the ceremony. He did a really great job – he was probably better than the person who was supposed to be playing too, so all is well that ends well. Apart from, you know, for me.

If I hadn't overheard Donnie on the phone earlier, I would probably be on top of the world right now. It's not that I'm not happy, or that I'm not having a good time, it's just that – as naive as it sounds – I was really hoping that I might actually get a win this time. Just a straightforward, easy day with not only lots to celebrate, but lots to be excited about too.

The marquee, where the reception is taking place, is so elegantly decorated. Fairy lights twinkle like stars, casting a warm glow over the tables adorned with white tablecloths, vases of vibrant flowers, and candles ready for the night to properly draw in.

I'm at the top table, front and centre, where I can see everything – well, just about, because this marquee is packed with more flowers than a botanic garden.

It also means I haven't really spoken with Donnie since earlier, as he's sitting at one of the guest tables. I've been watching him, though – I haven't been able to help myself. He's sitting with Sunshine, and the two of them are chatting away like old friends, now that calm has seemingly been restored.

Nathan is currently centre stage, microphone in hand, in the middle of his best man speech. So far he has been delivering the usual crowd-pleasing combination of jokes and embarrassing stories. I can't say I'm a fan, but tradition is tradition.

'The wedding almost didn't happen,' he continues. 'These two lovebirds managed to get themselves locked in a beach hut. I mean, why not use the room they paid a small fortune for, right?'

Everyone laughs – even Lucy and Rick can see the funny side of it now.

But then Nathan's tone shifts, and his face takes on a more serious expression.

'But, if I'm allowed to be serious for a moment,' he says. 'I stand here as the best man today, but to be honest with you all, I haven't always been the best man in life. I've stumbled, made mistakes, and I've hurt people. But Rick makes me want to be better.'

He gazes at the newly-weds with a genuine warmth in his eyes.

'Seeing what Rick has with Lucy, it's not just a celebration of their love, it's a reminder of what's possible. Rick, you inspire me, mate. You inspire me to be a better man every single day.'

A hushed silence falls over the crowd as everyone sits with Nathan's words.

'Okay, mood ruined,' Nathan says with a laugh. 'Insert a joke here about how he's going to be too drunk to get it up tonight.'

And just like that, the room is laughing again.

'So, let's raise our glasses,' Nathan declares, lifting his own. 'To Rick and Lucy, who've shown us that love is not just a word – it's a journey, an adventure, and sometimes, a sneaky shag in a beach hut. Cheers!'

Everyone laughs, claps, cheers and clinks their glasses. Nathan returns to his seat, smiling happily, pleased with his performance.

Lucy stands up, a mischievous glint in her eyes, and the room falls into a curious hush.

'I wasn't going to say anything – in fact, I was relieved that I didn't have to make a speech,' Lucy quips, her words drawing chuckles from the crowd. 'But I would like to say a few words. Things have been rocky, for all sorts of reasons, but I would like to raise a toast to the two people who deserve extra thanks, for making today go ahead without a hitch, and that is my amazing sister, Gigi, and our new friend Donnie. To Gigi and Donnie!'

Another cheer ripples across the room as glasses are raised and clinked for a final time.

I smile, caught off guard by her words, but touched that she would raise a toast to me on her wedding day. Then I look over at

Donnie, to find his eyes already on me, as he raises a glass in my direction. He looks so happy, so at home here with us all. I wonder what his deal is, and if what it is could be so bad that we might be over before we even get started.

With a gap between key wedding moments, I decide to nip to the loo, while I can, because I know how jam-packed the day is, and if I don't go now, I'll be holding it in until after the first dance, which I know is imminent.

There is a small building, next to the wedding marquee, which I'm assuming is purpose-built for outdoor events like today, because it houses a fully stocked bar and toilets, to save guests from trailing back to the hotel if they want or need something.

I step into the ladies' and the first thing I do is check my dress in the mirror. Lucy had these beautiful long but lightweight yellow bridesmaid dresses made, so that we wouldn't be too warm, but ensured that we still looked like bridesmaids. Yellow is not a colour I would usually go for but Lucy was right, it works. It's such a flattering fit too, somehow knowing where to cling, and where to hang loose. This dress is doing a lot of legwork today, that's for sure. I wonder if I can get other clothes made by the designer who made the dresses, so that I always feel this comfortable in my skin.

I take a step back, as the cubicle door opens, to let whoever it is pass me to get to the sink, only to find myself face to face with Sunshine.

There is a heavy awkwardness in the air as she passes me to wash her hands. She doesn't say a word, and I don't know what to say to her, so I head for the cubicle.

'Wait,' she says, stopping me before I can close the door.

I stop in my tracks. I'm surprised to see Sunshine's expression soften. She even smiles – dare I say genuinely.

'Do you have a minute?' she says. 'Can we have a quick chat?'

'Sure,' I reply – well, what can I say?

Her gaze drops for a moment to her feet as she seemingly examines her shoes, as though she's struggling to spit out what she wants to say.

'I wanted to say sorry,' she tells, her eyes meeting mine. 'For anything I might have done to hurt you.'

I can see something in her eyes, in her body language, and I can hear it in her voice too, something I don't think I've seen before – I think it's sincerity.

I'm taken aback by the unexpected apology. I was expecting her to make some kind of bitchy remark, or humblebrag, or even be angry with me.

'Sunshine, you don't have to—'

'No, I do,' she interrupts me firmly. 'I really do. And, I swear to you, I didn't know Nathan was still with you when we first got together. When I found out last night, genuinely, it hit me hard. I do love him, so I'm going to try to forgive him, and make things work, but if I feel like this then I can't even imagine how you must be feeling.'

Now I really am surprised. I've certainly never known her show any kind of sympathy, or consider how anyone else might be feeling in a situation. She's usually the kind of person who, when a celebrity dies, posts an anecdote about the time she met them on a plane and they told her she was the most beautiful woman they had ever seen, or similar.

'Nathan and I were over, we just needed one of us to be brave enough to end things,' I tell her. 'And what he did wasn't right. But I'm past it now. I just want to get on with my life, and I'm sure he just wants to get on with his and, even though he betrayed me, I'd never known of him doing anything like that before so...'

My voice trails off. I know it seems crazy for me to defend him, but we all make mistakes. I'm sure I would feel very differently if he were the love of my life, but now that I know that he wasn't, it changes things. It's hard to miss something, when you realise you didn't want it in the first place. As ridiculous as it seems, I feel more disappointed by the fact that Donnie is keeping a secret from me than I do by finding out that Nathan cheated on me when were together.

'Thank you, Gigi,' she says with a heavy sigh. 'You don't know how much better I feel for hearing that.'

I smile, making a move for the cubicle, but Sunshine stops me again.

She takes a deep breath, preparing herself to say something else. I should have known I wasn't getting off this easy.

'Gigi, I owe you another apology,' she tells me.

Oh, God, what now? There's more than that? I don't think I can take anything else.

I raise an eyebrow, puzzled but curious nonetheless.

'Another apology?' I repeat back to her. 'What for?'

She looks down at the tiles, then up at the ceiling, almost as though she's embarrassed.

'For not being nice to you,' she finally admits. 'I... I felt threatened.'

Oh... I don't know what I was expecting her to say but definitely not that. Sunshine Greene – *the* Sunshine Greene – threatened by me? With her hundreds of thousands of followers, and her perfect everything, and she was the one who ended up with Nathan so...

'Threatened? By me?' I blurt. 'Sunshine, that's... sorry, I don't understand.'

She lets out a sigh, pausing to choose her words carefully.

'Nathan talks about you all the time, Gigi,' she confesses. 'And so many of his memories seem to involve you. The things he owns, the thoughtful presents, they're all from you. It's like I can't escape from you, and then the icing on the cake is the fact that you're still around.'

I'm a little annoyed at first because how does she think I feel? I have to be around him and her. But, as I process her words, I start to feel sorry for her. Me having to see my ex with his new girlfriend sucks for me so, for Sunshine to be trying to enjoy her new relationship, but for her boyfriend's ex to still be on the scene, must be a similar kind of weird.

Perhaps we have more in common than we realised.

'Sunshine, I feel the same way about Nathan being around,' I tell her. 'I'm very much of the opinion that once someone becomes an ex, they should just... disintegrate – or appear to, at least. But I've stuck it out for Lucy and Rick, so that it doesn't mess up their wedding.'

'You have?' she says. 'You don't want him back or anything like that?'

'I absolutely do not want him back,' I say firmly, trying my best not to sound too much like I can't think of anything worse, because he is her boyfriend, after all. 'I'm here for my sister and Rick. And, come on, you... you're Sunshine Greene! Why would you feel threatened by anyone?'

She sighs, a vulnerability in her eyes that I not only didn't expect, but I didn't think possible.

'My Instagram is the version of myself and my life that I want to show people,' she tells me. 'But real life isn't what you see on Instagram.'

I mean, I knew that, but Sunshine has always made it seem like her perfect online presence was a genuine representation of her real life. Wow, so Sunshine Greene is human after all, and feels insecure just like the rest of us. If someone as bright and sparkly as Sunshine can feel insecure, then maybe I shouldn't be so hard on myself the next time I'm feeling down.

'Like, this morning, I posted a photo of my dress, and I started getting all of these replies, and not all of them were complimentary, but it was too late to do anything about it, so I've spent the whole day wondering if I really do need Botox in my armpits...'

Wow, I don't even know what that would do there, and I certainly hadn't realised I needed to be self-conscious about my armpits. Then again, with me at least, I'm sure there is plenty that a person might criticise before they looked that closely – not that I'm going to let myself feel all that bothered by it (hopefully) any more.

'We all feel insecure sometimes, it's just human nature, there's no shame in it,' I tell her. 'You and Nathan really do seem great together. Perhaps, now that you know that I don't want him back, and that he doesn't want me back, you can just focus on that, and enjoy it?'

She nods, looking almost relieved that I understand.

'You're right,' she admits. 'Sorry, I know it might be hard to believe, but I'm not usually this crazy.'

I do find that hard to believe – I watched *Welcome to Singledom.*

'Shall we hug it out?' she suggests.

'I'd like that,' I reply.

I step forward, offering her a reassuring hug.

'You look beautiful,' I tell her. 'Get out there any enjoy yourself – and don't worry about what anyone thinks – especially not about your bloody armpits.'

She laughs as hugs me back, and for a moment, all the tension between us seems to evaporate.

'Let's go enjoy the wedding together,' she suggests. 'I'm not taking no for an answer.'

'I do still need to pee,' I admit with an awkward chuckle.

'Okay,' she replies, laughing too. 'Come and find me later. We'll have a nice, normal chat.'

'Sounds great,' I reply.

Sunshine heads for the door before quickly stopping in her tracks again.

'Gigi,' she calls after me.

I turn around. I really do need to pee, but I don't like to stop her, when she's being nice.

'You look beautiful too,' she tells me.

'Thanks,' I reply.

I arrive back out under the marquee just in time.

'Ladies and gents, the bride and groom are about to share their first dance as husband and wife, and they would love it if you all would join them on the dance floor,' a voice announces, amplified by the microphone.

Lucy and Rick, a mixture of excitement and nerves, make their way to the centre of the dance floor. I know that they've been practising this, again and again, because neither of them is an especially good dancer naturally (it definitely runs in the family) but they want it to be as close to perfect as possible. I suppose sometimes, realistically, close to perfect is more than enough.

As the soulful sound of Lewis Capaldi's 'Pointless' fills the air, couples form on the dance floor, ready to join the newly-weds.

I always find, when I'm at a wedding, that I can never quite picture myself being a bride. I would like to, don't get me wrong, but on a day like today, when everything seems so perfect, it's hard to imagine it ever being for me.

Lost in my thoughts, I feel a tap on my shoulder.

'May I have this dance?' Donnie jokes, a touch of faux formality in his tone.

Unable to resist, I laugh.

'You may,' I reply.

Donnie envelops me in his arms, and we sway gently to the music, momentarily forgetting the world around us. Then I feel him tense up a little.

'Listen, about last night,' Donnie begins. 'It doesn't have to mean anything. We can just chalk it up to one of those holiday moments of madness and forget all about it.'

My body stiffens, bracing for the expected. This is the moment when he'll tell me I'm just a holiday fling, and I realise I was just a fleeting distraction to fill his boring days while he's been here alone. A pang of embarrassment washes over me, as I wonder why I let myself believe this could ever be something more than a holiday romance.

'Okay,' I reply coolly – someone give me an Oscar.

'Really?' Donnie replies, genuinely surprised.

I pull a face, my Oscar-worthy performance over as my frustration surges to the forefront.

'What do you want me to do, beg you to change your mind? If that's what you want, fine,' I tell him.

I shrug in his arms – but still carry on dancing, of course. It's one thing to be here without an impressive date, it's another to have a row with your mate-date in the middle of the dance floor, during the first dance.

'It's not what I want at all,' he tells me sincerely. 'I assumed it was what you wanted – you've been so weird since last night.'

I sigh. Should I tell him the truth, should I try to smooth things over for now, or should I scorch the earth? If I push him away now, I won't get hurt later. Sadly, that's never been my style.

'I woke up on top of the world this morning,' I confess. 'It was only after we found Lucy and Rick, and I overheard you on the phone, talking about keeping secrets from me, that my mood changed.'

'Oh,' Donnie says simply. 'I can explain. I was talking to my s—'

'Here's the thing, I don't think I want you to,' I interrupt him.

'Honestly, I'm sick of men lying, sneaking around, of me catching them out. I'm sick of the burden being on me.'

'You're right, it's not fair, and I'm sorry that you overheard what you did,' he admits. 'But I promise you, it's not what it sounded like. There is something I want to talk to you about – and it's nothing to worry about – I just wanted to tell you in my own time.'

Okay, now I feel bad. The last thing I wanted to do was push him in any way.

'Look, I'm sorry,' I say. 'And I'm being ridiculous. So long as you are actually single, of course, and you're over your ex, then whatever it is you've got going on, I want you to tell me in your own time. It's been a long week – but it has only been a week. Perhaps we just need to slow things down a bit.'

'First of all, I am single,' he confirms, rubbing my back reassuringly with his hands. 'And the break-up I told you about, well, it was more like the end of a relationship that was never romantic, so you have nothing to worry about there. It has been a long week, but it's been one of the best weeks of my life. Maybe we should slow down, but I don't want to. I really like you, Gigi, and I think we've got something special here. When I go back to London, I don't want you to be just some girl I cross paths with when I'm strolling around museums, I want you to be there with me.'

'I would really like that too,' I admit, a genuine smile breaking through. 'And I do too – really like you, that is.'

Donnie takes my face in his hands, sealing our fate with a kiss just as the song reaches its end.

The crowd cheers. Let's be real, they're probably cheering Lucy and Rick – because of course they are, it's their wedding – but it only adds to the moment for me.

With the first dance finished, everyone gets back to partying. Some guests continue swaying on the dance floor, now that a DJ has taken over, while others gravitate toward the bar to grab a drink. Other people return to their seats, to rest their feet – Lucy being the first one to plonk herself down and kick off her heels.

She's back at the top table, sitting with our mum and dad, so Donnie and I drift over there.

'Here he is, the man of the hour,' my dad announces with a cheeky wink. 'Well, after Rick, of course.'

We all laugh.

'You really did save the day, Donnie,' Lucy adds. 'I really hope we get to see a lot more of you.'

'I think you might,' Donnie replies with a smile, taking me by the hand, squeezing it tightly.

'So, come on then, are you taking his name?' Dad presses Lucy.

Lucy, sighing in good-natured resignation, nods.

'I am,' she tells him.

Our dad claps his hands together, laughing to himself.

'Giving you the world's funniest initials,' he announces proudly. 'Lucy Olivia Leeming. Aka: LOL.'

'Oh, God, I'm never going to hear the end of it,' Lucy tells us all with an exasperated chuckle. 'It was almost worth keeping Marsden, just so that he couldn't crack that joke for the rest of my life.'

'There are worse surnames to have,' Dad continues. 'Just imagine – Donnie's last name could be Trump. It isn't, is it?'

Donnie laughs wildly. I don't think he was expecting that.

'Er, no, actually,' he replies. 'It's Marsden.'

'Really?' Mum squeaks in disbelief.

'You never told me that,' I say to him.

'It never came up,' he replies, shrugging it off.

'Donald Marsden, that's a strong name,' Dad reasons. 'You sound like a Scottish laird.'

'I'm not a Donald, actually,' Donnie tells him with an amused chuckle. 'I've always gone by Donnie, because the kids at school never let me forget what an uncool name they thought I had.'

'So, what's Donnie short for?' I ask.

'He's not short, he's well over six foot,' Dad jokes.

'Gordon,' Donnie manages to say, as he laughs at Dad's non-stop jokes. 'Gordon Graeme Marsden.'

My jaw is on the floor.

'Yeah, we'll stick with Donnie,' Dad says with a chuckle, oblivious to the huge secret that he has just inadvertently unearthed.

I look at Donnie, who just grins at me. He knows that I know.

Suddenly I think I might know the secret that Donnie has been keeping and I laugh to myself. It's funny, because no one will know, but I may have brought the most impressive date to the wedding after all.

42

It's Friday the 13th – unlucky for some so, naturally, the perfect day for a big wedding.

I wouldn't say I was a superstitious person, but I'm *not* not a superstitious person either, if you know what I mean. Well, why chance it?

I was already feeling terrified, about walking down the aisle, never mind having to contend with the idea of doing it on Friday the frigging 13th, so as I'm sure you can imagine, my nerves are getting the better of me right now.

I'm excited too, though, don't get me wrong. I've spent hours getting ready today, so hopefully I'm looking good, and needless to say I've been practising my walk. I know, I always just thought it was a case of 'one foot in front of the other' and 'try not to fall' too, but it turns out that aisle walking is a whole thing, with a rhythm, and a pattern, and is yet another thing that I can get wrong today – yay!

'Okay, Gigi, time for you to go,' the wedding coordinator tells me.

'Okay,' I reply, puffing air from my cheeks.

264

PORTIA MACINTOSH

Oh, boy, here we go.

I begin my journey down the aisle, which seems to be an extra-long one, but it might just feel that way because the church is overflowing with guests and I'm terrified I'm going to embarrass myself. I don't need to worry about that right now – about how many eyes and cameras are on me, watching if I make a mistake – I just need to focus on putting one foot in front of the other, one at a time, in time with the music, until I safely reach my destination. Once I'm there, it's all pretty straightforward, right? Vows, photos, party. Genuinely, this is the only part I've been stressing about, but I'm nearly there. It's almost over. Then, perhaps, I can enjoy myself.

At the front, Nathan stands in a smart black suit – complete with a black bow tie – but, as great as he looks, he can't seem to stop fidgeting. I can tell he's a bundle of nerves about getting married – I do think it's just the wedding part, though, not the idea of marriage that is freaking him out. He's never been one for standing front and centre, with all eyes on him. I give his arm a reassuring squeeze as I smile at him. Then I take my place next to Lucy, the other bridesmaid.

I reach my mark right on cue, just as the music starts for the bride's grand entrance.

We are fondly gathered here today to witness and celebrate the joining of my ex-boyfriend, Nathan, and the woman he cheated on me with, Sunshine, in marriage and, honestly, I'm cool with it.

I steal a glance to the side of the church where the musicians are stationed. There he is, Donnie, my wonderful boyfriend, playing the guitar. God, he looks good. I have to admit, when I heard that Sunshine and Nathan were having an all-white wedding, and that guests were going to have to wear white evening wear to the church, in the a.m., and then keep it on all day, I was sceptical about how practical it would be. Not only does it feel kind of silly, wearing such formal outfits in a church, but it's not exactly summer wedding wear, and the fact that we're all dressed in white has me convinced I'm going to spill on myself, or someone else, or everyone – somehow. But now that I see Donnie in his white tuxedo, looking like an absolute dreamboat, I couldn't care less; I'm just basking in the fact that he's mine and looking beyond fit in that tux.

Sunshine gracefully takes her place beside Nathan – her big white dress impressively somehow even more white than what everyone else is wearing – and they exchange nervous smiles. Don't laugh, but it's kind of cute.

As the vicar begins the ceremony, I can't help but smile to myself. It's funny how things turn out sometimes. If someone had told me, at the start of last year, that I would be a bridesmaid at my ex-boyfriend's wedding, I would've laughed in your face. And yet, here I am, a part of the wedding party no less, smiling like I mean it – and I really do mean it.

The drama surrounding Lucy's wedding unexpectedly brought us all closer together, and gave me the closure I needed to finally move on. No, I'm not happy that Nathan cheated on me, and Sunshine really did treat me terribly, but what's the point in harbouring bad feelings and resentment? There is a lot to be said for choosing to look at things in a different light. Looking back, I actually feel sorry for Sunshine, knowing that she felt so insecure – that my presence was torturing her, making her into the supervillain she became. I don't ever want to be anyone's origin story, I can say that for sure. And as for Nathan, well, he did me a favour. I probably would have stayed with him, bored out of my mind, enduring the nights alone while he was busy working and the occasional, soul-destroying exclusively horizontal sex. That cycle needed breaking, and boy did he break it, but it led me to the love of my life: Donnie – or Gordon, as it turns out he's actually called. And to think, he had the audacity to make fun of Geoff's name, although I guess in hindsight he was just jealous.

When we got back to London, Donnie and I, despite floating the idea of taking things slow, absolutely did not take things slow at all. We've been pretty much inseparable ever since then – not that I'm complaining.

I couldn't believe it, when I found out that he was G. G. Marsden all along. In fact, I couldn't even bring myself to mention it to him, I was terrified to speak. But later that night, after the wedding, it was him who brought it up, asking me if I had something I wanted to ask him. Naturally I had a million questions and, to be fair to him, he answered every single one – including the fact that it was a solicitor who I overheard him on the phone to, the person who has been helping him keep all of this under wraps. One of the things I did find out, which is actually hilarious, is that the suite I ended up staying in was actually the suite that Donnie had booked. However, seeing as though he used an alias, hotel staff were quick to eject him from the suite, sticking him in a cheap room (which was obviously the one I booked) so that I could have the fancy suite. I can't imagine, if I were in Donnie's shoes, keeping quiet while someone else lived it up in my suite – although I suppose he did get to sleep in it eventually.

Wow, it feels like we've been through so much. When we arrived back in London, Donnie had the matter of his late, estranged dad's fortune to contend with, but one thing was clear, he didn't want to be involved in the family company, and he definitely didn't want the fame that came with it. All he wanted was a nice, quiet, happy life – something we both have in common, and something that is a lot easier to do when you've got money in the bank.

I'm happy that he took the money, and not the fame or the power at the top of the company, because – don't get me wrong – I enjoyed being G. G. Marsden for a week, but I couldn't put up with it for much longer, it was exhausting.

So, Donnie decided to cash in his shares, selling them off to his siblings for one hell of a decent payout – but you would never know. You know when people joke that if they won the lottery they wouldn't tell anyone, but there would be signs? Well, with Donnie, you really would never ever know. He's still playing guitar, happily admitting that it's a lot more enjoyable now that the pressure of making a living from it is off his shoulders. He's still the same kind, sweet, caring man – still with absolutely zero entitlement. As for me, I'm still working at the salon, making the world a more beautiful place, one haircut at a time. Well, I've got a whole list of customers who would be without a regular therapist if I quit, and you know what it's like, when you find a stylist you can trust – it ruins your life, if they move on.

We have been talking about our future, though, mapping out our next adventures. We've been making plans, and lists of places to explore, and it's amazing to think that we might actually be able to do them. We've also been talking about getting married, which… I can't quite believe I'm saying. At first it was just the concept coming up, now and then, but more recently Donnie has been dropping the kind of hints that make me think it might be sooner rather than later, claiming he's just waiting for the perfect moment to pop the question. Honestly, the most exhausting part of all of it is trying to keep on top of my manicures, so that my nails are camera-ready if he does spring it on me out of the blue. I'm sick with nerves, any time we go to a restaurant, or he takes me somewhere scenic for a stroll.

There are worse problems to have, though, right? Honestly, I couldn't be happier – and I certainly didn't think I could ever be this happy, that's for sure.

My life feels so different now, in so many ways, but in others, it's like nothing has changed, which I love.

And hey, if I do decide to say 'I do' to Donnie when he asks, at least I won't have to change my surname if I want to share one with him. You can't put a price on that, can you?

ACKNOWLEDGEMENTS

Thank you to everyone at Boldwood Books – especially my lovely editor, Nia – for their work on this book. Here's to another one.

Huge thanks as always to everyone who takes the time to read and review my books. Your support means so much to me. I really hope you have enjoyed reading *The Suite Life*.

None of this would be possible without the love and support of my wonderful family. My incredible mum, Kim, and my dad, Pino. I'm so fortunate to have been given the best brothers – James and Joey – who are so supportive and helpful. I'm also so fortunate to have my amazing gran, Aud, and my sidekick, Darcy.

Finally, thank you to Joe, my husband, who I couldn't do this without – I love you all so much.

ABOUT THE AUTHOR

Portia MacIntosh is a bestselling romantic comedy author of over 15 novels, including *My Great Ex-Scape* and *Honeymoon For One*. Previously a music journalist, Portia writes hilarious stories, drawing on her real life experiences.

Sign up to Portia MacIntosh's mailing list for news, competitions and updates on future books.

Visit Portia's website: https://portiamacintosh.com/

Follow Portia MacIntosh on social media here:

 facebook.com/portia.macintosh.3

 x.com/PortiaMacIntosh

 instagram.com/portiamacintoshauthor

 bookbub.com/authors/portia-macintosh

ALSO BY PORTIA MACINTOSH

Just Date and See

Your Place or Mine?

Better Off Wed

Long Time No Sea

The Faking Game

Trouble in Paradise

Ex in the City

The Suite Life

LOVE IN EVERY CHAPTER

WHERE ALL YOUR ROMANCE
DREAMS COME TRUE!

THE HOME OF BESTSELLING
ROMANCE AND WOMEN'S
FICTION

 WARNING:
MAY CONTAIN SPICE

SIGN UP TO OUR
NEWSLETTER

https://bit.ly/Lovenotesnews

Boldw**oo**d

Boldwood Books is an award-winning fiction publishing company seeking out the best stories from around the world.

Find out more at www.boldwoodbooks.com

Join our reader community for brilliant books, competitions and offers!

Follow us

@BoldwoodBooks

@TheBoldBookClub

Sign up to our weekly deals newsletter

https://bit.ly/BoldwoodBNewsletter